Margaret R. King

Memoirs of the Life of Mrs. Sarah Peter

Volume 1

Margaret R. King

Memoirs of the Life of Mrs. Sarah Peter
Volume 1

ISBN/EAN: 9783337335472

Printed in Europe, USA, Canada, Australia, Japan

Cover: Foto ©Andreas Hilbeck / pixelio.de

More available books at **www.hansebooks.com**

MEMOIRS

OF

THE LIFE

OF

MRS. SARAH PETER

BY

MARGARET R. KING

VOLUME I

CINCINNATI
ROBERT CLARKE & CO.
1889

"He who makes a faithful picture of only a single important scene in the events of a single life, is doing something toward painting the greatest historical piece of the day."

CONTENTS.

CHAPTER I.

Early Life—Chillicothe, 1800–1831.................................... 5

CHAPTER II.

Cincinnati, 1831–1836 29

CHAPTER III.

Cambridge, 1835–1840.. 47

CHAPTER IV.

Philadelphia, 1840–1853.. 59

CHAPTER V.

First Visit to Europe, and Travels in "The East," 1851–
1853—Removal to Cincinnati.................................... 77

CHAPTER VI.

Second Visit to Europe, 1854–1857......................... 264

CHAPTER VII.

Third Visit to Europe, for the Sisterhoods, 1857–1858.......... 341

CHAPTER VIII.

Works of Mercy during the Civil War, 1860–1867 425

CHAPTER IX.

Fourth Visit to Europe, 1867................................. 445

(iii)

CHAPTER X.

Fifth visit to Europe, 1869–1870.. 471

CHAPTER XI.

Intellectual and Art Culture—Religious Life...................... 499

CHAPTER XII

Later Life, 1870–1877.. 519

CHAPTER XIII.

The Close, 1877.................................. 549

INTRODUCTION.

After many years' hesitation, I have finally taken upon myself the work of writing a memoir of the life of Mrs. Peter. I undertake it because I believe there is no one left who so thoroughly knew her in all the most important stages of her life, and who entered so understandingly and with such true appreciation into her varied work, and who sympathized with her in important steps she conscientiously took, though differing with her in some of her conclusions.

If Mrs. Peter's life were to be written simply as a pleasing record for loving friends to read, each year of hesitation has lessened the importance of the undertaking, and now, twelve years having passed since her work on earth was finished, few personal friends are left, at least of her contemporaries, to take an interest in these details. But such a life as hers is so full of lessons, and the work done so vast in its importance, that a merely personal interest in the subject of the memoir is not of paramount consideration.

These are footprints which may guide and give courage to others in their own weak efforts, by seeing what has been done, and how good can be done.

(v)

Mrs. Peter's whole life, in its growth and development, forms a profitable study to those who would fulfill the doctrine of Christ and follow in his footsteps. Forgetfulness of self, a never-ceasing effort to do for others, were impulses of her character, but her daily occupations increased these tendencies, and as one travels with her through life the power of her influence must be felt. In all her long life, it is impossible to believe that a day ever passed in which this good woman failed to do a kind action to some one.

Exercise in the moral as well as the physical nature causes growth, and this combination with her of the natural desire and the strong sense of duty, made her lengthening years a blessing and an example to others. If the morning of her life shed blessing and hope in its brilliance—if the noonday glowed with all the fervor of beneficence—far more beautiful and helpful is the contemplation of the evening glow, and the coming out of the brighter stars of the beyond, as the light of this brief day of existence closed. We would impress the lesson of these closing years by glimpses into that useful life, and give courage to those whose hearts may prompt them to live for the good of others—if only by touching the human chord of desire for a peaceful and blessed end of mortal life.

With a true love and admiration for my husband's mother, and with an earnest desire to record faithfully what I know of a remarkable life, I make these pages a loving tribute to a noble son, upon whom she has left her impress, and whose wise and judicious early training shows itself in an unselfish beneficent manhood.

MARGARET RIVES KING.

CINCINNATI, *December*, 1888.

EARLY LIFE,

CHILLICOTHE,

1800–1831.

(v)

" The childhood shows the man,
  As morning does the day."
                    —MILTON.

" Life is a sheet of paper white
  Whereon each one of us may write
His word, or two.   .   .   .
Greatly begin, though thou hast time
But for a line, be that sublime—
Not failure but low aim is crime."
                    —LOWELL.

(vi)

CHAPTER I.

PARENTAGE—CHILDHOOD—SCHOOLS—MARRIAGE—VISITS TO NEW YORK AND NEW ORLEANS—CHILLICOTHE AS DESCRIBED BY THE DUKE OF SAXE-WEIMAR—CHURCH AND CHURCH WORK—SOCIETY AND FRIENDS.

THE early life of this remarkable woman, whose beneficent career we wish to trace, was passed in the town of Chillicothe, Ross County, Ohio. She was born on the tenth of May, of the year 1800. Her father, Thomas Worthington, afterward Senator and Governor of Ohio, removed from Virginia to his new home in the year 1797, with his young wife, freed slaves, and all that was necessary to make comfortable a new settlement in the wilderness. A man of strong will, noble character, and vigorous health soon overcame the difficulties of the pioneer life, and formed a home of comfort for his family and became a power in the formation of a new state. The father of Thomas Worthington, a man of wealth and social influence, died when the boy was of tender years. By the death of the mother he was left an orphan under the guardianship of General Darke, who filled the responsible position most kindly and fully, giving the boy a good education and the training of foreign travel, nursing his fortune so carefully that when the youth set forth in life he found himself in comfort and affluence, and prepared with confidence to ask the hand of the beautiful and sensible Miss Eleanor Van Swearingen, who graced his home and comforted his life for so many years, sharing so cheerfully with him the unavoidable hardships of a pioneer life. Of material comfort they were able to provide in their new home a full supply, but many of the privileges and luxuries to which they had been accustomed in their Virginia home were not to be had. As yet, the provision for education was not as ample as could be found in the older and more advanced adjoining state, Kentucky. So, at the early age of eight years, the child Sarah Worthington was sent to the boarding school of Mrs. Keats, an English lady of high cultivation and character, who had established herself not many miles from the town of Frankfort. This step, hard to parent and child, was wise, which was fully proven by its results. All through life might be traced, and was acknowledged by her, who was most benefited, the wisdom of the sacrifice for the principles of duty, of activity, of truth, which were the foundation of the plan of the excellent teacher, never forgotten by her faithful and grateful pupil. It was beautiful to listen to this venerable woman as she approached the close of her life, referring to the early teaching and principles instilled by her revered teacher, in her almost baby life. The soul that could thus impress itself, must have been full of the spirit of goodness and truth.

Hardly two years had gone by when the young girl was recalled to her home by the failing health of her mother, who desired, in the uncertainty of continued mortal life, to have her children around her. Sarah did not return to Kentucky, as circumstances had rendered it necessary that Mrs. Keats should give up her school, and her devoted pupils, with saddened hearts returned to their homes.

As Mr. Worthington was at that time United States Senator from Ohio, and passing a large part of the year in Washington, the two elder daughters were placed at school near Baltimore, where they had every advantage in intellectual development. The privilege most dwelt upon in after years by her of whom we write, was the opportunity of knowing in their Virginia homes, during vacations, the family friends from whom they were separated by a removal to Ohio.*

This opportúnity of seeing life in an older and more civilized community, and among people of the highest refinement and cultivation, was to the highly organized child, ever looking up, ever anxious to learn, an opportunity which, even as a child, she was grateful for, and profited by. In later years, she often referred to its benefits. The experiences of those days molded much of her thought and taste in after life. The memories of the old-time aristocratic hospitality of Virginia gave much of the charm to the genial open-heartedness which characterized the manners all through her life of a lady whose home spread sunshine wherever it was planted. Sarah Worthington was but sixteen when she became the wife of Edward King, fourth son of the Hon. Rufus King. Mr. Worthington and Mr. King were Senators from their respective states at the same time, and became warm friends during their residence in Washington. Through Mr. Worthington's account of the growing west, Mr. King became persuaded that no field could offer greater advantages for a young lawyer just setting out in life than the rising State of Ohio. Having come to this decision, Mr. King wrote to his friend in Ohio, Governor Worthington, asking for necessary information. A satisfactory answer being returned to this

---

* The homes of Mrs. Shepherd and Mrs. Bedinger, aunts of Mrs. Worthington, were the visiting places most enjoyed for their old-time elegance and hospitality.

letter, it was decided that Mr. Edward King, who had just completed his studies at the Litchfield Law School, should at once remove to the west, and Chillicothe, then the seat of government of the state, was chosen as his future home. In September, of the year 1815, he set forth, on what at that time was considered a serious undertaking, a journey across the mountains, bearing with him a letter of introduction to Governor Worthington.

One can not be surprised that a mother's tenderness should regard with some apprehension the removal of a son still untried in life's ways, to so distant a field, far off from family influences and care. The following letter will show how the mother's tender interest followed her absent son :

My Dear Edward:—If it were not for my invincible objection to writing, I might inundate you with letters at the public's expense, and thereby interrupt your grave and learned studies, but, fortunately for you, their is no apprehension on that score, for I will very frankly acknowledge that this is the first time I have taken my pen to write to you. There is less cause of regret on this account, as your father has become so regular a correspondent, and keeps you so well informed of all that is important in state affairs. I do not know whether he has communicated *one very important* piece of information, as it regards his increasing honors, and lest you should not have timely notice of this event, I will take it upon myself to announce it, that is his nomination for Governor of the State of New York (don't laugh, I beg). The step was taken without previous consultation with him, for he believed, with others, that Judge Van Ness was to be the Federal candidate, and was much surprised, and somewhat indignant, at seeing his name in the papers, as candidate for Governor, without ever having one word on the subject. The papers will give you the particulars. After mature deliberation he has yielded consent to become the candidate, and to this he was driven by the urgent entreaties of his friends, who thought he was the only man that, to use their own language, could rally and save the Federal party in the state. I must confess my patriotism is not sufficient to induce me to congratulate or wish him success. He probably has or will mention the subject himself. And now, my dear son, I should be glad to know with more particularity than your letters express, how you are, what you do, and what prospects for the future. I hope and trust the answer will be satisfactory to all these questions. With the exception of Governor Worthington's family, you say nothing about the female society of Chillicothe. Are there many females whose manners and conversation will compare with those you have been accustomed to? I like female society for young men; it softens and polishes the manners, even if the ladies themselves are not very refined. Have you any amusements, such as dances, not to dignify them with the name of balls, tea parties, etc.? I should suppose Mrs. Worthington's residence here, and at Baltimore, would have given her a taste for this kind of amusements, and that she would be induced to promote them there. In some of your first letters, you spoke of the indisposition of Mrs. Worthington, but as you have not mentioned it latterly, I hope she is entirely recovered.

I observe by the papers that the seat of government of Ohio is to be removed to Columbus next fall. This will deprive you of some society in the winter. The marriage of Miss Worthington * is certainly to take place, as I understand from the young gentleman's sister, who is passing the winter here, and she will probably reside at Detroit. This will be a loss to your society for a while, but others will soon supply the place. Washington, I am told, for I can not speak from my own knowledge, has been, and is very gay. One of your

---

* Miss Worthington, here mentioned, was the older sister of the future Mrs. Edward King, and became the wife of Mr. Macomb.

Litchfield belles has been much admired here, Miss Talmadge. I have not yet seen her, but Mrs. Gore thinks her very pretty. Speaking of Litchfield acquaintances, do you ever hear of a certain lady who lived not far from thence, or is that business deferred for the present. I have not heard one word on the subject since you left us. It is for my own information that I make this inquiry, and with no other view. I should like to be informed respecting your wardrobe, whether all your clothes arrived in safety, or if any were left by the way, whether you wish any addition to it this summer, or if it will do till you make a visit; if you will recollect my advice in having things timely repaired, you will find the benefit of it. We have no account of Charles since November, though we daily look for arrivals from England, James has leased his house for five years to Mr. James McEvers, the partner of Leroy D. Bayard, and is going to lead a country life, but has not decided yet whether it shall be at Jamaica or Greenwich. He would prefer the former if he could buy Colonel Motley's place, but I do not know if that is for sale; however, he must soon make a decision, as the first of May is not far distant. Before this reaches Chillicothe, you will have attained your twenty-first birthday, and with it I trust an increase of wisdom and prudence. I congratulate you with the most heart-felt sincerity on arrival at man's estate, and wish you may live to see many and prosperous anniversaries, and that you may be enabled to fulfill all the wise and good resolutions you have formed for your own government, ever walking in the paths of rectitude and virtue, is the ardent prayer of your affectionate mother.   M. KING.

Make our compliments to the Governor's family.

It would not require a prophet to foresee that a handsome, brilliant youth and a beautiful, intellectual young maiden would soon find a warm interest each in the other; so, on the 15th of May of the following year, 1816, the announcement was made of the marriage of

"Sarah Worthington, second daughter of Thomas Worthington, of Adena, to Edward, fourth son of the Honorable Rufus King, of New York. The ceremony was performed by the Rev. John McFarland. The youthful bride was a few days past her sixteenth birthday; the fortunate bridegroom just twenty-one.

The wedding had been hastened in consequence of the infirm condition of the health of Mrs. Worthington, which pointed to so speedy a termination of her mortal life that she earnestly desired to see a union consummated which seemed to promise so much happiness to the young couple.

The oldest daughter had already married, and her husband had made his home in the neighborhood of Chillicothe. The mother felt, in view of her departure, that the marriage of the two elder children would not only be for them an increase of happiness, but for her younger children there would be great advantages. Mrs. Worthington revived from this condition of ill-health, and lived for many years a bright and useful life.

When we contemplate the full fruitage of the life before us, we can but feel that every happy influence must have been brought to bear upon this perfect development, that nothing should be regretted, that every pain, every disappointment, every heart-ache, was a messenger from heaven to do the perfect work, and to bring about the results of this remarkable and full life. But one almost feels that a wrong is committed when the responsibilities of life are thus early thrown upon a child so tender in years, so innocent of the hard way. Yet for her it had many advantages. New fields were opened out for observation, new examples of worth to be imitated, and ambition to beckon on.

The first home of Mr. and Mrs. King was in Chillicothe, where fifteen years of their married life was passed, and where their children were born. Of the only two who reached manhood, one alone was left to mourn the death of the loved and honored mother. The first visit made by Mr. and Mrs. King to New York after their marriage was in 1819, when their first-born boy, then more than a year old, was introduced by the proud young mother to the illustrious grandfather whose name he bore. The visit was of duration long enough to establish a firm mutual affection, founded on respect and admiration.

Mr. King quickly recognized in his new daughter a rare and appreciative mind, which could sympathize with him in all the large ideas which so engrossed this distinquished statesman. At that time a young woman of only eighteen years, her natural powers and well informed mind drew forth much admiration, and surrounded her with an interest which justly excited the pride of those in whose hearts she had taken her place. The friendship and confidence established between the wife and the husband's parents continued unabated through the future years of intercourse. Many valuable recollections of Mr. Rufus King's life and thought were stored in the mind of his daughter, and it was her greatest delight to dwell upon the memory of this pure man, and to instill into the minds of her boys a reverence for their honored ancestor.

The position of Mr. and Mrs. Rufus King in New York was in every way calculated to place their children amid the most favorable environments. The glamour of a successful political career as ambassador to the Court of St. James and Senator in his own country at a time when great men were considered alone worthy to guide the affairs of the young republic, an ample fortune with

all the accessories which high birth only can give, and
without which wealth becomes a burden to its possessor,
living in a home of refinement, they could offer the young
daughter many opportunities which at that time no western home could afford.

Mrs. Rufus King was daughter of Mr. John Alsop,
a wealthy merchant in New York, who endowed his only
child on her distinguished marriage with a large fortune.
An innate sense of what was fit and proper in those
holding high political and social position, led Mr. and
Mrs. King to continue the same mode of life which had
been so gracefully carried out in the ambassador's home
in England. Mr. King was sent to England during the
administration of General Washington, and remained
abroad five or six years. He was sent a second time in
1825, but was compelled to return on account of ill-
health, and died in the year 1827. This year brought a
double grief to Mr. and Mrs. Edward King, for Governor
Worthington passed from this mortal life a few months
after his friend, Mr. King. Thus they were called to
mourn the loss of both fathers, and with their grief was
mingled the sorrow of a nation for two men whose lives
had been passed in valuable service in the interests of
their country. Their children may justly recall these
two ancestral names with pride. The impress of the
work performed by these two statesmen will not soon be
obliterated, Rufus King in the councils of the nation,
Thomas Worthington in the interests of his adopted
state.

Much of the elevation of Mrs. Peter's thought was due
to the early contemplation of characters so pure, so
worthy of study. She has left a beautiful and faithful picture of the life of her own father, which has been
made accessible to all his descendants by the thought-

ful devotion of her son. The life of Mr. King is a
work which both as a duty and a pleasure will be written by one of his descendants, not only as a valuable
study of a man noble, intellectually and morally, but
as a period of the country's history with which he was so
closely identified.

"Mrs. Rufus King was remarkable for personal beauty;
her face was oval, with finely formed nose, mouth, and chin,
blue eyes, a clear brunette complexion, black hair, and fine
teeth. Her movements were at once graceful and gracious,
and her voice musical. She had been carefully educated,
and her quick faculties seized advantage from every opportunity for cultivation; all the indulgence of a parent wholly
devoted to her as an only child was lavished upon her without spoiling her character. Few women in the city were
more carefully educated than Mrs. Rufus King, though she
possessed little of that fondness for display which made others
far more conspicuous. She was daughter of John Alsop, an
opulent merchant, whose large abilities, patriotism, and well-
known integrity had secured his election to the Continental
Congress which made the colonies independent."

This sketch of Mrs. King is taken from "The Republican Court or Society in the Days of Washington,"
by Rufus Wilmot Griswold. In the formation of character we well know how powerful as an aid is environment; as much to do in making the man as heredity, and
fortunate in both these " accidents of life " was the lady
whose life we record. Not, however, do we nor would
she admit it the work of chance.

"It chanced,
Eternal God that chance did guide."

The gentle birth, the early training by wise and judicious parents—the first teachers—the surroundings of

the new life which opened upon her in marriage, each contributed to the final full development.

In the early years of the century, no city of the west could more truthfully boast of its cultivated and excellent society than Chillicothe, the early seat of government of the State of Ohio. Settled generally by Virginians of education and antecedents, and who in coming to Ohio had brought with them and freed their trained servants, they were able to continue the well ordered and hospitable mode of living they had been accustomed to in the home they had left behind them. Their descendants were well disposed to keep up a life so full of interest, and even yet lingers in this pleasant town much of the former life which entitled it to its high rank socially. Among the most distinguished for tasteful and graceful hospitality were Mr. and Mrs. King.

The residence of Governor Worthington had for years been the center of much style and elegance in living. Distinguished men of the olden time often found themselves under the hospitable roof of Adena, and quaint anecdotes were heard from the lips of the venerable mistress, in her latter years, of queer visitors. Sometimes, the grand Tecumseh, with his wild followers; then the polished and suave Aaron Burr, interesting himself in all the gentle pursuits of the fair mistress. Much thought was given by Mrs. Worthington to the cultivation of flowers, also the more practical and necessary care of the vegetable garden. Mr. Burr entered with great interest into these occupations, and gave many valuable hints on a subject with which he seemed to be entirely familiar. Tecumseh was a natural gentleman, a man of stately presence, fine intellect, and wonderful command over the less civilized of his subjects. Still, when they came, all had to be treated with equal attention. On one occasion, a party of braves visited the governor on some affair of moment, and arriving early in the day, it was necessary to break their fast, and politic to see they should be treated as equals. So they were all seated at the family breakfast table—a fine set of young warriors, with Tecumseh at their head. The dignified mistress took her place at the head of the table, to do her part in the hospitality, with much trepidation. All went well, until suddenly a dark cloud passed over the brow of a young brave, and in a moment he and several near him arose with flashing eyes and angry gestures, placing their hands upon their weapons. As quick as thought, Tecumseh rose and commanded order, and the storm passed, and the placidity of a May morning was over all. It seemed that the fair hostess, in dispensing the coffee, had neglected thoughtlessly a young chief, who took it as an insult. But the action of the noble Tecumseh instantly silenced what might have been a more disagreeable scene. As it was, it was sufficient to disturb the nerves of the gentle lady, who often, in after years, told the tale with a perceptible tremor in her voice. Such scenes were not frequent, but were sometimes encountered by those who were dignitaries in the land, still the habitation of rude savages. Homes like Governor Worthington's were as oases in a desert, and men like Tecumseh ruled the more savage men; so that life was not without many of the pleasures and gentle ways of older communities. The stately residence of Governor Worthington was built on a large scale, well fitted in all ways for the gracious hospitality for which it was noted. It was of stone quarried from the hills of the Scioto, planned by the architect Latrobe; situated on a wooded hill overlooking a valley, through which the graceful river wound its way; the wide hills beyond filled with the game of the primeval forests—the deer, the bear, the wild turkey. From this home went forth the young girl to begin life at the head of her husband's house.

The blight of all settlements in the west was over the beautiful valley. The fever of the alluvial lands of newly cleared regions laid its destructive hand over the fair town; and in no instance was the energy of the young wife shown more fully than on the breaking out of the fatal disease in the absence of her husband. She took her children and went off to the wild hills, where was no fatal miasma, and there, in the unbroken solitude, superintended the cutting down of trees, the hewing of the logs, and the building of a snug log-house, which, on the return of her husband, she was occupying in health and comfort with her children. All through life this lady showed herself equal to any position in which she might be placed. She was quick to survey the circumstances and decided in action. This promptness was at the root of her real success in all her undertakings. To see the right was to do the right. No thought of ease, of self-interest, ever staid the active foot, the ready hand, of this good woman, inspired through all her being with the mission of mercy. All Mrs. King's children, four boys and one girl, were born in Chillicothe, and the shadow of her young life was the death of two while yet their home was in her native place. The little Edward lived but a few months, but Mary brightened the home for more than a year, and as she was the only daughter, it was a life-long wrench and sorrow to the mother's heart, and the brothers never ceased to regret the loss of a gentle sister's influence.

In the year 1825, Mrs. King accompanied her father, who was in ill-health, to New Orleans. She must have

been, at that time, a very beautiful and attractive woman.
She was of the medium height; expressive steel-gray eyes,
shadowed by dark lashes; soft, light-brown hair, inclin-
ing to flaxen, with a touch of gold; fair, pale complexion; manners simple, earnest, and graceful. Her great
beauty, through all her life, must have been the shining
forth of the beautiful soul within. She was greeted in
New Orleans with great *eclat*, not only on her own account, but, at that time, Governor Worthington was one
of the marked men of the country. Mrs. King was one
of three ladies who were invited to act as hostesses in
a reception to General LaFayette, who was to arrive as
guest of the city. We can well imagine how entirely
well the graceful lady performed her part.

At that time, to make a voyage to New Orleans, was
what a visit to Europe is to-day, and no part of the
country was so advanced in the elegance and luxuries
of foreign lands as this wealthy metropolis. A large
portion of the population were of French descent, and
entirely French in all their mode of thought and ways of
living. Many had come directly from La Belle France,
and many of the sons and daughters were sent to their
former homes to be educated. Paris was itself not more
of a French city than was New Orleans.

In the year 1825, the creole sway was predominant,
and so charming was their philosophy of life, that the
more sober American yielded naturally to its influence.
They led their bright lives of gayety and culture, of
dance and song, with happy hearts and gracious ways.
Long before the northern cities dreamed of opera, these
gay people brought over from France and encouraged
the best artists. As always with the French, manners,
and dress, and expression, in every way, was an impor-

tant study, and the creole gentleman was a wonder of elegance and a model for all to admire and copy.

It was like a tale of fairyland, as one listened to the fortunate who had escaped the ice-bound northern lands, and basked through the winter months in this land of flowers and song. They brought back fresh life with them, and the aroma of the rose, and the jessamine, and the violet still seemed to surround them, and they had caught the sparkling freshness of the gay science among whose votaries they had lingered. The beautiful climate still remains, but dark shadows have fallen over this joyous race, and the creole life and the creole homes are not what once they were.

Monsieur Levasseur, secretary to General LaFayette, gives, in his history of this distinguished man's travels through the country in 1824 and '25, a charming account of the above-mentioned reception in New Orleans. He speaks of the "beauty and grace" of the women, the "courtly and gracious manners" of the men, the magnificent arrangements, in all their detail, as being equal to any thing he had ever seen. This, coming from one whose life had been in Paris, amid the splendors of the Napoleonic days, is an important testimony to the advance which had been made in the refinements of life, at least, in one portion of this country, during the early years of the present century.

Mr. and Mrs. King enjoyed, with great zest, all the pleasures of social and hospitable life, and not only in their own home extended courtesies to strangers, but were important adjuncts to Governor and Mrs. Worthington in taking care of distinguished persons, many of whom in those days visited Chillicothe.

Among others a very interesting acquaintance was
2

made with his Highness, Bernhard, Duke of Saxe-Weimar Eisenbach, who so pleasantly writes of his visit to Chillicothe, and gives so accurate a picture of what he saw that we are tempted to give our readers the same pleasure which we ourselves have enjoyed from his book, "Travels in North America during the years 1825 and 1826." We extract the following:

"The 10th of May we rode nineteen miles from Circleville to Chillicothe, formerly the capitol of Ohio, situated on the right shore of the Scioto. Our way led through a handsome well cultivated country. We saw fine fields, good dwelling houses, orchards, and gardens, also several mills turned by the waters of the Scioto and several other little creeks. Some of these mills are at the same time fulling, flour, and saw-mills. The forests are chiefly of sugar maple, plane, and different kinds of nut trees. The road was tolerably good, the weather fine and warm. There is a covered wooden bridge which crosses the Scioto near Chillicothe. This bridge runs at least five hundred paces on piers over a meadow, which is sometimes inundated by the Scioto. We were comfortably lodged at Watson's Hotel, in Chillicothe. This town, like Philadelphia, lies between two rivers. The Scioto may be considered as the Delaware, and Paint creek takes the place of the Schuylkill. The streets are large and at right angles, and are without pavements, but have sidewalks. Great part of the houses are built of brick. There are several fine stores. Over the whole prosperity and liveliness seem to reign. Chillicothe is the chief town of Ross county. It contains a court-house built of freestone, which, at the time it was the seat of the state government, was used for the Senate house. The representatives met in the building now used for the court offices. There is also in the city a jail and a market-house of brick. I received visits from several of the most distinguished inhabitants, among them a lawyer, Mr. Leonard,

Dr. Vethake, and Colonel King,* son of the celebrated Rufus King, the American Minister to London, and son-in-law of the former Governor of the state, Mr. Worthington. The latter lives at a country seat two miles from Chillicothe, where he enjoys his rents and the revenue of a considerable property in the midst of an amiable family and an agreeable old age free from care. This son-in-law invited us to his father's house. We accepted his invitation and rode, in company with Mr. Leonard and Dr. Vethake, toward evening to the country seat. Our road led us through a beautiful and well cultivated valley near a little Indian mound, and through the forest of beech, maple, and hickory trees. Finally, we rode through handsome fields where here and there we saw groups of white thorn. The Governor's house is surrounded with Lombardy poplars. It is constructed in the style of an Italian villa of freestone, with stone steps on the exterior; is two stories high; has two wings, having a court in front of the center building, containing honeysuckles and roses. On one side of the house is a terrace with flowers and vegetables. This garden was arranged by German gardeners, who keep it in very good order.

"Behind the house are large clover-fields, and to the right the farm buildings. Governor Worthington occupies himself with the raising of cattle, particularly sheep. He had a flock of one hundred and fifty merinos. I understood they were numerous in the State of Ohio. Colonel King and his highly accomplished lady came to meet us. The governor and his lady soon appeared. He had traveled a great deal, had been long in public office, and was for several years a member of the United States Senate. His eldest son was traveling in Europe, and another son was in the Military Academy at West Point. He has ten children, on whom he has expended a great deal for education. The evening passed

---

* Mr. King had received a commission as colonel in the Ohio militia, at that time more complimentary and honorable than at present.

rapidly in interesting and instructive conversation. The hospitable governor insisted on our passing the night at his house.
The house is very commodious, the furniture plain, but testi-
fies the good taste and easy circumstances of the owner. I
arose early next morning, and took a walk in the governor's
garden. I ascended to a platform on the roof, to take a view
of the surrounding lands, but there is as yet nothing but
woods covering the greater part of the country. Fires that
were burning in some places were proof of the fact that new
settlers were clearing the woods. From this platform the governor can overlook the greater part of his property, containing five thousand acres of land. By this means he has the
greater part of his workmen under his control. The ground
consists of low hills, and it is only toward the east, in the direction of Zanesville, that more considerable elevations are
perceived. I took breakfast with the worthy governor and
his family, and observed here, as well as at Governor Morrow's, that the father of the family had the laudable custom
of making a prayer before sitting down. After breakfast, we
took leave of this most respectable family, whose acquaintance I consider as one of the most interesting I made in the
United States, and returned to town. Chillicothe contains
from two to three thousand inhabitants, who subsist chiefly
by farming, raising cattle, and retail commerce. They had
also commenced establishing woolen factories, and possessed a
bank. It was formerly a branch of the United States Bank
but, doing little business, was suppressed by the mother
bank in Philadelphia. We visited two churches, one Methodist and one Episcopalian; the former was large, both of
them plain, and contained nothing worthy of remark. We
paid a visit to Mr. Hufnagle, a native of Wurzburgh, an
elderly man, who had experienced misfortune, and who is now
established as a butcher and trader in cattle, and finds himself in easy circumstances. He appeared very much delighted at my visit, and received us very heartily in his well
arranged house situated in an orchard. Between two and

three o'clock the stage took me to Colonel King's house, where we dined, in order to drive us eighteen miles to Tarleton. We took leave of him with grateful hearts for so much kindness and hospitality."

Many pleasant reminiscences are recounted of those early days of the pleasant, well arranged social reunions, and the little circle of cultivated women yearning for an increase of knowledge, meeting daily for their readings and interchange of thought, of the determined efforts to help the suffering and those less fortunate than themselves, and in every way to develop the church idea in all its beautiful possibilities. A record of Mrs. Peter's life at this time would be incomplete without the mention of two names identified with her daily occupations and unswerving affection. The trio was Mrs. Douglas, Mrs. King, and Miss Eliza Claypoole, afterward Mrs. Carson and mother of Dr. William Carson, the eminent physician of Cincinnati. She was a daughter of a Philadelphia gentleman of family and high social position, who came at an early day to Chillicothe in the interest of the United States Bank. His daughters were all lovely and accomplished, but the affections of Mrs. King seemed to incline her especially to the second daughter. Their tastes were similar and their hearts were in accord. Their love for reading and their love for the church drew them closely together, and the same strong bond attached to them the cultivated and admired Mrs. Richard Douglas. The three were in daily intercourse, and the friendship was only interrupted by the removal of Mrs. King from Chillicothe, and finally by death.

Without any positive knowledge as to the early planting in the heart of the young child that love for a church

of order and liturgical system, which became more and
more developed with her soul's growth, we can but feel
that the influence of the excellent English lady, her first
teacher, Mrs. Keats, made the impression on her young
life which was to come to perfect fruitage in after years.

Though Governor Worthington and his wife were
brought up under the influence of the Anglican Church,
at the time of their removal to Ohio, there being no
Episcopal, the one became a Methodist, the other a Presbyterian.   The daughter afterward found her happiness
in the Episcopal Church, and when the first parish was
formed, she threw all her energies into the work.   This
parish was organized in 1818 by the Rev. Mr. Searle.
In 1820, the first church edifice was commenced, and the
building consecrated by the Right Rev. Philander Chase,
first bishop of Ohio.   Although parishes had been established in divers places throughout the state, this was the
first Episcopal church consecration which had been made
in the diocese.

We find the names of Mr. and Mrs. King prominent in
all the work of the parish during their residence in Chillicothe.   Mr. King frequently represented the parish in
convention, and Mrs. King, though full of the cares of
the young wife and the young mother, was foremost
among the women workers in all beneficent church work.

The first regularly installed rector of the parish was
the Rev. Ezra Kellogg.   The congregation continued to
occupy the first erected building till the year 1836, when
the little edifice became unequal to the accommodation
of the increased number of parishioners.   It was sold to
the Right Rev. Bishop Purcell, and was occupied for
many years as a Catholic ·church.   Since then, it has
fallen into less worthy hands and is used for more unholy
purposes.

We have dwelt long, perhaps tediously, upon these early years, but it was the formative period of a character, which in after years, by its strong individuality and strength of purpose, was enabled to conquer adverse conditions and to bring all circumstances in subjection to her own good will, to effect her own benevolent plans.

It is not without its lesson for those who would work as she did. Self-forgetfulness, except in the cultivation of every power with which she was endowed, untiring zeal for the welfare of others, an earnest and systematic mode of life, were nurtured by every event of her early life. Even the "discipline of sorrow," that most potent of teachers, came to her as to all, in ways seen and unseen, for there are dark chambers in every life which the stranger may not enter, but which may become the Holy of Holies and the guest chamber for angelic visitors.

CINCINNATI,

1831–1836.

" So should we live that every hour
May die as dies the natural flower,
A self-reviving thing of power ;
That every thought and every deed
May hold within itself the seed
Of future good and future meed."

—MILNE.

"And all may do what has been done."

—YOUNG.

(30)

CHAPTER II.

FIRST HOME IN CINCINNATI—DEATH OF A SON—CHURCH INTER-
EST—ORPHAN ASYLUM—PICTURE OF CINCINNATI BY CHARLES
FENNO HOFFMAN—SOCIETY LIFE—SEMICOLON PARTIES—NEW
FRIENDSHIPS—ILLNESS OF GEN. KING—MRS. KING'S VISIT TO
CAMBRIDGE—DEATH OF GEN. KING.

IN the year 1831, Mr. and Mrs. King removed to Cincinnati, then a city of thirty thousand inhabitants, noted for its cultivated and refined society, the beauty of its surroundings, and the cleanliness and loveliness of its external appearance.

A few years later, Charles Dickens made his first visit to this city, and speaks with enthusiasm of the beautiful homes, their little front yards filled with flowers, and the purity and cleanliness of the atmosphere, a singular contrast to the present sooty atmosphere and badly kept streets. It was late in the thirties when the work began of cutting down the magnificent forests which swept in all their primeval splendor down the slopes of the surrounding hills into the valley, where the prosperous little city clung close to the banks of the beautiful river, the only outlet for its commerce. The extensive, well-graded, well-paved quay was the city's pride—made always gay by the floating palaces which swept the Ohio river from its source to its union with the still vaster Mississippi, thronged with those monarchs of trade from the great Falls of St. Anthony to the Gulf of Mexico.

Before the introduction of railways, the rivers were

the highways of travel, and cities resting on the shores
of the rivers were marts of commerce and centers of
civilization.   All ways of transportation by water commanded more attention and more lavish expenditure than
now.   The steamboats which plowed these great waters
were truly floating palaces, and excursions which were
then made are now as tales of wonderland.   Great parties would be formed, from Pittsburgh, Cincinnati, Louisville, St. Louis, for a voyage to New Orleans, to be a
gala of festivity, where dance and song would reign su-
preme for a week or more, before reaching that gayest
and most fascinating of all cities, New Orleans, which
was to be the climax of mirth and happiness in the enjoyment of the opera and all the charms of that region
of flowers and mirth.

The return voyage would be equally delightful, and
longer; full two weeks would be passed in steaming
against the rapid current of the Mississippi.   Stops long
enough at all the principal towns would be made for
friends to meet and kindly greetings to be exchanged.
The peculiar and strange plantation life, so unfamiliar to
northern eyes, would furnish many pictures and throw
much variety into the voyage.   It was not a time of
bustle and haste, as now.   Railroad cars were not to be
boarded on the minute, to rush, like inexorable fate, to
the journey's end, but the wave of a flag, or the signal
of a hand, would bring the graceful steamer to the lovely
shore, where, if aught might come up of interest, the ac-
commodating commander was always ready to delay an
hour or two, and many charming little detours could
thus be made.

Cincinnati, at this time, proudly and deservedly bore
the name of " Queen of the West," for she had no rivals,
neither in commerce nor in culture.   The sister cities of

Louisville and St. Louis claimed no rivalry, and Chicago was not known even in dreams. The site where she now asserts her grand individuality was still the sparsely-settled, wind-swept shore of Lake Michigan.

So graphic and truthful a description is given of Cincinnati in the book of Mr. Charles Fenno Hoffman, "A Winter in the West," in 1834, that we are tempted to use this observant writer's words rather than our own, as they express so pleasantly a very faithful picture.

"It was a still, sunny morning, when in rounding one of those beautiful promontories, which form so striking a feature in the scenery of the Ohio river, we came suddenly upon a cluster of gardens and villas, which indicated the vicinity of a flourishing town, and our boat, taking a sudden sheer from the shore, before the eye had time to study out their grouping and disposition, the whole City of Cincinnati, embosomed in its amphitheater of green hills, was brought at once before us. It rises on two inclined planes from the river, the one elevated about fifty feet above the other, and both running parallel to the Ohio. The streets are broad, occasionally lined with trees, and generally well built of brick, though there are some pretty churches and noble private dwellings of cut stone and of stucco. Of the latter, there are several with greater pretensions to architectural beauty than any which I remember in New York. The first impression upon touching the quay in Cincinnati, and looking up its spacious avenues, terminating always in the green acclivities which bound the city, is exceedingly beautiful, and your good opinion of the town suffers no diminution when you have an opportunity to examine its well washed streets and tasteful private residences. Of the rides and walks in the suburbs, I can not speak too warmly. The girdle of green hills already spoken of, on some of which the primeval forest still lingers in the aged trees, command some of the most beautiful views you can imagine, of the opposite shores of Kentucky, with the two pretty manufacturing vil-

lages on either side of the Licking river, which debouches opposite to Cincinnati.   Cincinnati herself, with her twenty
gilded spires gleaming among gardens and shrubbery, lies, as
if spread upon a map, beneath you, while before attaining
this commanding height, you have been rewarded when winding up the steep ascent by a hundred charming glimpses of
groves and villas scattered along the banks of the beautiful
Ohio.   Verily, if beauty alone confer empire, it is in vain for
thriving Pittsburgh, or flourishing Louisville, bustling and
buxom as they are, to dispute with Cincinnati her title of
' Queen of the West.'   The population of the place is about
thirty thousand; among them you see very few but what look
comfortable and contented, though the town does not wear
the brisk and busy air observable at Louisville.   Transportation is so easy along the great western waters, that you see no
lounging poor people about the large towns, as when business
languishes in one place, and it is difficult to find occupation,
they are off at once to another, and shift their quarters
whither the readiest means of living invite them.   What
would most strike you in the streets of Cincinnati, would be
the number of pretty faces and stylish figures one meets in a
morning.   A walk through Broadway here rewards one hardly
less than to promenade its New York namesake.   I have had
more than one opportunity of seeing those western beauties
by candle light, and the evening display brought no disappointment to the morning promise.   Nothing can be more
agreeable than the society one meets with in the gay and elegantly furnished drawing rooms of Cincinnati.   The materials being from every state in the Union.   There is a total
want of caste, a complete absence of selfishness, if I may use
the word.   If there be any characteristic which may jar upon
your taste and habits, it is, perhaps, a want of that harmonious blending of light and shade, that repose of both character
and manner which distinguish the best circles in our Atlantic
cities, and so often sinks into insipidity, or runs into a ridicu-
lous imitation of the impertinent nonchalance which the

pseudo picturer of English 'high life,' in the novels of the day impose upon our simple republicans as the height of elegance and refinement. It is in the highest degree absurd to speak of Cincinnati as a provincial place, when the most agreeable persons here hail originally from New York, or Philadelphia, Boston, or Baltimore, and are very tenacious of the styles of living in which they have been educated.

"I have been here now nearly ten days, and scarcely an hour has passed without some gay and agreeable engagement. The acquaintance of Mr. King and Mr. Pendleton, both formerly of New York, and now distinguished members of the Ohio bar, inducted me at once into all the society of the place. My table was covered with cards on the morning of my arrival, and I see no end to the hospitalities should I prolong my stay. A literary soiree and a sporting club dinner would perhaps be two of the most characteristic circles into which I could carry you, but description would be nothing without the music that gave variety to the spirit of the one, or the delicious birds that lent a relish to the jokes of the other.

"The principal buildings of Cincinnati, besides more than twenty churches, some of which are very pretty, and several fine hotels, one of which, the Pearl Street House, would rival the best in New York, are the Cincinnati College, a couple of theaters, four market-houses, one of which is five hundred feet in length, a court-house, United States Branch Bank, Medical College, Mechanical Institute, Catholic Atheneum, Hospital, High School, and two museums.

"The collection of one of these museums is exceedingly interesting, embracing a number of enormous organic remains among the curiosities, with antique vases and various singular domestic utensils, excavated from some of the ancient mounds in Ohio," etc.

Thus does this pleasant writer go on giving entertaining and truthful pictures of the city which was to be the home of Mrs. King through many future years at different periods of her life.

Such was the place when General and Mrs. King arrived, in 1831, and such the cultivated society in which she at once took her place among the most admired and best loved.

Mr. King, or, as he was called, General King, from the position he held in the state militia, came to Cincinnati, as a larger field in which to exercise his acknowledged talent in his profession. He soon took and held a high place as barrister, and as one of the founders of the Law School. This same school has as one of its professors now Mr. Rufus King, eldest son of General Edward King. Mrs. King was at this time well known as one of the leading intellectual women in the country. Her frequent visits to the eastern cities, and her elegant hospitality in her beautiful home to strangers, made her reputation more than provincial. The rare gifts with which nature had endowed her had not been neglected in the calmer life she had led in the more quiet town of Chillicothe, and when she appeared on the larger field that Cincinnati offered, her advent was hailed with delight, and she soon became prominent in the highest circles which at that time, more than at any subsequent period in the city's history, was characterized by intellectual cultivation, gracious hospitalities, and gentle manners.

Their fortune enabled Mr. and Mrs. King to live in a style to extend such hospitalities as placed their home at the head of hospitable mansions. Music, in which Mrs. King excelled, both as critic and as a proficient, gave character to many of her assemblies, and at that time a literary tone brought out wit and humor, which gave zest to charming entertainments, to which Mrs. King was not alone in her graceful contributions. The charming Caroline Lee Hentz, so well known as novelist and dramatist, was at that time, a teacher of young ladies in Cincinnati, and one of the most useful and ornamental members of this fine society. Her beauty, her grace, and her ready pen were important elements in the society in which she moved. Her impress may be traced in the culture and taste of those who profited by her instruction and wide yet womanly views—Catherine Beecher, the accomplished and well known writer, and her still more distinguished sister, Harriet Beecher Stowe. It would be impossible to mention all the bright minds and gracious hearts uniting to make a complete whole. But it is impossible to give a full idea of Mrs. King's surroundings without mentioning some of the marked minds with which she came in contact. No man was more noted in the earlier history of the west, and in laying the foundation of Cincinnati's prosperity than Dr. Daniel Drake. "The able writer, the skillful practitioner and teacher in his profession, united with a devotion to public interests, made him a marked man." His social qualities were equally admirable. Then also there was James Hall, the author of "Sketches of the West" and "Border Tales and Legends of the West." He had distinguished himself as an officer in the army, and was prominent for his gallantry in many of the early, hard-fought battles against the British forces in 1812. After his marriage, he studied and practised law, retiring to a quiet life, and amusing himself with his pen, which he so skillfully wielded. His knowledge of Indian character, of early pioneer life, which his graphic pen so well portrays, the purity of his style, the expression of a highly poetic mind, will cause his works to be read as classic lore a hundred years hence, when the ephemeral literature

3

home of Mrs. King through many future years at different periods of her life.

Such was the place when General and Mrs. King arrived, in 1831, and such the cultivated society in which she at once took her place among the most admired and best loved.

Mr. King, or, as he was called, General King, from the position he held in the state militia, came to Cincinnati, as a larger field in which to exercise his acknowledged talent in his profession. He soon took and held a high place as barrister, and as one of the founders of the Law School. This same school has as one of its professors now Mr. Rufus King, eldest son of General Edward King. Mrs. King was at this time well known as one of the leading intellectual women in the country. Her frequent visits to the eastern cities, and her elegant hospitality in her beautiful home to strangers, made her reputation more than provincial. The rare gifts with which nature had endowed her had not been neglected in the calmer life she had led in the more quiet town of Chillicothe, and when she appeared on the larger field that Cincinnati offered, her advent was hailed with delight, and she soon became prominent in the highest circles which at that time, more than at any subsequent period in the city's history, was characterized by intellectual cultivation, gracious hospitalities, and gentle manners.

Their fortune enabled Mr. and Mrs. King to live in a style to extend such hospitalities as placed them at the head of hospitable mansions. Mrs. King excelled, both as critic and character to many of her assem' literary tone brought out w to charming entertainme

alone in her graceful contributions. ████
line Lee Hentz, so well known ████
was at that time, a teacher of ████
and one of the most useful and ████ ██
this fine society. Her beauty ████
pen were important elements ████
moved. Her impress may ████
taste of those who profess by ████
yet womanly views—████
plished and well known ████
guished sister, Harriet ████
possible to mention all ████
hearts uniting to make ████
possible to give a full ████
without mentioning ████
which she came in ████
the earlier history of ████
tion of Cincinnati's ████
"The able writer ████
his profession ████
made him a ████
equally ████
the author of ████
Tales and Legends ████

l
s
d-
rt.
rcle
and
The
wn in
fellow
uinnati,
a gentle
u interest

Cincinnati, ████ ne a
the death

which has now supplanted them will have run its course and will have passed into oblivion.

These brilliant minds, and many more, contributed to the entertainment of the "Semicolon parties," as they were oddly called, literary parties which combined the *conversazione*, the reading club, the musical recital, and the dance. Only in the youth of a city, before society began to crystallize into set forms, could these informal, unique assemblies exist. Their existence, too, must depend upon conditions of good taste. The Semicolon parties were begun in the home of Mrs. Samuel Foote, a graceful and gracious lady, who enlisted with her Mrs. Charles Stetson. Both ladies were noted for good taste, kindliness of manner, and hospitable inclinations. These homes, even in these days of luxury, would be considered centers of art and elegance. Fine paintings adorned their walls; beautiful statuary filled the niches; and flowers, winter and summer, were spread lavishly around.

There was then in Cincinnati a remarkable degree of culture in every direction, and a combination of wit and education rarely to be found. These parties were to be carried out on strict æsthetic principles. A glass of fine old wine, with its accompanying delicious sponge cake, the cup of fragrant coffee, and sandwiches, at the close of the evening, was all that could be allowed to minister to the grosser nature. Never was present a larger number than could be made comfortable in the capacious drawing-room. The thoroughly social and unceremonious nature of these parties was shown by the busy fingers of the ladies employed in pretty fancy or knitting work.

A certain number of original pieces, essays, poems, stories, were expected on each occasion, running through all the scale of pathos and humor. Mr. William Greene, whom all old Cincinnati people will remember as the

genial, accomplished, intelligent gentleman, was by general consent chosen reader, and well did his sympathetic
nature, ever ready for a smile or a tear, satisfy the authors of the various effusions. After the readings were
closed came the music, always rendered by masterly
hands; then the close was the joyous dance —the social
quadrille, and the merry Virginia reel, for then the
round dances were whirling their dizzy courses in far-off
lands, and had not yet ventured upon America's more
puritanic shores.

The reel closed the evening, always led by the jovial
reader and a merry hearted young girl over whose evening of life is cast the beautiful afterglow of those sunny
days.

As time went on, other homes were opened to alternate with Mrs. Foote and Mrs. Stetson in these charming entertainments. Mrs. Greene, Mrs. King, and Mrs.
Springer were among the privileged, but Mrs. Stetson's
name is the one most closely identified with the Semicolon parties, and in her beautiful home were extended
warm hospitalities which have gladdened many a
stranger's heart, and under the patronage of this excellent lady was developed much of Cincinnati's early art.
There are so many names to recall in this brilliant circle
that silence is our best refuge. Over all the bright and
winsome spirits, Mrs. King held a queenly sway. The
grandeur of her character, however, is best shown in
her active interest in all that could benefit her fellow
beings, and the foundations made not only in Cincinnati,
but in Philadelphia, remain to speak of what a gentle
woman may do by a loving heart and an active interest
for the unfortunate of her race.

During the second year of the residence in Cincinnati,
a great grief came to Mr. and Mrs. King in the death

of their third son, the little James, a bright boy of five years. In the new home, surrounded by comparative strangers, it was a hard blow to the young mother, but in all the sorrows of her life we shall find that her grief was only a key to unlock the deeper fountains of love for all, and to give her new strength to fulfill the duties broadcast around her. So we see her again soon in the discharge of the active obligations of her position. It was after this grief that they established themselves in the commodious and beautiful home at the corner of Fourth and Vine streets, which was to become the center of such gracious hospitality.

A saying of Goethe, that he never had an affliction which did not turn into a poem, so, if we observe whenever the heart of this dear lady was crushed, it sent out more abundant blessing and beneficent work.

Mrs. King's work was not confined to the church with which she had connected her religious life, though there her work was constant and efficient—of this we shall speak under another heading—but she identified herself with the band of active spirits who first planned and carried out the foundation of the Cincinnati Protestant Orphan Asylum, an institution which has grown with the growth of the city, and which is still pointed out as one of the ornaments and blessings of Cincinnati.

In the more than fifty years of existence thousands of helpless children have been cared for, and have gone forth from its protection to be useful citizens. With Mrs. Burnet, Mrs. Davis, Mrs. Staughton, Mrs. Bates, Mrs. Young, and other benevolent women, Mrs. King worked efficiently in this enterprise. A lot of ground, comprising about ten acres, was offered to the managers for the uses of the asylum by the city authorities, and accepted. On a part of the ground was a building sufficiently adapted to a temporary occupation. This ground had been used for the burial of the poor— the "Old Potter's Field," which may be remembered by our older residents as occupying a part of the city now known as the "West End." A portion of it is the beautiful Lincoln Park. At that time all this part of the city was but the low marshy borders of Mill creek. After remaining a few years in this place, they were again approached by the donors with a proposition to exchange the ten acres for a lot of about one acre in a more central and eligible situation, being on Elm street, where now stands the Music Hall and Exposition buildings. This offer was considered favorably by a majority of the managers, Mrs. King being in the minority, who opposed the proposition. A commodious house was erected on the new ground and occupied for many years. It was finally bought by the city, and the asylum was removed to Mt. Auburn. This was the only public institution in which Mrs. King was actively engaged during her first residence in Cincinnati, but church work in all its interests, of Sunday-school, church music, looking after the poor, etc., engaged her unceasing efforts. The great interest of her life, that into which she threw her whole soul, was for the benefit and elevation of women. It was not until she became a resident of Philadelphia that the way was opened to her to carry out her benevolent wishes for her own sex.

Ever eager to do for others, especially for those bound closely by family ties, Mrs. King had always found abundant opportunities for offering advantages to the younger members of her family. While in Chillicothe her home was the center of attraction to her sisters and brothers, and in many ways she sacrificed her own comfort for them. Mrs. King, finding better schools in Cincinnati than were in Chillicothe, gave her youngest sister, then a girl of fifteen years, the opportunity of availing herself of these higher advantages in education, and Miss Elizabeth Worthington was for two years an inmate of her sister's beautiful home. A niece, too, the daughter of her older sister, whose husband had removed with his family to the wilds of Texas, was brought back from this border life and lived under her aunt's kindly influence, with every advantage that could be bestowed upon her for three or four years; grew up to a useful womanhood, and became the wife of a gentleman from the south of influence and respectability. These would be trifles scarcely worthy the attention of the reader, but as indicative of the spirit within, ever ready to extend the hand of help, a spirit which never rested in the desire to do for others.

It was in the beginning of the winter of 1834, that General King began to feel the first inroads of what was to be his fatal malady, and to avert the ill results of an illness from which he had suffered, his physician advised a winter in the south. It was not necessary, nor would it have been best in every view that Mrs. King should accompany him. Home affairs needed supervision, and the oldest son was recalled from Kenyon College, to go with his father on a journey which would be highly advantageous to a boy of his age, apart from the comfort he would be to his father as a companion. The change was beneficial, and afforded father and son much pleasure.

During the following summer, it was determined to place their son Rufus at Harvard, for the superior advantages he would have there over Kenyon, and as General King's health, though improved, was not strong

enough for him to undertake so hard a journey, it was
thought best that he should avail himself of the quiet
home of Mrs. Worthington, at Adena, and that Mrs.
King should accompany her son, and see that he was
properly entered upon his course of study. As her own
health was not very vigorous, and depressing anxiety had
worn upon her, she planned the tour for one of benefit
to herself, as well as to her son. This was before the
days of railroad travel, and the journey was to be made
through the picturesque mountains of Western Virginia
by stage-coach. After accompanying General King to
Adena, and remaining long enough to find that he improved in the healthful surroundings of this beautiful
country home, Mrs. King and her son set forth on their
journey to take the steamer at Portsmouth, which would
carry them to their entrance into the Virginia mountains.
On the boat they had the good fortune to meet a charming party of friends who would be their *compagnons de
voyage* through the mountains. The party consisted of
Mr. Robert Rives, of Virginia, and his daughter, and
Mr. William C. Rives, former minister to France, and
United States Senator from Virginia, who had been visiting friends in Cincinnati, Dr. Landon C. Rives, and
Mrs. Rives, who were among the nearest and most cherished friends of General and Mrs. King. With this delightful party, the journey was commenced with antici-
pations of great pleasure. Among other enjoyments suggested, as Mrs. King had expressed much interest in Mr.
Madison, and admiration for his character, Mr. Rives
urged her to stop for a day at Montpelier, offering her a
letter of introduction. He well knew how much delight
Mr. and Mrs. Madison would have in receiving this brilliant, gifted woman, whose charming society he so
thoroughly appreciated. Every moment of the journey

was a pleasure to be remembered by each member of the
party, and a bond of friendship was established which
was strengthened in after years by delightful intercourse,
and by the forming of family ties. Mrs. King and her
son were received warmly and hospitably at Montpelier,
where they spent the day and dined, and had a most satisfactory chat with the venerable ex-president, who
seemed only to regret that a longer visit could not be
made. The impression made upon Mrs. King sustained
the high respect she had always held for the pure and up-
right character of this dignified statesman. The steps
of the travelers were then turned toward Washington,
where a delay long enough was made to see the public
buildings, and to make a call of respect at the White
House. The president, General Jackson, was not at
home, but their curiosity was gratified by the courtesy of
those in charge, who, with great civility, opened the
doors for the visitors. Passing through Baltimore and
Philadelphia, New York was reached, where family visits
were to be made. Mr. Charles King, afterward president
of Columbia College, at that time lived in the city. To
his house Mrs. King and her son were first invited ; from
there they visited Highwood, the residence of Mr. James
G. King, and Jamaica, at that time occupied by Mr. John
King, later Governor King, of New York. Jamaica was
the ancestral home, the residence of Mr. Rufus King at
the time of his death.

After a pleasant and satisfactory visit to New York,
Mrs. King continued her journey to Cambridge, by way
of New Haven, where she was hospitably entertained by
the family of Mr. Hillhouse, poet and littérateur, living
in beautiful style in that delightful city of cultivated
men and women. From thence they proceeded by way
of Worcester to Boston—and it was at Worcester they

entered the first railroad car they had seen. On arriving at Cambridge, Mrs. King took lodgings at Mrs. Newell's, where she remained a week or ten days making necessary arrangements for the comfort of her son.

After every thing was satisfactorily settled, Mrs. King started on her homeward journey, which in those days was far more tedious than now, and as her mind was not entirely free from anxiety on account of Mr. King's health, it was necessarily a long and lonely journey. She found, too, on her arrival at home, that her husband's health had not improved. Surrounded by kind friends he had needed nothing that kindness and love could give, and there was no reason for Mrs. King to regret the step she had taken, but on the contrary a duty had been performed which was equally satisfactory to husband and wife, and the journey had brought health and strength for the trials which were in store for them.

The illness which preceded General King's visit to the south was thought to have been the result of overtaxing his strength, in a political contest into which he was persuaded to enter by those who knew his power as a public speaker and the magnetic influence he had over men. With all the enthusiasm of his nature he entered the field only to find, after the excitement was over, that he had done himself an irreparable wrong. The apparent benefit which had come from the southern tour was but of short duration. Nothing that skill in medicine, nor in the watchful care of a loving wife and friends in kind nursing, seemed to check the rapid strides of the fatal malady, and, after much suffering with entire composure and submission, he passed from this mortal life February 6, 1836. A correct idea may be formed of this distinguished man from the subjoined extract taken from a journal at the time of his death:

" In contemplating the character of Mr. King, there was much to admire. He possessed a fine and versatile genius. His mind was quick and acute in perception, his imagination vivid and playful; his elocution chaste, rapid, and impressive. As a successful and eloquent advocate he enjoyed throughout the state of his adoption the reputation of standing among the first of his profession, of which he was an ornament.* His attainments in his profession were varied and extensive. He was ardent, impulsive, and kind-hearted, with great urbanity of manner, unvarying cheerfulness of disposition, and colloquial powers of the first order. He was always a welcome member of the social circle, in which his absence will long be felt and lamented. General King was buried in the family burying-ground of Governor Worthington, at Adena, which was finally transferred to the public cemetery at Chillicothe."

Thus sadly closed the first residence in Cincinnati of the lady of whom we write.

Quick to arrive at conclusions, Mrs. King at once decided that her life's interest should be thrown with the two sons who were left her, and we next find her settled in Cambridge, to be a guide and help to those so dear to her heart, and who lived to be a reward to her for all her anxieties and care.

---

* While engaged in the practice of his profession General King was several times returned to the House of Representatives and Senate of Ohio, and in two sessions was Speaker of the House.

CAMBRIDGE,

1835–1840.

" The crags of Duty scaled
Are close upon the table-lands
To which our God himself is Sun and Moon."
—TENNYSON.

"She was ever mindful of the primal duties which shine aloft like stars."

(48)

CHAPTER III.

REMOVAL TO CAMBRIDGE—EDUCATION OF HER SONS—A NEW HOUSEHOLD — LIFE AND SOCIETY — CIRCLE OF FRIENDS — STUDIES—VISITS TO MAINE—CLOSE OF CAMBRIDGE LIFE.

MRS. KING, having decided upon her future course in reference to her sons, determined to arrange her affairs as speedily as possible, and establish herself at Cambridge, that she might in every way protect and advance the interests of her boys. In the fall of 1836, she found herself at Cambridge. For several months, she remained in lodgings, that she might look around and advantageously settle herself for a residence of several years. She was fortunate in the selection of her boarding-house, especially for the pleasant association she immediately formed with the Misses Davis and their sailor brother, who afterward became Admiral Davis, of the United States Navy.

Through these ladies, Mrs. King made the acquaintance of their sister, Mrs. William Minot, of Boston, a lady of rare good sense and acquirements, who became to Mrs. King the most familiar and congenial friend of this period of her life. Through Mrs. Minot, Mrs. King made other valuable and charming friends. The ladies of President Quincy's household were among her earliest visitors, and the friendship she made with the president himself proved not only a delight to her but a valuable aid to her sons, who, even after they left college, had many evidences of the continued interest of their hon-

(49)

ored friend. During the later life of President Quincy, after he had retired to the seclusion of his loved home at Quincy, visits of respect were made by Mr. King's sons, and with delight does the writer recall a visit to the venerable sage in company with her husband, when the shadows of evening were closing around the path of the wise old man, but like a grand monument of worth, he stood erect, unmarred and undimmed by the conflicts of the day. The courtesy and gallantry of the old school gentleman still marked his manners, and the brightness of the eye and the readiness of speech betrayed no evidence of the old man approaching his ninetieth year. Set in the quaint, beautiful surroundings of his home of many generations, it was an impressive and glowing picture, full of the lessons of a well-spent life.

Mrs. King found in Mrs. Quincy the traits of a very remarkable woman, whose friendship she was proud to secure, but a more familiar intercourse was established with the daughters, who were nearer her own age.

The strong feature, however, of Mrs. King's character was reverence—a looking up always, that led her through all her life to seek the companionship of those who had gone through the experiences of life and profited by their teachings. Thus, the society of President and Mrs. Quincy was eagerly sought by the still young woman, and she was frequently and always a welcome guest at the president's house.

Mrs. King allowed but little time to pass before she turned her attention to the interests of the church of her love, at that time the Protestant Episcopal Church. A large number of her friends were Unitarians, but she found in the family of Judge Fay a delightful congeniality in her church work. The young and beautiful Miss Maria Fay became a charming worker in her band, and the sons always retained pleasant memories of the days over which Miss Fay had thrown such luster.

Mrs. King at once identified her church life with the Christ Church parish, organized in the year 1761. In this old church she worked heartily during her residence at Cambridge, and it is a curious fact that three young rectors who ministered in this parish through four years of her residence there became bishops of the church— Bishop Williams, Bishop Vail, and Bishop Howe. The beautiful shade-trees which now surround this church are due to her taste and energy.

Mrs. King soon found that the life for her sons could be made brighter, the attractions of home greater, by going into a house of her own and enlarging the family circle. So, with the desire to do good in its widest sense possible, she decided to arrange for her nephews, James and Gracie King, sons of Mr. James G. King, to become inmates of her home. She also persuaded her mother to allow her youngest brother, a youth of about the age of her own sons, to come to her for the advantage of a course at Harvard.

Thus she established herself with five boys, with the determination to stir them up to the development of all that was good within, and to make them happy in their outward life. This was no easy task, but success rewarded her determined will. Her home was a center for all their friends. Youths from far off southern and western homes, among them the son of her early friend, Mrs. Douglas, who was always especially welcomed to the home circle. These were gladdened, perhaps, saved from many reckless ways by the sunny influence of this good woman, with all her kindly and attractive manners. Although the style of this charming home was simple and unostentatious, there was no home in Cambridge more delightful nor any place where so great a number of brilliant spirits might be found. Among the many friends who contributed to the happy life of Mrs. King and her family of boys, was the charming household of Major Lomax, at that time the officer in command at the Arsenal at Watertown. The residence was a beautiful and attractive one, situated on the Charles river, with a fine outlook, but still more charming and attractive were the ladies of the family—Mrs. Lomax herself being a highly accomplished daughter of Virginia, with all the dignity and attractiveness of the southern woman. The young ladies were worthy of the mother, and their graceful and gracious ways gave great charm to the lives of our young students. One was made most happy by becoming the husband a few years after of the beautiful and brilliant Jane Tayloe Lomax, whose genius and early development of talent too soon passed from earthly scenes, for her death as Mrs. Francis Worthington occurred when she was but twenty-five years of age. Her gift of ideality and power of expression was of a high order, as is shown by exquisite gems of poetry which remain to tell of her talent. The pleasant evenings with Mrs. Storrow and Mrs. Higginson, mother of Thomas Wentworth Higginson, the distinguished littérateur, were always remembered by Mrs. King with pleasure, for these were coteries where were assembled men and women of brilliant wit and intelligence. Those were days when men like Longfellow, Ticknor, Prescott, Pickering, Quincy were authoritative representative men.

Wherever Mrs. King held her sway, music was always a power in her hand, herself a cultivated and critical pianist. Her sons, too, were both lovers of music, and with voice and on instrument were proficients, so that music always lent its cheering influence at her assemblies. Mrs. King had the satisfaction to see all these youths become useful and respectable men, adorning and benefiting the circles in which they moved.

After her first object, the welfare of her sons, had been provided for, the next thought was given to the employment of her own leisure hours. Quick to seize the·opportunity at the right moment, Mrs. King felt that in this environment of intellect was the proper period for her own self-culture. Her recent affliction rendered an entrance into the frivolities and gayeties of fashionable life distasteful, even impossible for her, and further than to contribute to the cheerfulness of the young lives about her, the disposition was to be quiet and secluded. Language had always been a favorite study of Mrs. King, and here excellent masters were to be readily secured. She had already made progress in French and German, but to these she now added Italian, and became interested in a wanderer from sunny Italy, poor and friendless, the since notorious Mariotti, to whom she showed important kindnesses in many ways, which were misconstrued by this man full of conceit and vanity, who rewarded his kind patroness in after years by recording in a book his impertinent misapprehensions.

He, however, was a very good teacher, and at that time behaved himself with respect and modesty, and Mrs. King profited much by his teaching.

This determination to make herself mistress of the modern languages seemed to evidence an almost prophetic sense, for the facility she had acquired in speaking the different languages of Europe served her well in the travels of later life.

This period in Cambridge might be characterized as the time of intellectual growth, for in the very atmos-

4

phere seemed to be the spirit of advance, and the constant contact with men of intellect gave bent to the entire life.

Mrs. King's residence at Cambridge was always remembered by her as a period of special interest in the formation of many friendships, and bringing her in close interchange of thought with strong and cultivated minds. At that time there were many men of great superiority clustering around this center of learning and good taste, with all of whom Mrs. King found congenial association. No one had a higher place in her regard than Mr. John Pickering, whose character and scholarship is too well known to need notice here. As the oldest son of an honored father (Colonel Timothy Pickering), every advantage came to him that birth and heredity could give. He was a man of learning, fine taste, and a philanthropist in the widest sense. It is not wonderful that a strong friendship should spring up between two persons of like nature and aim.

A fine miniature of himself, which Mr. Pickering gave to Mrs. King on parting, gives the expression of a most pure, gentle, and noble nature. It has been a pleasure to Mrs. Peter's son since her death to restore this fine likeness to a member of Mr. Pickering's family.

In no part of Mrs. King's life do we find her less preoccupied by outward charitable work. Not that this strong element in her nature was dormant—only turned in different and quieter channels. With the aptness which marked this lady's desire to seize opportunities, was combined a penetration in selecting, a rare judgment in deciding what was best among many good things. In Cambridge much was offered in many ways, but her wisdom told her that not again in her whole life might she have the same opportunities given for the cultivation

of her intellectual part—always would occasions arise for
the exercise of her charitable nature which for the time
could be subordinated without injury.

Was she not absorbed in the greatest of all her life
work—the training of those five youths to be mighty
powers in the battle of life? Well might she rest from
other works of charity!

The class of 1838, of which her oldest son was a
graduate, proved to be a mine of rarest ore. Men came
from the class who have made their mark in the world;
whose names stand among the foremost of their generation. The genius of Story will be known as long as lasts
the adamant which has embodied the noble ideas; and as
poet, statesman, cultivated man of letters, the name of
James Russell Lowell will be known through generations
to come. The church, the bar, the healing art, the army,
all had marked men from this class, who have adorned
their adopted professions. The longevity of the members of the class, too, is something remarkable; so
many are yet active in life, as their late semi-centennial
celebration has proved.

Mrs. King had always indulged a desire to visit the
native state of her children's distinguished grandfather,
Mr. Rufus King, and in a vacation a visit was planned to
the last remaining brother of this honored gentleman.
Governor William King, of Maine, was yet living, and
Mrs. King and her sons determined to pay a visit of respect, and to see some of the revered old homes and
haunts of their ancestors. A voyage had to be made
from Boston to Bath, which at that time was the only
communication, except by the toilsome, fatiguing journey
by stage-coach. The weather proved stormy, the waves
ran high, and the "rock-bound coast" was somewhat
appalling; but the voyage was made in safety, and the

voyagers were landed in good time at Bath, the place of residence of the former governor of the state, the Honorable William King. They were greeted with great warmth by a majestic, ruddy-faced, genial old gentleman, with one of those deep-toned, resonant bass voices so characteristic of the northern New Englander. The home was of the best class of large, comfortable old mansions in New England, situated not far from the sea, on the Kennebec. This beautiful river spread out in majestic width for some miles above the point where its waters were lost in the great ocean. From every window in the house, charming picturesque views were to be seen, and the deep, tranquil river's flow was suggestive of thought high and ennobling to the mind.

One may well understand how those boys, after their shut-up life with their studies, enjoyed the freedom of this fine old home and the genial heartiness of the old uncle. Mrs. King received great pleasure and satisfaction from the familiar chats she enjoyed with a man who had been so distinguished in his day, and had been in such close association with the greatest men of those days of great men, himself the brother of the most distinguished among them. He retained the full vigor of his mind, and still occupied himself in active duties. One of the most pleasant excursions made was the result of the still active interest of Governor King in matters of education and advance. He was one of the overseers of Waterville College, and it was on the occasion of a commencement that an excursion was made of several day's duration, and the young Harvard junior was honored with a seat on the platform, one of those attentions to youth never forgotten. While at Portland, where Mrs. King went, on suggestion of Mr. William King, to visit family friends, the families of General Wingate and Dr. Merrill, the

near town of Scarborough, the birthplace of Mr. Rufus
King, was also visited. Several delightful weeks were
passed in this vacation recreation, and to Mrs. King no
part was remembered with more pleasure than the hours
of intercourse in familiar chat with this vigorous, hearty,
sensible man, full of delightful reminiscences of the past.

The warm friends made during her residence at Cambridge filled Mrs. King's life while there with a constant
flow of genial, social enjoyment, which was varied by an
occasional visit to Boston to a concert or to a lecture;
but it was an earnest life, with a determined purpose, to
which every thing else yielded. Even had the life been
without the genial friendship and friendly intercourse,
the one object would have been attained and the mother's
desires would have been satisfied. As it was, every day
brought pleasant incidents, and happy memories were
stored up and life-long friendships formed. So, when
the time came for another life elsewhere, there were
many regrets and many sad partings.

PHILADELPHIA.

1840–1853.

"The reason firm, the temperate will,
Endurance, foresight, strength, and skill,
A perfect woman nobly planned,
To warn, to comfort and command."
—WORDSWORTH.

"Im ganzen guten Schönen,
Resolut zu leben."
—GÖETHE.

(60)

CHAPTER IV.

REMOVAL TO PHILADELPHIA—VISIT TO CINCINNATI—VISIT TO WASHINGTON—WINTER IN NEW ORLEANS AND CUBA—VISIT TO VIRGINIA—IMPRESSIONS OF OLD TIME LIFE IN VIRGINIA— MARRIAGE TO MR. PETER—RETURN TO PHILADELPHIA—CHARITABLE WORK—CHURCH LIFE—FOUNDATION OF SCHOOL OF DESIGN—BRILLIANT SOCIETY LIFE—DEATH OF HER SECOND SON.

IN 1840, Mrs. King, having completed her work of superintending the education of her sons, left Cambridge, not having fully made up her mind as to her future permanent abode, thinking, perhaps, to be influenced somewhat by the decisions of her sons. She had wished to make a visit to Philadelphia, invited by a friend of her earlier life, and this interval in which all work seemed to be suspended was a time to carry out her wish. Mrs. Lewis, a younger sister of Mrs. King's early friend, Mrs. Carson, had married a gentleman of Philadelphia, and was living very charmingly in that beautiful city. It was the invitation of this friend that Mrs. King accepted, and the result was that she was so delighted with the cleanliness, the order, the cultivation, and high tone of every thing in Philadelphia that she determined, so far as her own inclinations were concerned, that this must be her future home. She desired much that her oldest son, who had finished his law studies at the Harvard law school, should decide upon Philadelphia as his residence, but the son's desires were for his native state Ohio. With her interests he felt it to be a duty to

(61)

identify himself, and he chose Cincinnati as his residence. The mother was too wise to urge her own desires, for she had so thorough a respect for the judgment and discretion of her son, that after the first suggestion she left the decision to him.

Mrs. King made a visit to Washington at the time of the inauguration of the new president, General Harrison, who was to enter upon his duties on the 4th of March, 1841. Mr. King accompanied his mother, and it was a time of much festivity and social enjoyment. Mrs. King was still a young woman, handsome, gracious, and highly intelligent. The life at Cambridge had tended to her intellectual development, and time having softened her sorrows, she entered with zest into all social enjoyments. She made many new acquaintances at Washington, and renewed old friendships. Among her valued friends were General and Mrs. Totten, at whose house, one of the most hospitable in Washington, she met a constant flow of entertaining people. It was the great gathering point for the army and navy officers; indeed, all celebrities who might be in the capital were to be met in the salons of this gay genial family. At this period began the part of Mrs. King's life, which might be characterized as her worldly life, not in the obnoxious sense, for never were the frivolities of society in accordance with her tastes, but the elegancies, the refinements, the intellectual intercourse were full of attractions for her, and we find, for some years, her position, especially in Philadelphia after her marriage to Mr. Peter, was that of a leader in society.

During all this time, however, her charitable nature was active, and there were always hours for reading and study.

Before Mrs. King had finally fixed her home in Philadelphia, she returned to the west to visit her mother in Chillicothe, and to renew her friendships in Cincinnati, thus giving herself an opportunity to judge of the advantages to be gained by her son in his decision.

While in lodgings in Philadelphia, which she had fortunately obtained with a very refined lady who by loss of fortune had been compelled to exert herself for the support of her family, Mrs. King met Mr. Peter, who was then British consul in Philadelphia. Mr. Peter was a man of extraordinary learning, a graduate of Christ Church College, Oxford, a fine writer, a scholarly man in its widest sense. The two were mutually attracted, and became fast friends. Mr. Peter belonged to an old family in Cornwall, dating back to the time of William of Normandy. He was a man of singular refinement and gentle ways. He had represented his county in Parliament as a Whig of very decided political views. Politics not turning as he desired, he became disgusted with the bustling life, and decided to follow the quieter impulses of his literary tastes.

After the death of his wife, his children all being grown and settled in life, he accepted the offer of a foreign position, which would afford leisure for his intellectual pursuits. He found himself in Philadelphia soon in most congenial companionship. Mr. Peter was a thorough classical scholar, and with a poetical mind which made him fully appreciative of the vast wealth of poetry among the Greeks and Romans. It was a work of love for him to translate and arrange one of the very best books which had ever been compiled in the English language of the " Poets and Poetry of the Ancients." His own fine poetical talent enabled him to place before those not so fortunate as himself in classic lore beautiful gems never before translated. The work is of rare value. Mr. Peter was also a fine German scholar, fully enjoying and comprehending the highest poets of Germany. His translations are very fine of Göethe's "Egmont," Schiller's "Marie Stuart," "William Tell," and "Joan of Arc." He also translated much from other authors. Rarely have two minds been brought together more appreciative and more helpful. It was after Mr. Peter's marriage to Mrs. King that the great literary work of his life, the "Poets and Poetry of the Ancients," was commenced, and the dedication will show his estimate of the helpful powers of his wife:

TO

MY WIFE,

AT WHOSE SUGGESTION THE WORK WAS UNDERTAKEN,

BY WHOSE ENCOURAGEMENT IT HAS BEEN CONTINUED, AND

WITH WHOSE AID IT IS NOW COMPLETED,

THESE SELECTIONS

FROM THE POETS OF GREECE AND ROME ARE WITH SINCEREST AFFECTION

INSCRIBED.

Mrs. King's second son, Thomas, who bore the name of her own father, Thomas Worthington, decided upon mercantile pursuits as his life work, and he commenced his commercial life in the counting house of Mr. Richard Alsop, in Philadelphia, and through Mr. Alsop's influence he was offered an opportunity by N. and G. Griswold of going on a voyage in their clipper ship, "Helena," to South America and to China. This he accepted, and the experience thus obtained widened his views of life, and in every way expanded and strengthened the young merchant just entering upon his chosen work. Thus both of Mrs. King's sons were settled in life in the employments of their preference, and this part of her work, fitting her sons for the duties of life, had been successfully done. Mrs. King passed the winter of 1842–3 with her son in Cincinnati, and remained until after his marriage, which took place in May, to the writer of these memoirs, who was at once taken to the loving heart of the young husband's mother, and who for years was the happy daughter and congenial friend of this noble lady.

During Mrs. King's residence in the severe climate of New England, she contracted a bronchial trouble, from which she suffered at intervals through all the years of her life. The only alleviation seemed to be found in the general strengthening of her system, which was brought about by a periodical visit of several weeks at the seaside. For many years Newport was her favorite summer resort, and the life she led of free, untrammeled enjoyment with friends of like mind with herself, continued until fashion invaded and made as years advanced the place irksome and wearisome to her.

After this result came, Mrs. Peter made experiments amid the numerous bathing places of the Jersey coast, but finally found all she wished in the retirement and pure air of the eastern part of Long Island. The last summer of her life she passed in this tranquil spot, so congenial to her in every way.

The autumn following her son's marriage, Mrs. King returned to Cincinnati, to be with her daughter and to comfort her in a great sorrow which had fallen upon her. In the latter part of the winter, she decided to visit the south, to go to New Orleans and to Cuba. Mrs. King had never, at that time, traveled outside of her own country, and the voyage across the gulf to Cuba, the residence of some weeks in Havana, with an occasional excursion into the interior of the island, was a new experience of enjoyment for her, and she returned widened and invigorated. Her nature was so receptive that what might be passed unnoticed by the less observant would be eagerly taken in by the earnest woman ever anxious to learn.

During this visit to Havana, an incident occurred so illustrative of Mrs. King's character that it should not be omitted. She had not been many days in the hotel when she discovered that a young Englishman was in the house, in the last stages of a fatal disease. He was there without friends, a stranger, and dying. She immediately found him, and with a mother's care tended him during the days that his life slowly ebbed away. She relinquished all her plans for the time, and gave herself up to the suffering stranger, and he so grateful that his last hours were rather of joy than of suffering. Mrs. King received all his last instructions and messages to his sisters, and when at last the spirit departed, with a mother's love and tenderness she made every necessary arrangement, and broke the sad tidings to his family, far off in England. One may well imagine the words which came in return from their sorrowing hearts, so full of gratitude to the angel of mercy who had soothed the dying pillow of their loved brother.

Of course, many plans had to be given up which had been formed for her own pleasure by the occurrence of this sad interlude, but yet time enough remained for very satisfactory investigation. Mrs. King's letters show that she was not favorably impressed with the Spanish character as developed in Cuba. Had she made the visit after she had entered the Catholic Church, she would have understood much which at that time she was dis-

posed to criticise. So she thought herself, as in after
years she expressed oftentimes in speaking of these experiences.

As the spring advanced, the heat and prevalence of
disease warned her to leave this tropical region, and she
returned to her son and daughter in Cincinnati, with
whom she made a delightful summer's visit to friends in
Virginia, and saw again and enjoyed those beautiful old
homes which had delighted her so much in her young
life. One of the finest old homes in Eastern Virginia
was the residence of Mr. Robert Rives, the grandfather
of Mrs. Rufus King, a gentleman of large wealth and
fine tastes, whose home was noted for its elegant hospitalities. Nothing could have been more charming than
the life in those days on the great plantations of the
Southern Atlantic States. The excellence of the service
of the well trained slaves, taking as much interest and
feeling as much pride as the courtly master whom their
effort was so closely to imitate, afforded leisure for all the
arts of luxurious living, and the cultivation of intellectual and æsthetic tastes. After a full enjoyment of this
charming life, which Mrs. King expressed herself as finding the most perfect system of luxurious home-life and
perfect housekeeping she had ever seen, the little party
passed on, to separate after a few more pleasant experiences, to consummate their separate plans.

It was in October of the year 1844, that Mrs. King became the wife of Mr. Peter. The wedding took place at
Chillicothe, and the ceremony was performed in St. Paul's
Church, the same to which Mrs. King had given so much
thought and work in her earlier life. The wedding
breakfast was served, too, by some of the old servants
who through years had done good service in the hospitalities of Chillicothe. Mr. and Mrs. Peter returned im-

mediately to Philadelphia, where they were so fortunate as to secure for their future home one of those fine, ample old houses, whose large rooms had echoed with the gay laughter and jovial festivities of the days of the Republican court.

This winter began a life of great social enjoyment, which was to continue through a period of ten years. Mr. Peter had already become a great favorite in the highest circles of Philadelphia, and Mrs. King had been long enough resident there, admired and caressed, to be received as Mrs. Peter with open arms and congratulations. Their home became a great center for all that was highest in intellect and good taste. Mr. Peter's connection in England brought to his house, in familiar association, many people of rank and distinction who might come as travelers to the United States. Every thing combined to make Mr. and Mrs. Peter perfectly fitted and adapted to the high position they filled. Their house was furnished with exquisite taste, and Mrs. Peter may be regarded as a pioneer in the fancies which now exist for old furniture. Rare opportunities were presented for indulging her quaint tastes, for the idea of gaudy and tawdry decoration had been introduced, and beautiful old chairs with claw feet and carved back, and tables and old bureaus and escritoires and buffets with brass ornaments had been relegated to the garrets and back alleys to give place to their garish successors of ormolu and velvet. The writer remembers, with much delight, the frequent excursions in which she was the companion of Mrs. Peter, to sequestered old houses, where were found rickety ill-used battered relics of the fine old days, which Mrs. Peter's antiquarian eye soon discerned to be rare gems, and under the skillful hands of cleaners and polishers would come out things of real beauty and value. Even before Mrs. Peter's visits to Europe had given her opportunities to collect so many objects of value, she had never lost an apportunity of picking up rare and beautiful things, and her naturally artistic eye was not often mistaken in her quick discernment.

This Philadelphia home was certainly a charming abode of good taste and refinement. Many musical parties and receptions were given this winter, but both Mr. and Mrs. Peter enjoyed best the hospitalities of the dinner party, which in the then existing society of Philadelphia could be so perfectly arranged for the highest social enjoyment. At their dinner-table were to be met such men as Horace Binney, John Sargent, Mr. Duponceau, the brothers Henry and William B. Reed, Clement Biddle, Ingersoll, Tilghman, Wharton, the brilliant young Wallace, so soon to pass away—a circle too large to enumerate often called together to meet strangers of note. The famous Mrs. Rush and her sister, Mrs. Barton, the lovely Mrs. Willing, the cultivated Misses Tilghman, beautiful Mary Wharton, and the graceful Mrs. Montgomery, with many others, were bright stars in this galaxy. In all this time of brilliant society life, Mrs. Peter did not silence those inner suggestions which were ever present in her nature urging her to the mission of mercy. She seemed to have always sounding in her ears "the still sad music of humanity." We find her already interested in carrying out the plan always nearest her heart for the help and elevation of her own sex. With a number of earnest women, a majority of them belonging to the "Friends" or "Quakers," a society was formed to build up and put into active operation an asylum for degraded women. This was the "Rosina house for Magdalens," which is still actually and efficiently working

5

in the good cause for which it was founded. Another
and still greater work in its results was then commenced
by this untiring lady. In her own house she appropriated a room and engaged a teacher of drawing to begin
the initial steps of a school of design for women. This
was carried on with great vigor during all her years of
residence in Philadelphia, and the work grew into vast
proportions. It was not long after the beginning that advance enough was made to authorize a systematic arrangement of the school in its different practical workings.
Teachers in the several departments were secured, and
orders were obtained for patterns in iron work, for paper
hanging, for calico prints, etc. No industry but might now
be supplied by this valuable school. After Mrs. Peter's
removal from Philadelphia, this school still continued to
grow in size and usefulness, and we copy, from a recent
circular, facts which will show that the school, after passing through forty years, still grows in magnitude, and is
carrying out the good work designed by its charitable
foundress:

"PHILADELPHIA, *February* 28, 1887.

"The Philadelphia School of Design for Women asks your
attention to the following statement:

"It began as a private enterprise under the auspices of Mrs.
Sarah Peter, and entered upon its career of usefulness in her
house on the west side of Third street near Spruce street,
more than forty years ago. From this small beginning it has
grown continuously, until it has reached its present large proportions indicated by its plain, yet large and well-adapted
building, south-west corner of Broad and Master streets. The
school was moved to this point when the exigencies of the
Pennsylvania Railroad drove it from the corner of Merrick
and Filbert streets, where it had long dwelt in its own house,
and out of debt. The movement occasioned a large outlay, as
will be readily understood by any one who visits the building

now occupied by the school, one of the largest, if not the largest, and best appointed structures for the purpose in the country. . . . We have now upward of two hundred and twenty pupils in attendance, etc.

"MISS EMILY SARTAIN, *Principal.*"

"P. PEMBERTON MORRIS, *President.*

"JOHN SARTAIN, *Vice-President.*

"GEO. W. HALL, *Secretary and Treasurer.*"

We find, too, that Mrs. Peter organized an association for the protection and advancement of tailoresses, but its history is lost, and we must suppose it was among the very few of Mrs. Peter's efforts which were not marked with success. Some papers remain, but it is evident the enterprise was full of difficulties, and at last other works of more practical good seem to occupy the thoughts of this charitable lady.

One of the noble acts of Mrs. Peter's life must be mentioned here. A young southern girl of birth, education, beauty, brought up under all the protecting influences of a luxurious country home, had married hastily and unfortunately a man in every respect her inferior, but wealthy, who took her to a city home of luxury, surrounded by frivolity and all the snares of a life to which she had been unaccustomed. The glamour of this life dimmed the innocent, guileless senses of the young girl whose heart was unprotected by the talisman of love. Deception, illusions, secret correspondence, then at last a discovery by the infuriated husband, whose hand became stained with the blood of his rival. This poor child, the erring, forsaken wife, Mrs. Peter took to her home, where she remained for several years, and comforted the misguided but not sinful heart. The reward of the benefactress was infinite gratitude of one who was afterward a happy wife and mother, and a devout Christian in all her ways.

Long would be the list of such acts, but we feel that this one instance should be spoken of, for it shows the unmeasured mercy of this dear lady's unselfish heart.

The seaside, always the summer resort of Mrs. Peter, was at this time Newport. She found in the quaint old town a combination of quiet, simple life with a zest of pleasant society. Her son and his wife often joined her in these pleasant summer recreations. The writer remembers with great delight the annual visits which, with her husband, were made to his mother. They were occasions of both pleasure and profit, for the kind and considerate lady knew that these were interludes for storing up memories for after years. Mrs. Peter had a remarkable faculty of discovering, wherever she went, all that might be interesting and curious in her surroundings. A combination with her of desire to learn, penetration to discover, good taste and judgment to discriminate, enabled her often to make disclosures for those who had long been living in close proximity to objects of interest of which they had never known. In Newport, queer old houses, where had reveled many a gay company of French and English officers and ladies of high degree; indeed, some of the stately dames still remained who could tell of those days. Treasures of old furniture, antique china, and oddities of all sorts, brought from foreign parts to this once important seaport, were to be seen in these venerable houses. I know not whether they still remain, for treasure seekers have been dismantling all the old abodes in the land, and the spirit of veneration seems to have died out in the present generation among the descendants of those who held on with pious tenacity to all which was connected with the past.

There was no place, however, where so much was offered in the way of investigation and revival of the past as in Philadelphia; no place in the whole country where there had been so much of elegance and style in living, such grand old houses, not in decay, still kept up by those bearing the great names of which they were so justly proud. The Willings, the Chews, the Mifflins, the Morrises, and a host of other names connected with continental times, still appeared, and were on Mrs. Peter's visiting list. The writer was always taken, during her visits to Philadelphia, to make visits of respect to quaint old ladies, who could boast that their mothers had danced the stately minuet with the Father of his Country, or could speak in touching accents of the unfortunate but accomplished Major André, of the magnificent Meschianza festivities which were given during the occupation of Philadelphia by the British.

Among the most interesting reminiscences of these days are what might be called pilgrimages to Burlington, visits of compliment and respect to Bishop Doane and to Mrs. Bradford, a venerable lady, the last left of that Republican court which had held such regal sway in the grand early times immediately following the Revolution. Mrs. Bradford, in the forties, was a lady of more than ninety years of age, the widow of the attorney-general in the cabinet of General Washington. She occupied the same grand old home, a large, square house, in the midst of fine old trees; the same furniture, carved and inlaid; the massive old plate, and the venerable butler, a negro man, silvered and bent with age.

Mrs. Bradford was medium height, but still, even at her advanced age, plump and erect, with quite a glow in her face and fire in her eye. On the occasion of the visit above alluded to, this venerable lady appeared dressed tastefully in satin and lace and a white turban, entering the room with the elastic step of a woman of forty. It was only on near observation that the wrinkled skin and the film over the eyes suggested the woman of ninety years. Her conversation was bright, and bore quaintly on the by-gone days. The venerable butler, during the visit, came several times into the room, and in a respectful attitude, seemed to await the mistress's orders; finally, as if suggested by his own hospitable ideas, he entered, bearing upon a massive silver salver cake and wine, the richness of flavor of the wine suggesting that it had without doubt had the approval of the great Washington himself, who, as our hostess had told us, was often a guest in the very room we then occupied. We departed, at length, with a dazed feeling that we had been in companionship with the ghosts of those long since gone, and; though full of delight from our visit, not sorry to breathe again the open, fresh air, and to see the sights of the more modern days.

At no period of Mrs. Peter's life, did all its accessories cluster around her so favorably as during those years in Philadelphia. Health and affluence, a beautiful home, a congenial friend in her husband, the consciousness of having performed her part toward her sons, and seeing them prosperous and happily settled in life—all combined to give her a freedom in thought and action she had never before experienced. She was happy in the present, and in all the results of her labors. She felt her power and her influence, and looked out to a future of usefulness as durable as her strength of purpose; but sadly and suddenly did this happy period of her life close. The death of her youngest son, to whom she had gone when

the startling accounts of his serious illness reached her,
threw new responsibilities into her life, and she was to
take up other work, and not again was this life in Philadelphia, with all its interests socially, to be resumed.
In other paths and other fields her efforts were to be
spent.

FIRST VISIT TO EUROPE

AND TRAVELS IN "THE EAST."

1851–1853.

*Herder says, very beautifully and truly, " that deep and hidden strength comes to light in man which could never have become active unless the individual had gone through much trial." I can say that it is in this view alone that life has any importance for me—it is quite incalculable what strength can be called forth by the varying circumstances of life. The development of every germ which lies in the individual nature of man is the true aim of earthly being.—*WILLIAN VON HUMBOLDT.

  Oh deem not they are blest alone
   Whose lives a peaceful tenor keep ;
  The Power, who pities man, has shown
   A blessing for the eyes that weep.

  And thou who o'er the friend's low bier
   Sheddest the bitter drops like rain,
  Hope that a brighter, happier sphere,
   Will give him to thy arms again.
       —BRYANT.

(78)

CHAPTER V.

PART I.—DEATH OF MRS. PETER'S SECOND SON—VOYAGE TO EUROPE—LETTERS FROM ENGLAND, SCOTLAND, BELGIUM, GERMANY, SWITZERLAND. PART II.—LETTERS FROM FRANCE AND ITALY. PART III.—LETTERS FROM EGYPT, SYRIA, TURKEY, GREECE—RETURN HOME.

THE year 1851 brought to Mrs. Peter a grief which it seemed impossible for her to bear with the submission with which she had already borne so many bitter sorrows. Her second son, Thomas Worthington King, had died in January of the year 1851, leaving a wife and three boys, the oldest but six years of age. It was a crushing blow to the mother, and an event which seemed to change the whole current and object of her life. For the time, at least, her thoughts must be centered in those who were the tender objects of the love and interest of him whose watchful care would have guarded their young lives, and from whom they were now separated for all this mortal life.

Mrs. Peter, in the intense love she bore for her departed son, felt that she could do his work and show her love best by giving herself in unlimited devotion to the widow and the fatherless, and without hesitation she took to her heart these dear ones, and her whole soul seemed to be given to them. She took them to her home in Philadelphia, and when the first bitterness of grief had passed, and thought began to assert itself amid the hitherto absorbing feeling, it was decided best for all that a great change in the life must be made. Other scenes and other lands must be sought to attract the minds of the mother and the wife from their all-absorbing grief, and it was determined that a year should be passed in Europe. Preparations were accordingly made, and as neither Mr. Peter nor Mrs. Peter's only son, Mr. Rufus King, could accompany them, the voyage was undertaken by the two ladies with children and nurse. It was thought at the time that they would soon be joined by Mr. Peter; perhaps by Mr. and Mrs. King. The following letter will show how successfully the voyage was accomplished:

ON BOARD THE SHIP WYOMING, FROM PHILADELPHIA.

A DAY ON SHIPBOARD.

A little bell at $7\frac{1}{2}$ o'clock warns those who have not long before risen from their hard beds, that it is time to prepare for breakfast at $8\frac{1}{2}$. Before this hour most of the passengers have been on deck to inquire of the speed of the night and to assure themselves of the state of the weather, which in these seas, the captain says, "rains nine months of the year, and drizzles the remaining three." Be this as it may, we are now in our twentieth day, and have seen but one sunset. Breakfast being announced, by a repetition of the little bell, all tumble down the narrow stairway, and, like a jovial set of bacchanals, totter as they can into their accustomed places. A variety of liquids, called tea, coffee, and chocolate, are handed about in mugs, which the luckless seekers after food seize with one hand while they endeavor with the other to secure the more solid viands within their reach. At length a lull ensues, and all apply themselves diligently to their task, when, incontinently, a sudden heavy lurch overtakes them in the midst of cups and dishes, every thing pitches headlong in the laps of the unhappy occupants of the

lee side. I could not but laugh this morning at the dire dis-
comfiture of two neat and tranquil Quakers of the City of
Brotherly Love, male and female, who suddenly found their
laps the recipients of the breakfasts of their *vis-a-vis* neighbors. What scrambling and cleansing! what distressed
visages! Well, all things have an end, and so has breakfast, our most perilous work of the day. This over, the men
betake themselves to the deck, and taking refuge from the
passing showers in the wheel-house, busily occupy themselves
in filling the whole vessel with the nauseous fumes of tobacco,
and then, the deck being dry, commence their sole and elegant amusement of shuffleboard. Two squares having been
marked on the floor by the carpenter, the play consists in sliding along the floor by means of a wooden pole, flattened at
one end, circular discs of heavy wood some five inches in diameter. He who continues to enter oftenest by counting the
number on which his disc lodges is the winner, a part of the
play being also to dislodge the disc of his antagonist. This
rude play brings sad headaches to those who prefer to remain
below, but the prevailing notion aboard seems to be that
each had a right to amuse himself in his own way. At 11
luncheon is announced. After this some write, a few read,
and others doze. Then a repetition of shuffleboard and
smoking, inquiries about the log, lounging, chatting with the
second cabin passengers, who, by the by, from appearances,
are decidedly more intelligent than the "*upper ten.*" Dinner
comes at 3; sufficiently good chicken every day, turkey,
ducks, beef, mutton, etc., pies and puddings, raisins, oranges,
etc.. Smoking and shuffleboard and dawdling till night. At 9
taffy (burnt sugar and butter), and the yawning circle withdraw to bed. At ten no one is to be seen. Fresh bread is
baked daily, and rolls are always on the breakfast table.
Crackers, butter, and eggs, are abundant. The second cabin
is separated from us only by a thin partition. Among them
is a young Presbyterian minister, just from Princeton, going
on a visit to his mother in the North of Ireland, before set-

tling himself in his future duty as missionary to Texas.
The weather being fair, he held service last Sunday under
the awning on deck, which was attended by all his fellow-
passengers in the second cabin, some from the steerage, and
as many from the first cabin.   The second cabin passengers
sing well, and employ every evening in singing a great variety of hymns, very beautiful hymns, in which four or five
parts are sustained.   I often feel inclined to join them.

When you come bring winter garments with you, and the
shabbiest you have, for the sea water will soon make all alike ;
especially you will need heavy shoes and one or two good pil-
lows or cushions, on which to recline on deck, will add greatly
to your comfort.   It is on deck only you can escape sickness,
or in any way enjoy the voyage.   We found our life pre-
servers very comfortable to bolster us up when there was a
heavy sea.   Bring warm hoods and caps.

After beating about most uncomfortably in the Irish
Channel, the Wyoming arrived in port at Liverpool, after
a voyage of nearly four weeks.

Mrs. Peter's life may now for a while be most satisfactorily followed by her own letters, of which we shall give
only detached portions.   Soon the good health of the
whole party seemed to restore healthful views of life and
interest in the new objects which attracted at every
day's advance of the journey.   In many ways Mrs.
Peter was enabled to see objects of interest which are
not usually opened out to travelers in England.   Her
letters of introduction gave her an insight into homes
and home life, and Mr. Peter's high social position in
England gave her opportunites not usually afforded to
strangers.   Such letters will be selected as will give
views of unbeaten tracks, and though all Mrs. Peter
writes has originality, it might be recounting a twice
told tale.   We shall omit descriptions of notable places

always visited and so often described. After the voyage
is finished, and England in all her beauty of nature and
art lies spread before the traveler eager to see and to
enjoy, Liverpool, smoky commercial bustling Liverpool,
is a place to pass through, and few stop to see the many
objects of interest in and around this important place.
Mrs. Peter's letters will show that she observed well, and
lost neither time nor opportunity to investigate.

LIVERPOOL, *June* 19, 1852.

It rained all day yesterday, but we are resolute travelers,
and were on foot all the afternoon, having first deposited our
trunks on receiving them from the custom-house officers at
our lodgings. The people in the shops are intelligent and re-
markably attentive and well bred. It is not difficult to discern that taste in dress is not indigenous; the millinery, especially, is positively as ugly as can be imagined, but in
architecture they are altogether in advance of us. Sculptures are common on the exterior of almost every good house,
and there are many more beautiful public buildings in this
one city than I have seen in our whole country.

Having made an appointment to see the town hall with
Mr. Crittenden at eleven, I went after an early breakfast to
see a collection of paintings presented by Roscoe, whose statue
adorns the stairway. Along the stairway are crayon sketches,
some of which are of high merit. At the entrance is a picture of West, King John, receiving his crown from the
Pope. This is a very curious collection, consisting of a series
of pictures by the most renowned artists of the age from
A. D. 1500 to the present time. These are the first paintings
by the old masters I have ever seen, and I find I should be
quite likely to become enthusiastic if I indulged my impulses;
they have afforded me very great pleasure. There is also a
fine gallery attached containing marbles and sculptures,
among which is a complete set of casts of the Elgin marbles, excellently executed, from which several students, male

and female, were making copies. The collection of antiquities is very good, and must tend to improve the public taste.
The mayor was giving a state dinner to-day, and none could
be admitted without his special permission.   We were among
the fortunate, for it is only on these festive occasions that the
state apartments have the furniture uncovered, and besides,
the tables were laid out for the banquet and covered with
massive plate, all together with the rich china adorned with
the heraldic emblazonments of the corporation.   The state
entrance is through an apartment but little elevated from
the street about twenty-five feet square, floored with bright
colored encaustic tiles of gay patterns.   Opposite the entrance
door another opens upon the grand staircase, which is very
wide below and divided into two a little way up.   On the
landing at this division stands a colossal statue of Canning
in marble.   These flights of stairs are seen from the entrance
underneath where they are finely carved.   The floors and
stairs are finely polished and magnificently carpeted; the rail-
ings are of brass.   This grand entrance has a truly grand
effect.   Ascending (above you is a wide and loftly dome exquisitely wrought in stucco) you enter a suite of apartments
wide and high, and, as far as I could judge, some sixty feet
by forty, three rooms of this size in a line furnished with
magnificent damask hangings and chairs, carpets, and chan-
deliers to match, with full length portraits of Canning, Huskisson, George IV, William III, Duke of York, etc., and
busts of the Queen and Prince Albert.   Two ball-rooms of
equal splendor are at right angles with the drawing rooms,
and overlook the area of the Exchange, in the center of which
is a group in bronze representing the death and apotheosis of
Nelson.   It was the hour for assembling on Change, and the
area was full of busy men.   After walking through street
after street, and finding every-where objects well worthy of admiration, we returned, wearied in body but not in mind, to
dine at 5 o'clock.   The days at this season are long, for at 10

o'clock P. M. it is not dark, and I sallied forth to see other sights.

June 20th. This has been a wet day for sight-seeing. We took a long drive through noble streets, some of them nearly as dingy as Pittsburgh, passing by the University and several beautiful parks to the Necropolis, prettily planted but not very remarkable, to the Zoological Gardens, which are very extensive and beautifully laid out, with beasts and birds scattered here and there among shrubs and flowers. There are some pretty pieces of water, on which are sailing in all their stateliness, swans, black and white, but who condescend to pick up the bits of cake thrown to them. On another little lakelet is arranged the most curious optical illusion, representing mountains and valleys, a city and numerous boats are floating over it—all the effect of paint. After wandering an hour amid these sylvan scenes, we proceeded to the botanical gardens, about half a mile distant. These were both pretty and extensive, with long ranges of green-houses; but we found less rarity than in the former. Our next progress was to St. James Cemetery, the most wonderful and curious of the whole. Here was the excavation of a stone quarry, some one hundred feet deep, which, had it been left as it was found, would doubtless have been a nuisance and a misfortune to the community. Now it is the most remarkable object in Liverpool. One side had been walled up with terraced walks; the others are precipitous, but covered with verdure, except at one end, which is wild rock, through which the ascent is by a tunnel, smoothly cut. On the top of this rock is a mortuary chapel, containing some beautiful marbles in groups or statues and mural tablets, executed by Chantry and other world-renowned artists. One of Mr. Ewart is in a sitting posture, and clad in dressing-gown and slippers, is so life-like as to startle the beholder. The principal monument, at the bottom of this pit or quarry, is a temple inclosing a statue of Mr. Huskisson, who was killed at the opening of the

6

Liverpool and Manchester Railway. Another statue of this gentleman, in bronze, stands in the town hall.

21st. A note was brought in at an early hour from our Greek friend, Neroutzos, announcing his intended visit to us. To-day another came from Professor Harvey, to say he had written letters of introduction for me to Glasgow and Dublin.

We have had a storm tempestuous enough for the tropical latitudes. It was a thunder-storm of remarkable violence, but has cleared away much of the smoke. It looks strangely to us to see ladies, nearly at midsummer, using furs. The nine o'clock sunset is strange, too. I am surprised to find the bricks so inferior in appearance. They resemble those we use for partition walls, and being rough and not painted, are soon begrimed with coal soot. When any attempt is made to build a fine house, there is far more of ornament than with us. Sculptures and reliefs abound. All public buildings are lavishly decorated. The streets are cleaner than in Philadelphia. Most of the streets are macadamized, and as it rains generally a part of every day, they are not dusty.

Well, I have seen the mansion of an English nobleman of the highest family rank and historical association, whose name will not pale before any duke in the realm. In reply to my note—"Will the Earl of Derby kindly give permission to two ladies, Mrs. Peter, and her daughter, Mrs. King, to visit the house and grounds of Knowsley, on Monday morning?"— there came a polite reply, written at some length, which I shall preserve for you, in his lordship's own handwriting, though suffering from partial paralysis, in which he tells me that he has given special orders to his servants to show us every thing, and that he regrets extremely that a severe attack of illness will prevent his appearing in person to congratulate the ladies on their safe arrival in England. We found all as he had said, and refreshments, too. The house is very large for our ideas, containing, I dare say, from sixty to eighty rooms. It is a long range of two stories, in the form of an ∟, filled with pictures and books, and every thing that wealth and taste and time can accumulate. The great Countess of Derby, whom Scott commemorated in, I think, "Peveril of the Peak," is represented in an historical painting, as she receives the officers of Cromwell. But the most remarkable attraction of Knowsley consists in the prodigious collections in natural history. There are some ten or twelve rooms of stuffed specimens, minerals and other curiosities, larger than any public collection I know of, except that of Philadelphia, besides the still larger wonders in the green-houses, and the acres upon acres covered with live animals and birds in the most perfect cleanliness, inhabiting by turns open fields or stalls in pretty houses, and acres of aviaries covered with net-work, and ponds with rocks and houses for water-fowl. In the poverty of our own country in objects for comparison, I can give you no idea of the proportions of this magnificent collection, and no other individual in England approaches it. The park contains seven thousand acres, covered with forest trees and shrubberies and flowers, and every-where beautiful lawns and walks in perfect keeping. One would think it an establishment for public use of some powerful prince, which in fact the Earls of Derby have ever been, and they were formerly, as you know, kings of the Isle of Man.

You will remember the "heir apparent," of whom I formed so high an opinion, when we introduced him to you a year or two since, Lord Stanley. I am glad to hear he is esteemed by all who know him for the same qualities which I admired so much—his earnest purpose to improve and to do his duty. Truly, his future position needs preparation—fearfully great, because undivided, is the responsibility of one who thus holds in his hands the weal or woe of such a multitude of dependents. I must not forget the boat-house, a pretty Gothic cottage, built on an inlet from a beautiful sheet of water. It contains a large room (apart from the head boatman and family rooms) entirely covered with antique carvings some thousand years old, and culled from ancient monasteries and wherever they could be found, and brought together to form a complete whole. The furniture (much of it) is of the same date, and then there are curious old chairs, once in the possession of Charles II. This is used for a tea and luncheon-room when they have boating parties.

In a letter from Chester, Mrs. Peter gives an account of a visit to the Bishop—

Dr. Graham—who succeeds Sumner, appointed Archbishop of Canterbury. I sent up my card, and was very kindly received; and on coming away, his lordship very politely thanked me for the honor I had done him, and regretted that his immediate absence would deprive him of the pleasure of seeing me, etc. I had shortened my visit by hearing some one say that he was on the point of departure for London, but my vanity was gratified by seeing that he was really unwilling to let me go. Of course, I was well able to tell him of the American Church and its progress, and to this I owed my welcome reception. This afternoon, we drove out some three miles to a show house, Eaton Hall, the principal country residence of the Marquis of Westminster. It is pronounced the most splendid specimen of the pointed Gothic style. It must already cover several acres of ground, yet extensive additions are now in progress, in consequence of which the house is closed to visitors, who see only the outside. It is impossible to give an idea to an American, who has not been abroad, of these great places. The park contains thousands of acres, through which the beautiful river Dee winds its way, here and there spanned by a pretty bridge, and there are drives of many miles in all directions. There are porter's lodges of various styles of architecture and surrounded by flowers and shrubbery. There were miles of apparently native forest, with fine-paved roads and the river every-where enlivening the scene with its placid surface. Truly, these nobles are princes in their generation. They seem to be very well liked by their dependents, who are proud of belonging to them.

I had resolved, in passing through this country, to seek for
some record of our family, a junior branch of which is native here; and by a singular coincidence, on being directed
by the verger to a pew at the Cathedral, the first object on
which my eye rested was the escutcheon over the pew, and a
Bible marked in gold letters, W. D. Worthington. The
same lady, who so kindly accompanied me to St. John's
Church, pointed out to me the residence of the ladies of the
family. Unfortunately, they are all absent at the Isle of
Man, and the family seat is too far out of the way for a visit
to it.

Mrs. Peter visited Leamington, Manchester, Stratford
on Avon, with all the places renowned by connection
with Shakespeare; also, Kenilworth, Warwick, etc.; but
these places have been so fully described by other travelers that we shall not give any of her descriptions nor
impressions, but pass on to the lake region.

GRASMERE, *July* 13, '51.

We have found ourselves so very pleasantly situated in this
delicious little vale of Grasmere that we are reluctant to leave
it. Our duty, however, is onward, and to-morrow, after a
ten days' rest, we proceed northward twelve miles to Keswick.
We have availed ourselves of this blessed spot of retirement
to remove some of the soil of travel and set our house, *i. e.*,
our trunks, in order. Our hitherto ill-washed clothes have all
been bleached upon the pretty soft grass and restored to us
as sweet as new-mown hay. We are in one of those little
nooks the world has hitherto passed by. The rustic inhabitants have lived for ages, unknowing, and, but for tourists,
unknown. Their hills are bare and offer nourishment only
to sheep; and the spring is so late in their valleys that they
scarcely attempt any thing beyond a few garden vegetables
and grass. A more skillful agriculture would doubtless find
its reward, but the wants of the peasantry are too few to urge

them to further exertion. They are clean and neat in their way, and laborious, too, but they seem content to live as their fathers lived. I can not understand how it is that their population continues so thin. I do not hear of emigration, and yet the inhabitants are scarcely more numerous than when they followed their lords to Bannockburn. That their soil is not uncultivateable may be proved by the measure of a strawberry just brought to the table—five inches. To be sure, it is the largest in the dish, but generally they are not far below in size. L. assisted in the measurement, and vouches for its truth. These Goliaths are sold here for eightpence per quart, about fifteen cents of our currency. They are perhaps not quite so sweet as ours, but very juicy. There is scarcely one to be found that can be taken with less than two bites. They make cream cheeses, too, which are delicious. These delicacies are probably cheaper because of the extreme thinness in the ranks of the tourists this season. From one end of the vale to the other, the complaint resounds every-where—"The exhibition is ruining us; the exhibition is robbing us." Even our washerwoman made the exhibition an excuse (by what process of ratiocination I was unable to comprehend) for certain articles found deficient in the cleansing. It is quite possible that some who make but one excursion in the year may have turned their faces toward London, but it is amusing to listen to these primitive rustics, in their wooden-soled shoes and rude stockings and breeches, which look as if they might have slept with Rip Van Winkle, as they talk of the "Xibition" (exhibition), which, I dare say, they quite as often fancy to be a menagerie as any thing else. Most of the houses must be many hundreds of years old, and they are each of them strong enough to stand a siege. Here and there new windows have been put in, but the old ones are all composed of panes of some three inches by four, inserted in heavy frames and opening in the middle. The walls are usually two or three feet thick; the roofs slated, there being large

quarries of this material in the mountains. Sometimes a
thatched roof is seen, but of shingles, none at all.

Immense flocks of sheep graze on the hill-sides. Cold as
the climate is, the fuchsia remains in the ground all the winter,
and grows to the size of a large shrub, and I think I have
never seen one pour forth so rich a bloom as in these secluded
valleys. We had yesterday an opportunity of witnessing a
scene of painful interest. I mentioned, I think, in my last
letter, the death of Mr. Quillinan, the widowed husband of
Wordsworth's only daughter, Dora, who died just four years
since. Yesterday he was buried at her side in the little church
yard of St. Oswald, which is overlooked from our parlor windows. I was startled, at an early hour, by the unwonted toll-
ing of the bell; on inquiry, I learned that it was the passing
bell of "old John Watson," a villager of upward of ninety.
I had walked over to the church, however, to learn this, and
seeing two men employed near the tomb of Wordsworth, I
paused to observe their work. They were engaged in preparing the grave of Mr. Quillinan, and willingly answered my
inquiries, though in a dialect I could scarcely comprehend.
Dora Wordsworth's grave had been covered with flowers two
days before, which were yet fresh. This was done, they said,
on her death day, by the request of her husband, who had
earnestly desired to depart on the same day, but expired some
twenty-four hours earlier. He leaves, by a first marriage, two
daughters, who attended him to the grave, each leaning on an
arm of Mr. John Wordsworth, the eldest son of the poet. I
should previously have remarked, that before the arrival of
the funeral cortege, friendly hands had been busy in strewing
the graves of the family with evergreens and flowers, a mark
of delicate tenderness which in such a spot was touching.
There was no display. The melancholy procession, headed
by the hearse, with its heavy black plumes, comprised some
eight or ten carriages containing the family and the friends.
They had come from Mr. Quillinan's residence at Foxham, near
Rydal, some three miles distant, in the order observed in our

country.   A few villagers had collected in the church-yard,
among whom we ranged ourselves. The clergyman, in surplice,
met the procession at the gate, and all entering, the service
proceeded as with us, and at the grave also.   The whole scene,
in all its details, was so entirely like what may be seen under
the same circumstances at home, that but for the absence of
familiar faces, we might easily have imagined ourselves at
home.   This little church-yard, where the " rude forefathers
of the hamlet sleep," contains few grave-stones of any description.   Long rows of grassy hillocks, whose form is carefully preserved, and often shaded by yew trees, alone indicate
the spots where tears have fallen on ruined affections, and
until within a day or two the long grass concealed these.

Lowther Castle, the seat of the Earl of Lonsdale, is said to
be one of the noblest castles in England.   The hall is far beyond any thing we have seen, in its architectural embellishments; as usual, it contains armour.   The library also is a
vast apartment filled with books.   Some of the apartments
contain cabinets of buhl, which belonged to Louis four-
teenth; pictures, and sculptures, and embroideries, and vases,
old china, and curious screens, are profusely distributed over the
apartments.   " My Lady's Boudoir" (the mother of the present Earl, who is a bachelor), is hung with buff silk, goffered,
and the furniture is covered with white satin, embroidered.
The castle was rebuilt in the early part of this century, and
the architect has well performed his part; but the guiding
spirit is seen in the furnishing of these splendid apartments,
and I fancy the lady chatelaine was commonplace in character.   ,

Brougham Hall, the hereditary residence of the eccentric
Lord Brougham and Vaux, is within sight of Mayborough.
This place should rather be called a castle since we have seen
few more worthy of the name.   It has no porter's lodge, and
the visitor drives at once to the massive arch which serves as
the entrance to the court.   Over the arch-way a covered
passage is constructed to lead to the chapel.   The hall is

neither so large as that at Lowther Castle, nor so full of architectural embellishments, but the "*genius loci*," is every-where
apparent.

Suits of armour of nearly every age since the Conquest,
family portraits for the same period, sculptures, bronzes, curiously stained glass windows, with German epigrams interspersed, form the principal attractions of this singular
entrance.

Midway on the right and left are small arched galleries
leading to other apartments, into which the ascent is by oak
stairs.   Our guide informed us that, when they had parties,
dinner was served in the hall, there being another entrance at
the grand staircase. We next entered the ordinary dining-
room, which is paneled in dark oak with curious carvings.
As we were examining them, Lord Brougham passed a door
in returning from a walk. I had heard that this singular
person was much gratified by the visits and admiration of
strangers, and seeing on a side-table writing materials which
had been lately used, I took the liberty of writing a very
brief note to his lordship, which immediately brought him to
us.   He expressed much pleasure in seeing us, and immediately led us out on a terrace to see the views, which are said
to resemble Windsor Castle; but Windsor can not have Hel-
vellyn to bound the horizon. I have seen castles finer to look
at, for instance, Warwick, but not one which had views so
extensive, so beautiful. Every thing here differs, like its
master, from any thing elsewhere; but, though curious, there
is nothing grotesque. A salon of large proportions was hung
with Gobelin tapestry of the very finest manufacture, and in
better preservation than that at Warwick, though it is probably not less than two hundred years old. The carvings are
of the time of Elizabeth. We were shown, also, a suite of
bed-rooms. One is the Saxon chamber, with oak furniture
of that era; another is the Norman chamber, hung in stamped
and gilded morocco, and finished in rudely carved black walnut. A state bed-room was hung in Gobelin tapestry, nearly

equal to the first in beauty and preservation. A long, well-lighted corridor had paintings on the walls, filling both sides in a double line, a fac-simile of the Baxeaux tapestry, done by the order of Lord Brougham himself. Descending the noble staircase, we crossed the hall to the library, a spacious apartment, filled with books on carved shelves, and piles of new books not yet released from paper wrappings laid pell-mell upon the table. A pretty room adjoins, of moderate size, which contains a portrait of Lord Brougham's father, his mother, and himself. He strongly resembles his father. In this house are few articles of *bijouterie*, or merely ornamental. Eevery thing indicates a purpose or explains a fact. The hall is paved with fine encaustic tiles, each bearing an initial or motto or a crest. Again traversing this apartment, we passed a long corridor paved with stone, which leads to the chapel, and here a new scene bursts upon us. It can not be less than one hundred and fifty feet in length, with well proportioned breadth, and rich beyond description in ancient carvings, many of which had been taken from the ruins of the old castle, a mile distant. It is all of black walnut, and the panels of the roof are each occupied by an escutcheon inclosing a coat of arms. The organ, the screens, the lectern, the pulpit, the pews, the chancel rails, are all exquisitely carved, yet no two pieces are so alike as to produce monotony. The short days always require lighting, and even the candlesticks are beautiful. We could have lingered here long, but as soon as we comprehended the beautiful whole, we took our leave. Lord Brougham is so well known that it is needless to describe him. His manner is like his writings, quick and pointed. I am sorry to see that time has done its work, and he is an old man, yet full of life.

EDINBURGH.

Through the kind attentions of many friends, especially of Lord and Lady Murray, Mrs. Peter was enabled to see and enjoy fully all the charming and attractive places

in and about this most grand and picturesque city. Her
descriptions are all glowing and graphic, but now we
have such familiarity with all old places of interest in
the Old World that it is a tedious story to go over again
and again the description of places, even those most
time-honored and sacred. We shall, therefore, satisfy
ourselves with experiences more of a personal character,
and those letters or extracts wherein are little touches
of individuality. Lord Murray was an early friend of
Mr. Peter, and the introduction thus given to Mrs. Peter
insured her the most cordial attentions.

EDINBURGH, *July* 30, 1851.

It is, I believe, quite as great a comfort to me as to you
that you have been at last relieved from your anxieties about
our sea voyage. It was utterly disgusting, and never to be
forgotten; but, as we escaped without any serious prejudice
to our health, I try to dismiss it from my thoughts. It is a
great comfort to have received your letter of the 13th yesterday, for this day completes the half year since our dear, dear
Tom was taken from us. There are certain wounds which
never close, and this is one of them. I can cover it over, but
it is always there, and my only earthly consolation is by hearing from you frequently and fully—to be constantly reminded
that I have still a child left to me.

31st. I was interrupted last evening by the entrance of
Henry Parker, who has just returned from his North Highland tour, and came to offer his services for to-day. I do not
know that I had mentioned in my last letter that he had
kindly pressed me to accompany him, which I would but for
the constant uneasiness I should have felt on L.'s account,
who would have been obliged to go to Glasgow alone, and find
lodgings, too. I was therefore obliged, most reluctantly, to
decline so advantageous an offer. I can not leave Scotland
without seeing more of it, and therefore think I shall hire a
maid, and set forth next week, leaving L. and the children

safely housed for five or six days without me. I engaged L. to finish my letter of Monday, while I prepared a dress for the evening at Lord Murray's—he and Lady Murray having called, in answer to Mr. Peter's letter, to invite us. L. preferred to decline the invitation, and so should I also as a matter of choice, but, as a traveler, I ought not to lose proper opportunities of seeing men and manners.

At this season, as in Philadelphia, it seems that "every body" goes out of town, and no large parties are given. The present was a small *soiree musicale* to hear some French artist, and Lady M. charged me "not to listen unless I liked it, for Lord M. would devote himself to me."

I was invited at 8 o'clock—broad day-light here—and at eight I went, and was shown into a large room, perhaps thirty-five by twenty-two feet, with musical instruments and pictures and books—every-where, in cabinets or on tables, articles of "vertu." One thing, I think, we may imitate—a cabinet of rosewood extended along the whole side of the room, about four or four and a half feet high, with doors of convenient width all along, composed of rosewood frame, inclosing gilded or brass bars some three inches apart. Some of these doors were lined with blue silk or velvet; others left the volumes which they contained exposed to view, and the whole range of the top afforded suitable places (which are tastefully filled) for busts, vases, etc.—not a toy shop, like Mrs. Otis', but objects either remarkable or beautiful—the width of the cabinet being only just enough for the arrangement of folio or quarto volumes. The piano was not unlike mine, and a pretty little instrument, resembling an organ, stood near it. Here I laid off my shawl, and was shown into another room, about twenty feet square, hung with pictures of great value. It was a back room, and the large windows looked on the valley of the little stream called the Water of Leith quite across to the noble estuary of the Frith of Forth, beyond which were the magnificent clouds of the approaching sunset. My hostess welcomed me very heartily as I entered, and after a brief survey of the beautiful views from the windows, she desired me to be seated by her. She is decidedly fat, fair, and sixty; good natured, etc.; a little patronizing, and very fond of music. Several others joined us at the tea table, and this being accomplished, the lady withdrew with the party to the adjoining music room, and again indicated to me that I was expected to entertain his lordship. This personage is one of the high lords of the courts. He is a very well informed man and a good talker, so that I considered myself as having decidedly the best portion of the company, inasmuch as I had a sensible and agreeable companion and could listen, if I pleased, to the music. At ten, we had slight refreshments, and at eleven, I took my leave, content with my quiet evening.

After a very charming drive this morning, I returned to prepare to dine with Dr. Greville, a friend of Mr. Harvey. He had invited two gentlemen of superior abilities to meet me, as I declined a larger number, and his wife and daughter made up the rest. All was very pleasant and both literary and artistic in character. Lady Murray had already invited me on this day, but Doctor Greville was first, and as they dined earlier, Lady M. pressed me to come to her at nine. Only two gentlemen were there—one a Highland laird, full of wit; the other, a French nobleman of the ancient régime, who has long been French Consul here; and I thus passed two hours very pleasantly.

After visiting many objects of interest, we returned in time to take some refreshment and to prepare to dine at 7 o'clock at the French Consul's, Lady Murray having sent me a note to say that she and Lord M. would call for me and bring me home. I am truly sorry that these kind friends are to leave town for their Highland home the next day. In due season, they called, and we went to No. 1 Torres street. M. le Baron de M—— received us very graciously, but began immediately in French to bewail his hard fate—that he had hoped to have given us an excellent dinner, but, owing to that maudite

whiskey, his cook had rendered himself entirely unfit for duty
"*et tout etait abyme.*" We tried to console him, and mean-
time there entered two young people (French *noblesse*), to
whom we were introduced, and the witty Highland laird of
Lady Murray's dinner. In due time, we were ushered into
the dining-room, where we found a table very neatly arranged,
which I shall describe for M.'s benefit. There was a supply
of three different wine glasses to each plate, and water goblet.
In the center was a large bouquet, placed in a glass of the
shape of an enormous champagne glass, with a coiled gilt
serpent around it. As we were but seven in all; the table
was small. A round china dish of peaches, and another of
grapes and two of strawberries, were arranged around it. A
tureen of soup was placed before the host, which he served
out himself; the wine was served as usual; then salmon
(fresh) broiled in large round cuts and codfish were placed, the
one before our host, the other before Lord Murray, who was
opposite; then champagne and oyster patties were handed
round; the meats were not brought on the table; chicken
which had been cut up and put together again and stewed,
was handed round; the lobster and lettuce (a little cooked, I
know not how); then *coutlettes de veau* in *papillottes*. This
being disposed of, a leg of roasted mutton, with a large silver
skewer at the knuckle, was placed before and carved by the
host. I think this concluded the series. Then little fruit
patties were handed around, which having been duly eaten,
two ices were set upon the table, one of strawberry, the other
seasoned with sweet grapes—very nice; little cakes were
served with this and fresh preserved peaches; then some
other French wines, and the ladies withdrew to the drawing-
room, where coffee was served, and the gentlemen joined us.
The servants were excellent. This all especially for M.
I took leave of Lord and Lady Murray with sincere regret.
They kindly invited me to visit them on Loch Fyne.

GLASGOW, *July* 11, 1851.

We occupied Monday at Glasgow in visiting the grand old crypt of the cathedral. This is considered the finest in the world, and I can not conceive how it could be finer or more grandly true to its purpose, *i. e.*, a subterranean burial place. How many are buried there no one knows, for, in the blind fury of the Knoxites to reduce every thing to the level of their own vulgar and fanatical ideas, no tomb was held sacred that bore evidence of being tenanted by a papistical dignitary. Most of the ancient churches were destroyed, and the sublime Cathedral of Glasgow would have shared their fate, but that the people of the town (then small) were attached to it, and resisted these fanatics by force of arms. If you will look at *Rob Roy*, you will find some notice of this wonderful crypt in the scene where Rob emerges from behind a pillar to tell Frank Osbaldistone of his danger, etc. We also went through the Necropolis, which occupies the most commanding position of any that I have yet seen. The monuments are also many of them exceedingly fine, but it is there, as well as in Edinburgh, that the trade or occupation is almost invariably a part of the epitaph, and sometimes even thus: "A. B., leather dresser, No. 11 Castle street," with a long list of virtues appended, together with the names of his afflicted wife and children, who have "erected this monument as a tribute of their affectionate veneration of such worth," etc. The very lowest trades are as common as the highest, indicating, what I believe is true, the remarkable prosperity of this thriving town. The fruits in season are very fine and abundant and cheap, and there is a general air of enjoyment. The town is the best built and handsomest that we had yet seen. Street after street of large and well-built stone houses, many having large shrubberies in front. The consul, Mr. Kellogg, and his wife, were exceedingly attentive. We went with Mrs. K. to one of the "sewed muslin" or embroidery manufactories, which is one of the "lions" of the town. Upward of seven hundred women were employed in this house

alone to make up the embroideries wrought all over Scotland
and Ireland.   The head man told me that not less than
twenty-five thousand persons were employed and derived support from this establishment (Mr. McDonald's).   Much of
this work is exquisitely done, and sold very cheap.

We left Glasgow on Wednesday.   L., having resolved to
accompany me to Iona and Staffa, was much delighted as the
difficulties seemed to diminish as we approached them.   We
began the journey in a little steamer which was to take us
to the outlet of the Crinan canal up the Loch Tyne.   This
canal crosses the long promontory of Cantire, near the northern end of the sound of Jure, and saved a long distance.
We had a very distinguished party of lords and ladies and
other aristocratic persons on their way to the Highlands for
sporting, but they were none of them particularly interesting.
A peeress sat next me at breakfast, but they dress so badly
they acquire a vulgar air.   The sail among the wild looking
islands was very fine.   The strongholds of the ancient highland chieftains rose up from many a prominent rock, but in
ruins, until we reached the Castle of Dernolly perched upon
a sort of rocky pinnacle, which announced the end of the
journey for to-day.   Turning into a beautiful inlet, the village of Oban appeared like a crescent at its inland extremity.
Here we landed and the boat went on to Fort William with
her passengers for Inverness by the great Caledonia canal,
which is navigated by steamers.   The Queen of France and
most of her family were in possession, as we knew, of the
whole of one of the three hotels which the village boasts, and
the Duchess of Orleans occupied a fair portion of the others,
so that no time was to be lost in securing rooms.   I therefore
ran on and was fortunate enough to bespeak two small rooms
at the top of the house.   It was half-past six P. M., but in
these northern regions the summer days seem to have no time,
and we make the most of them.   An ancient royal residence
of the earliest Scottish kings, Dunstoffnage Castle, lies in
ruins at three miles distance from Oban.   A carriage was or-

dered at the usual fare of a shilling a mile (one horse), and
a gratuity to the driver, and we trotted away among a line
of shops of tailors and shoemakers, rejoicing in the names of
McArthur, McDougal, McTavish, and McDonald, and the
town being left behind, the thatch covered hovels without
chimney, occupied by the rural relatives in kilts without the
luxury of breeks, *i. e.* pants, apparently as little disturbed by
civilization as their Pictish ancestors. Those medieval barbarians, however, though indifferent to modern ideas of comfort, never failed to give proof of an artistic eye for the
picturesque of which, as we neared the ivy covered walls of
Dunstoffnage, we had additional evidence. From this old
castle was removed the stone on which the Scottish kings
were crowned at Scone. Edward VI had it conveyed to
London, where it remains under the Coronation chair at
Westminster Abbey. Tradition reports that it was brought
originally from Ireland. This fine old ruin stands on the
shore of Lock Eten, an arm of the sea. The walls are yet
strong enough to afford a walk quite around them at the top
where they are some three feet or more thick, and the views
are beautiful from every point. There is also a chapel with
some fine old stones in an adjoining wood. The McDougals,
Lords of Lorn, built this fortress and warred against the
Crown in the time of the Bruce. We gathered some ivies
and mosses to take home with us, and returned to our lodgings well pleased with the excursion. At seven o'clock next
morning we were on our way to the steamer Dolphin, which
was to convey us to St. Columba's Isle, when, on stepping
from the wharf upon the deck of the steamer, a friendly face
beamed upon us, and that of no less a personage than Bishop
Otey. Judge of our mutual gratification and astonishment.
This had hardly been half expressed when up came Henry
Parker, brother of Mrs. Edmund Quincy, and still another
whom we only knew by name, Rev. Arthur Cleveland Coxe,
of New York. This was, indeed, a most unlooked for pleasure at this *Ultima Thule*, and we felt ourselves quite made

7

up. With these pleasant companions, and one of the loveliest days the sun ever shone upon, we visited the hallowed
Icolnskill (look for it on the map outside the island of Mull).
We wandered over the old church-yard, and the ruined nun-
nery, and the old, old walls of the noble cathedral, which was
once a light to lighten the heathen far and wide. Rich old
symbolic carvings surround each time-worn pillar, many of
which are yet sufficiently plain to be understood. It must
have been a magnificent pile. The ruins are of great extent, and show elaborate workmanship. There are rows of
Kings of Scotland and Ireland and Norway, each under
sculptured slabs, abbots and bishops with mitres on their
effigies, all lying exposed to the warfare of the elements. I
felt a disgust at the Duke of Argyle, who owns the island,
that he could permit such neglect; but he is a poor Duke,
and, perhaps, can not help it. Some two or three hours were
passed in examining these honored remains, and we re-
embarked for Staffa, nine miles distant. You have often
read descriptions of the grandest of nature's cathedrals as
well as myself, but the reality far surpassed my expectations.
The unusual conjunction of high tide, and a sea as smooth
as glass, enabled us to enter to the utmost limits, in little
boats, each of the caves, of which Fingal's is the largest, and
most frequently described. No drawing can give you an
idea of this wonderful structure. The island seems one con-
tinuity of basalt pillars having a heavy entablature of earth
and conglomerate through which also the basalt pillars have
forced themselves in fragments. In some parts of this small
island the basalt pillars seem to have been bent in curves,
and in others laid horizontally or piled up in fragments, yet
always with perfect regularity. The caves of entrance have
been washed out by the currents of the ocean that have detached the blocks of basalt piece by piece from the pillars to
which they had belonged, until the grand gothic arches
have been formed, which are now so imposing. We landed
in Fingal's cave, and Bishop Obey, animated to a state of re-

ligious enthusiasm in which all had a share, began in a loud
tone the Hundredth Psalm, "With one consent let all the
earth," etc., in which the whole company joined, consisting of
about thirty persons. There were several fine voices, and
the parts were well sustained, producing a harmony which in
such a place was truly sublime. We afterward ascended the
top of the island 140 feet, where I gathered bird's feathers
and plants as trophies. The sea-birds were greatly incom-
moded and evidently annoyed by our presence, and flew
screaming in every direction. The whole sea is covered with
basaltic islands, inhabited like Staffa by birds alone, and but
for the overshadowing grandeur of Staffa, they would be
sought by tourists for their picturesque beauty. Passing by
the large Isles of Tin and Coll, we entered the Sound of Mull,
so narrow that we could examine with care the numerous
ruined strongholds as we passed, each having its legend of
warfare and crime, and at seven o'clock reached Oban in
good season for tea.

On Friday morning we returned to Glasgow, and by the
boat I joined the Bishop and Mr. Coxe by stage and through
Loch Awe and Loch Lomond. This country is full of legendary
lore. "Its far to Loch Awe," was the cry of the clan as a
boast of their secure fastness, when the clan McGregor held
possession of it. One of Bruce's greatest victories was in Loch
Awe.

The Dutchess of Saxe Cobourgh, formerly Princess Cle-
mentine, Louis Phillippe's daughter, married to a brother of
King Leopold of Belgium, accompanied by the Duchess of
Kent, had been passing some time with her mother, the Queen
at Oban, and on this day she had engaged nearly all of the
coaches for her suite. She was accompanied by the Queen,
the Duke, and Duchess of Nemours, also a Cobourgh, and the
Prince de Joinville, all looking like a party of well-bred
ladies and gentlemen, neatly attired, and deporting themselves
precisely as well-bred people do. The queen is extremely
thin, and looks as if she had suffered much, but endured all

with Christian resignation. The two duchesses looked as if life to them had much to enjoy. All wore mourning dresses, but the Duchess de Nemours was without a bonnet, and wore only a pretty little black lace cap. Her husband is a noble looking man, and very handsome. The Prince de Joinville is less prepossessing. The Princess of Saxe Co-bourgh has four nice children, two girls and two boys, all under perfect control. The whole party was dressed in excellent taste, so rare in England, that it was quite a relief to my eyes, and with great simplicity. Her royal highness walked up a steep hill, an hour after setting out, with a spirit which M. could not have exceeded, and her whole demeanor was that of a most lady-like and lovable woman, full of energy, and resolved to do her duty in all things. We were together all day, and I was much interested in her. I found L. in the evening, and yesterday came on to this beautiful city, where we have lodgings opposite a fine park, to which the children have access by a private key at all times.

KENMORE, *August* 11, 1851.

Now that I have not L. and the little people with me to occupy my spare moments, I can more readily devote them to you. It was last night that I sent off my usual hebdomidal, and here in the pretty inn of the prettier village attached to the pleasure grounds of the great Castle of Taymouth (Bread-albane), while waiting for the dish of haggis which I have ordered for my dinner, I have a few minutes to recount the adventures of the morning. Mounted on the top of a coach, with several others (chiefly English tourists), I set out at six o'clock for the village, to see one of the great castles of Scotland. The castle is not usually exhibited to strangers, but, taught by experience, I can, with propriety, win an admission any-where by an application to the lady, if she be at home, since foreigners from so great a distance are never refused. One of the great entrance gates to the park opens across the end of the little street of the village, and as we drove up to the inn, three Highlanders, in the full costume of the Bread-albane Campbells stood in the gateway ready to act as guides to any who wished to see the grounds. Prepared with a proper note to the marchioness, who, fortunately for me, had returned only a few days ago, I engaged one of these men to accompany me, who proved to be intelligent and kindly disposed, speaking English well. The Gaelic is the common language of all the peasantry of this quarter, and they learn English as we do foreign tongues, and speak it, when ac-quired, with far more purity than the Lowlanders; they are also a much handsomer race, and there is a fine intelligence in their handsome faces which excites my surprise since it so very far surpasses that of the Lowlanders, who have, notwith-standing, proved themselves so much more capable of civiliza-tion. I constantly chat with the peasantry, and thus learn much of their characteristics. There is all the devotion to their chief in the clansmen of the Breadalbane, which has been imputed to the medieval Highlander.

I doubt not that every one of them would be ready to pour out his life's blood like water for his sake. My Highlander was as proud as a peacock to show me the grandeur of his chieftain, and he did it all with the air of a courtier. He pointed out the finest views here and there, showed me the trees which the queen planted, the pretty dairy, and finally the hall or entrance, regretting, on my account, that we could go no further. I, however, sent up my note, which soon brought the housekeeper to me with orders to show all that I wished to see. There is in this palace completeness beyond all others that I have seen—comfort united with princely magnificence —a new feature in the "Baronial Hall" which you would like. It is an immense room from sixty to seventy by forty to fifty feet, wainscotted and ceiled with the richest carvings. The entire ceiling is covered with the armorial bearings, each in its own compartment, surrounded with rich carvings illus-trative of each tribe composing the great clan of Campbells, with the mottoes and names of each inscribed in the most tasteful manner, and all along the sides are arranged the banners used by each of the tribes on the visit of the queen when some thousands, as you will remember, were assembled. Pictures of untold value cover the walls of the numerous superb apartments, the ceilings and walls of which are painted in fresco by the finest artists in the world. In the hall, which is ninety feet high, and rich in architectural decoration beyond description, are numerous specimens of ancient arms and armor of a thousand years ago. The billiard room is surrounded by Highland armory; in short, no description can give you any adequate idea of the reality.

If I had seen that princely residence at first I could not have comprehended it at all, but I am learning to discriminate. The marquis owns an estate here of more than one hundred miles in length and twenty miles in breadth, the cultivated lands yielding him £2½ to £3 per acre, and this territory is covered with thatched piggeries of his tenantry! men, women, children, pigs and cows and horses all under the same roof.

FORT WILLIAM, *August* 13.

I left Kenmore on Monday at 6 o'clock for Killinhead on Loch Tay, and passed the night there. This is an old Gaelic name, as I was informed by my very intelligent guide, Peter McAlpin, a descendant of King Alpin of apochryphal memory, and a near relative of the renowned Roderick Dhu. But to return to the etymology of Killin: these Scotch gauls have adopted English letters, which give strange pronunciations, this being really, as Peter says, Ke-ern, the grave of Fingal, which is shown by a stone, and which, until recently, a curiously shaped mound. The ruin of an old castle about a mile distant, he says, was the sometime residence of Fingal, and this castle was named his pass or stopping place. The ruin is beautifully preserved by the Breadalbanes, whose burial place is within a few feet of it. The scenery around is beauty exemplified. I should so like to give you an account of my pretty sail up the Lochy River to the castle with the "royal Peter," and tell you all his curious anecdotes, which I shall forget before we meet; but time presses. It never entered my mind before that there was any reality in Mc-Pherson's Ossian, but to see the traditionary grave and ruin, and also the birthplace of Ossian, handed down through long ages, makes one pause before accusing the translator of Ossian of being its author.

At 11 P. M. yesterday I again mounted a coach, and came here without once leaving the soil of the Breadalbanes. At one place, on a pretty lake, is situated a hunting-box of the marquis, where he usually passes six weeks of the autumn, containing bed rooms for sixty guests—a large box!—in the midst, too, of a park for red deer, forest, as it is called, though nearly destitute of trees, thirty miles in circumference. The soil is poor and cold, and has very few inhabitants. We also passed through the vale of Glencoe, of fearful historic memory, some ten miles in length, having the grandest, the wildest, the most savage scenery in Britain. In this glen is pointed out the birthplace of Ossian. Then we passed through a village, the houses being all exactly alike, viz: rough stone, about five or six feet high, and gables also of stone, with thatched roofs, about half of them having chimneys and stone floors, the other half only a hole to let out the stifling peat smoke, and floors of mud. For all the apartment occupied by cows and pigs when they are rich enough to have them, is separated only by a partition, and is always filthy to a fearful degree, children all bare-legged, winter and summer. It seems to me if the owners of the princely estate acted up to their duty that this could not be. It is frightful to witness, in such close connection, such boundless luxury and such squalid want. Granted the soil is poor, but judicious agriculture would make it better, and the enormous rent exacted, £3 per acre, as Peter told me, ought richly to repay the landlord for his outlay. The leases are only from year to year, and the tenants have no interest, if they had the ability, to improve either house or land. I have entered as many of these huts as time and opportunity have permitted to chat with the inmates, and to encourage them to emigrate. The Scotch are desirable immigrants for us, and I have suggested to a number of them the plan formerly used by the German redemptioners, i. e., to engage a captain to take them over and sell their time to pay their expenses of the voyage, for they are quite too poor to go in any other way, and the bare suggestion seemed to awaken nearly extinguished hope. They are now, they say, in their seventh year of famine, and their native soil refuses to support them, and their landlords growing poorer go to the continent to live cheaper, and come home only to collect rents, which they spend abroad, leaving these poor people destitute of manufactures, which might employ them, to this fearful strife with their barren rocky fields, which no longer afford sufficient to nourish them. There is not a negro in the slave states who would condescend to live in such wretched mud hovels.

This is the very heart of the Highlands, Inverness being considered the capital. Fort William is a poor little village clustering around a fortress built by General Monk, and strengthened by William III. to check the Highlanders.

The country is bleak and wild, soil and climate being too cold to ripen even oats with certainty. Ben Nevis rises just behind the village, and is never without a covering of snow around the crest. A fearful battle between Montrose and Argyle took place in 1645, just at its base. The clan Chattan and Glengary had strongholds near these, and the coast for miles below is called Lochabar. Achnorery, the fine residence of the unfortunate Lochiel, is a few miles up the Loch Lochy, which forms a part of the great Caledonian canal. All these names are strangely familiar in this far away land. The scenery throughout is grand and beautiful.

After leaving Scotland, Mrs. Peter turned her face to the south, and passing through York, Durham, and other places of note, which she thoroughly investigated and enjoyed, she found herself in the great Babel, London, where she remained, on this occasion, a very short time, knowing that she would return at a future day, to investigate its wonders more fully. She longed to get to Canterbury, in whose quiet shades she could repose for a while with home comfort, for Mr. Peter's children were anxiously waiting to receive her. In writing from Canterbury, Mrs. Peter says, "I wrote to Frances Peter of our coming, and she and George were at the station to meet us. Frances and Robert, the clergyman, live together in a small house, and as our party was large, I preferred taking lodgings."

George and his wife, from Antigua, are here on a visit, and like us are in lodgings. They are all singularly agreeable people. Frances and George are uncommonly lovable. All have been very kind and attentive to me as possible. We have comfortable lodgings, literally on the ancient walls, which has a deep embankment behind, and the old dry moat in front. This old, though not decayed town, is full of ancient churches, and much of the old wall is still standing and crowned with ivy. The venerable cathedral contains, besides the tomb of Thomas à Becket, the Archbishop Lanfranc, and Langton St. Dunstan, Cardinal Pole, and Edward (Black Prince), with his shield and helmet and surcoat, hanging above, Henry IV. and his second wife, and many other fine monuments of less renowned people. Being an Archepiscopal Diocese, the services are very grand and imposing. I should think the surpliced choir contained nearly sixty voices, most of them the boys of the charity school; and besides the ordinary daily services, there is always an anthem sung. The communion service is of gold, and very large and massive. There is a little church here of St. Dunstan, which interests me nearly as much as the cathedral, in which several generations of the Roper family repose. Margaret, daughter of Sir Thomas More, married into the family. You know how renowned a person she was, and how devoted to her father. She contrived to get his head after execution, which she brought here and had it buried in her vault. Only a few years ago, the vault was examined by authority, and the head was found in good preservation. Just behind the church door is a head in stone or plaster, said to have been modeled from Sir Thomas before interment. It is painful to see. The likeness resembles closely the prints.

The adjoining country is beautiful, and covered with hops. They are just beginning to gather. There are good plums and other small fruits, but peaches are rare. The vegetables, too, are fine.

Mrs. Peter, being anxious that her daughter should enjoy with her the pleasure and benefit of continental travel, she determined to set forth on her journey with Mrs. King, the three little boys, and nurse. Having procured a well recommended courier, they entered Europe at Ostend. The following letter will give an account of the departure from England, and the passage across the channel :

GHENT, *September* 8, 1851.

Here, in the birthplace and ancient capital of Charles V., in a noble bed-room adjoining L.'s, of equal dimensions, I am seated to recount to you the adventures of the last twenty-four hours. At half past five P. M. yesterday, I ascended a coach with a gang of British radicals. It is needless to say more than that we breathe more freely among the more kindly Belgians. We entered a Belgian steamer at Dover, about half past nine P. M., and waited for the tide until half past twelve. We reached Ostend at seven in the evening. The tide was too low to come up in the steamer, so we were taken ashore in little boats, and marched off in quite a procession to the Hotel au Bains, where we had a nice breakfast, and refreshed ourselves. I walked about the old fashioned town. The names of the people are very pleasant, after the English—the women, with the pretty little goffered French caps, and their cloaks and hoods fluttering about, offering picturesque groups at every turn. .

After attending to certain little matters for the boys, we set forth to the railroad station. Here the civility was most consoling and comfortable. We sent off our trunks to Cologne, keeping only necessities with us; we then moved on through a flat but cultivated country, passing frequent villages, to Bruges, the capital of Charles the Bold. Here we had an excellent dinner, *table d'hôte*, and enjoyed the blessing of seeing cheerful faces, and dining well at half past one o'clock. Then we set forth to see sights, viz.: the Church of Notre Dame, having a sculptured Virgin and Child, by Michael Angelo, the magnificent tombs of Charles the Bold, and his daughter, Mary of Bergundy, and multitudes of features of the highest merit, then to the Hospital of St. John, where two hundred and twenty sick or old people of both sexes are maintained, where is a small but fine collection of pictures. There is a curious reliquary, formed like a house, of four feet long, and proportioned width, with steep gables carved and gilded, being divided into three compartments on each side, each containing portion of the pictorial history of the blessed St. Ursula, and her eleven thousand virgins, their landing at Cologne, at Basle, at Rome, their Baptism, re-embarkation with Pope, Bishops, etc., return to Cologne, martyrdom there. At the ends are the canonization of the blessed martyr and her converts. The numerous heads are small miniatures of exquisite execution, and the coloring wonderful. It gives me great pleasure to find that I have a good and discriminating eye. The cathedral is grand, and full of paintings and sculptures. Belgium is immensely rich in all these things. It is a smiling land, and I have no doubt is well governed by King Leopold.

For the first time since we left home we had really good beds, and I slept soundly enough to do them justice. We had

arranged to begin early to-day with our sight-seeing, and we
went at six to attend the early service of the Beguin nuns
who have a considerable quarter to themselves, and at the
church we attended sometimes number six hundred. They
are a cheerful, healthy looking set of women whom you meet
in all quarters of the city, even among the crowds at the
railway stations. According to their rules, each has to purchase and prepare her own food, and you can see them chaffer-
ing at market and other places as busily as if each had a
dozen to supply. The large church is very fine, and the dress
of black contrasted with the white head dress, and a sort of
white linen shawl with which they cover themselves during
divine service, has a very chastened effect. We afterward
went to one of their convents and enjoyed our visit. We
next went to the magnificent church of St. Bavin, full of fine
pictures and sculptures. I have not time to describe them.
I am very tired and must go to bed. Some of these pictures
are world renowned, and I now begin to see something of
high art. Ghent deserves at least a week, but alas, we can
not spare it. At ten we left for Antwerp, where we saw in
the Cathedral of Notre Dame that greatest work of Rubens—
The Descent from the Cross. It is worth a voyage across the
Atlantic. We also ascended the tower of Notre Dame and
saw its eighty-two bells. The churches here are even more
full of works of art than those in Ghent, and I do not hesi-
tate to believe that the Church of St. Jaques alone, where
Rubens is buried, contains more sculptures and first rate
paintings than can be found in all the United States. There
is also a curious place to see called Calvary, made to imitate
the side of a mountain—our Savior on the cross at the top—
and sculptures of all the patriarchs, prophets, and apostles and
the sepulcher at the bottom. Near this is a representation
of purgatory in painted wood, in which men and women are
represented in flames and looking up wistfully. This reminds me that I forgot to describe a sepulchral monument
in Ostend, which is attached like a shed to the side of the

great church some ten feet by four, and represents a family
of several persons in marble also in purgatory with piteous
faces.   All is inclosed in glass with an inscription in Dutch,
"Do us good with your prayers and with your alms."   Can
you conceive a more painful monument?   The churches on
the continent, so far as I have seen, are infinitely better kept,
and the works of art are immeasurably beyond those in
England.   The sculptures in wood are wonderful in execution
as well as in quantity, and from some late works the art seems
still in the highest preservation.   The pulpits especially are
works of the highest merit, and are managed with a boldness
of design which astonishes.   I am bringing home to you some
fine prints which will show you their merit.   I must think a
higher civilization prevails here than in England, and taste
which has hardly an existence there.   The hotels are also in-
comparably better.   The country is well cultivated, and living
cheap.   We visited this evening a large gallery of pictures
by modern artists.   Among the rest one is painfully impressed
upon my memory both by the wonderful power in its execution and its subject—the Counts Egmont and Horn as they
were laid on the scaffold after decapitation.   The collection
contains many works of merit, and shows the remarkable advancement of these happy and industrious people.   The park
contains trees in great numbers worthy of America.   We
visited also the beautiful botanical gardens.   The lace manu-
factory employs more than 1,300 young women.   At 2 o'clock
we set out for the battle-ground of Waterloo, distant about
fifteen miles.   The road passes through a fine forest which
has lately been much cut away on one side.   The soil is fine,
and produces huge crops of buckwheat.   At the village of
Waterloo, twelve miles, we entered the little church to see
the monuments (very poor ones, mere slabs against the walls)
to commemorate many of the fallen.   At the village of
Mount St. Jean, two and one-half miles farther, we left our
carriage and walked half a mile to the monument raised by
the King of Holland in 1825 on the spot where the Prince

of Orange was wounded. It is a mound precisely like that of our Indians taken from the adjoining soil. It is two hundred feet high, and surmounted by a pedestal and lion of proportionate height. We passed on our way to it through a stubblefield, a man knitting and watching sheep, while a women, a little further on, was gathering a basket of buckwheat. After ascending the Mont du Lion, and seeing all the field which was duly explained, I called at the Bayard's at an early hour to have our passports vised, and was very kindly received by Mr. Bayard. In the evening they all called, but we were out and did not see them.

I write at a little mountain town between Basle and Soleure, having sent off a hasty note this morning to tell you of our safety. I now return to Coblentz, from whence I sent my last missive. I regretted that I had but little time to tell you of the Rhine and its various points of interest below Coblentz. The scenery is uninteresting until Bonn is passed, when the Sieben Gebirge, with Rolandseck (Toggenberg) and Nonnenwerth, all at once opened upon us. Nearly every height has its ancient fortress, but only above Coblentz does the scenery equal our expectations. We slept at the latter place, which is opposite Ehrenbreitstein. I arose at six the next morning, to examine the "Gibraltar of the Rhine." I mounted to the top. The views in all directions are beautiful. The Moselle enters the Rhine at Coblentz, and has a Roman bridge over it. I walked about the old town and entered the churches, where the people were at morning prayer. In fact, you can seldom enter a church at any time without finding men and women devoutly kneeling in different places, often at some shrine, where they have lighted a poor candle, all that their poverty can allow. We continued on our way, past many an old ruin tenanted only by its legend of the Middle Ages. Leaving Prussia, we entered the dominion of Nassau, and then Hesse-Darmstadt. At Mayence we took the railroad to Frankfort, and slept there. The town was full, on occasion of its annual fair, and

the streets were full of booths. We saw the cathedral and
Dannaker's celebrated Ariadne, which you know, and also
the old Rothschild house in the Jew quarter, and proceeded
to Heidelberg, a small town in the valley of the Neckar, but
having the finest castle we have seen in Germany. It is magnificent in its beauty and position. We first saw here tobacco
largely cultivated and very flourishing, looking better, I
think, than in Virginia; and all along the Rhine there are
patches of it, and sometimes stunted Indian corn. From
Heidelberg, we came through Carlsruhe to Baden-Baden,
where we passed the night. The situation is beautiful—a cup
among the lovely hills of the Odenwald, surmounted by two
old castles, having a medieval subterranean communication at
least a mile long, through which judges passed to try criminals, who were let down through a trap-door some one or two
hundred feet. The horrible cells still exist, and the instruments of torture are also there, but unused. Above these are
the magnificent salons of the Grand Duke of Baden, glittering in gilding and pictures. We also visited an old convent,
attached to which is an orphan house, the gift of the tailor
Schultz, who was a native of Baden. From there we passed
on to Strasbourgh, and entered the French territory. Every-
where the words in large characters—*Liberté, Fraternité,
Egalité*—met our view, and our trunks were examined. We
dined, and went forthwith to the noble cathedral, whose
foundation was laid by Charlemagne. This tower, you know,
is the highest in the world, and the most beautiful. It is one
hundred and fifty feet higher than St. Paul's, and the clock is
the wonder of the world. The stained glass is the finest we
have seen, and the sculptures are innumerable. Thence, to
see the admirable tomb of Marshal Saxe, by order of Louis
XV., and the statue of Guttenberg, the inventor of printing;
and then on by railroad to Basle, where we arrived last night
all safe. We found very pleasant company in the cars, which,
from Frankfort, are the best we have yet seen for comfort and
cleanliness; and the people are civil and polished; the man-

agers of the roads are really gentlemanly; the stations very
handsome and convenient buildings, surrounded by flowers
and shrubbery.   Heidelberg was embowered in flowers, in
honor of a visit the day before of their sovereign, the Grand
Duke of Baden.   During our stay of three or four hours, I
availed myself of the time to visit the grave of Mr. Peter's
wife, who died here in 1836.   At Basle, both taste and civilization are lower.   At the old cathedral (now Protestant) are
buried Erasmus and several other noted persons.   Holbein
was born there, and there is a small gallery of his paintings.
I am surprised at my success in languages, both in French
and German, and I doubt not I could get along well even
alone; but it would scarcely be safe to travel in these mountains with only a *vetturino*.

Our courier is not what might have been expected from his
high recommendation in England that he brought us.   I have
a written agreement, which will enable me to dismiss him if
we do not like him.   We have advanced some leagues, and
find the tops of the mountains already covered with snow.
The roads are excellent.   We turned aside a short distance
from Soleure, to see the tomb of Kosciusko, who passed the
latter years of his life at Soleure.   It is a square pedestal of
masonry, surmounted by a shaft some three or four feet high,
with a short inscription, almost covered with the names of
Poles, who have thus commemorated their pilgrimages.   We
reached Berne on the 18th.   I saw its bears—living, sculptured, and painted—for they are to be seen every-where.   We
passed the night in an excellent hotel.

We left Geneva, after a pause of one day, for Lausanne,
where we passed a day to see the town, the Gibbon House,
etc.

The party consisting of Mrs. Peter, Mrs. King, their
maid and the three little boys finally reached the beautiful Lanen about sunset.   The view was enchanting.

The water was covered with little boats filled with people singing with great glee.

" We slept at the village of Lanen where Melancthon lived, and passed next morning to Waldstallen Lake, where we found an English gentleman, Mr. Frederick John Wood, barrister in Chancery London and his wife, who proved very agreeable people. The steamer had stopped the day before, and we hired a little row boat together to cross over to Waggis at the foot of the Righi. The ascent required from three to four hours, and we could not expose the children, so Lizzie stayed at Waggis whilst I mounted the Righi with our new friends and passed the night, rising early next morning to see the sun rise upon the grandest of landscapes overlooking the Waldstellen, a lake of the four cantons—the center of Tell's country as it has been called, also the Lake of Zug, even the Lake of Zurich, with all the country between with its towns and villages. At the foot of the mountain, is the former site of the village of Golden overwhelmed with all its inhabitants by a fearful slide in 1806 from the Rossberg. Away to the south are seen the showy and broken peaks of the Jungfrau, Wetterhorn, etc., while Pilatus frowns upon us from across the Waldstellen Lake. The hotel Kulm, at which I write, is the highest point of the Righi, and is low in comparison with its neighbors, but its position as the advanced guard of the Oberland Alps gives it a pre-eminent landscape. After visiting Shaffhausen and the falls of the Rhine, which are very fine, and then here to Constance, the place where poor Huss and Jerome met their martyrs doom, I have seen the house near the gate, where he came under the emperors safe conduct to lodge, but was forthwith arrested and committed to prison. The place where Huss stood in the church to receive the monstrous sentence which was given by the council was shown to us, and also the place of execution. This church was enormously rich, and still contains an immense quantity of solid silver, I should think more than a thousand pounds

8

made up in candalabre images, etc. The vestments are also of immense value in gold embroideries and laces. We were shown some of the latter in guipure more than four hundred years old. All the services here are in Latin or German, and we could understand nothing of them."

MUNICH, *Oct. 7th.*

Arrived last night. Our first visit, having engaged a *valet de place*, was to the Glypbothek, a beautiful classic building of white, exquisitely decorated and filled with ancient sculpture, Egyptian, Greek and Roman, arranged in the most perfect taste. The Pinacothek is still larger and more highly decorated and filled with fine paintings from the thirteenth to the present century—containing some eighteen apartments, most of them very large and lofty, and lighted through violet colored glass from above. One immense room is occupied by the productions of Rubens, and is magnificent. Besides this there is a large and elegant building appropriated to modern painters and sculptors, an art union, etc. The royal palaces are all painted in frescoe, with designs from Homer, the Niebelungen Lied and other German historical legends; and sculptures, too, are every-where. The churches have the grandest frescoes of modern times—the floors are covered with marble and the walls with sculpture. It is positively inconceivable how one man, and he a king of a second rate power only, could have collected and executed so much and so well. During four days we were busy from morning till night, seeing the works created by his order, and yet many more left unseen. Munich is confessedly the center of modern European art, and we ought to have staid a month. You can have no idea of the grandeur of these productions, confined as they are in so small a space, for Munich is about the size of Cincinnati. I must not fail to speak of the great bronze statue of Bavaria—it is beautiful and of such gigantic proportions that eight people, of whom we were two, were easily seated in the head. It has nothing coarse, but exhibits a sweet womanly expression of face, combining vigor, good-

ness and gentleness. The artist Schwanthaler died in his
forty-sixth year, before it was quite completed. I wonder we
do not hear more of him in America. There is a sublime
moral grandeur in all his conceptions, which excel any other
artist whose works I have yet seen. I have a catalogue of his
works which are as wonderful in number as excellence. We
saw both King Louis (the builder), and King Max, his son,
every day driving about the streets. You remember the
father resigned during the troubles three years ago, and now
enjoys his retirement, it is said, in great happiness. I wish I
had time to write more about Munich, which place we left on
Saturday, passing through Augsberg and Donnenwerth to
Ratisbon, and about four o'clock we seated ourselves in a little
carriage to visit the Walhalla, some six miles below on the
Danube. This you know is another creation of King Louis.
It is copied from the Parthenon, and stands on a moderate
height, which is seen from the Danube for many miles. It is
dedicated to German greatness—and painters, philosophers,
statesmen and women, and a few warriors find a place and
commemoration there. The king every-where shows his
desire to commemorate the civic and moral virtues rather than
warlike fame. I can only say of this work, as of others, that
it is grand and beautiful, and it is admitted that there is
nothing in Europe so fine; but the Colonnade, beautiful
as it is, does not equal Girard College. It contains
many busts and tablets, and I suppose as years roll on
it will be filled. The difficulty of navigating the river
after sunset compelled us to stay over night at the little
village of Welshofen. Our accommodations were much the
same as in all German taverns—rooms without carpets, narrow beds with a small feather bed about the size of a large
pillow for covering, and great vulgar looking pottery stoves.
It is a surprise to me how these people sleep under such covering, unless they coil themselves up like snakes. We have
always asked for other covering but rarely got it. Here we
had the good fortune to get a blanket.

Throughout Switzerland, or wherever the German race prevails, we find a singular stolidity and consequent want of progress—they seem like the bears, capable of learning only to a certain point. I doubt whether they are really at all in advance of their ancestors of five hundred years ago—their governors doubtless advance, but not the people. Just opposite our house, last night, there was a ball, with quite tolerable music—of course it was a ball of the bourgeois and peasantry—the windows were all open and we could see everything. The men wore their hats and the women had their hair all falling over their shoulders. They kept it up all night, and it was riotous and unseemly. The more I see of Europe the more am I convinced in the belief which I have often expressed home respecting the foreign immigrants, that they are inferior to the American race, who have more just notions of right, and are less given over to their passions, and are altogether a finer, milder, and better constituted race" [This was Mrs. Peter's opinion of the Northern Europeans—she modified her views after she had extended her travels to Italy, and saw a marked difference between the German and Italian races]. "So far, I like the people of Belgium, and along the Rhine best, where the German is tinctured by an admixture of the French element. I sometimes remember, and I think the observation just, that you once made, 'that all the better part of the English character comes from the Norman.'"

VIENNA, *Oct.* 15th.

We passed the town of Passau, of historic memory, and its immense fortresses. It lies on two points of land at the juncture of the Ilm and Ilz with the Danube, and is one of the very finest points on this noble river, the scenery of which becomes finer as we descend. We passed many an old ruined castle, perched high upon the rocky summits overlooking the river, and among them the savage Dürrenstein, in whose aerial dungeon poor Richard, of the Lion Heart passed long and doubtless tedious years of captivity. We reached Lintz early in the P. M., and had time to enjoy the fine scenery and also to send a telegraphic dispatch, at the instigation of our friendly landlord, to bespeak rooms at Vienna, and a carriage to receive us at Nierdorf, some three miles distant, the landing of travelers. Before settling down in our hotel I ran off to the banker to ask for letters. They had not yet arrived, and have probably not yet had time. I wish longingly for the next letters, which I hope will give your ideas of our longer staying, although I desire most earnestly to be at home again, and dread a longer stay so much that it would be a positive relief to have the question decided; yet I know I shall always regret not having seen Italy. At Lintz, we saw in the house-book, the names of William Story, the Springers, Taylors, etc., with many other of our acquaintances who had been there. Having employed a *valet de place*, we duly set forth this morning to see sights; and first we went to the Augustine Church to see what is called the masterpiece of Canova—the monument of the Archduchess of Saxe F——, and in a subterranean apartment, to see ranged in a row the silver vases of various sizes, which contain the hearts of the imperial family — among them is that of Napoleon's son—the bodies being elsewhere. After driving through the city palace courts we set forth *en voiture* to Schönbrun, and walked through the forest gardens some two hours, then back to the hotel to look after the children and take a little refreshment, then to the regal palace of Lichtenstein. The architectural decorations here exceed any we have seen any where, and Windsor sinks into a common country house in comparison. There is, however, no gallery of pictures—only think.

The doors of the grand salon are twenty feet high, and from five to six wide—one side rosewood, the other solid plate glass (mirror), made to turn on a pivot which a child can move. There are a great number of grand apartments, and almost if not quite every one is hung with brocade of exquisite colors and patterns, and ornamented with fringe of the most delicate patterns, finely gilt—the ceilings are elaborately

wrought in stucco, and the floors are all of the most tasteful
and delicate patterns of wooden mosaic. When lighted it
must present a fairy scene—but, alas! for the poverty without. We called to see our charge, Mr. McCurdy, who has so
well sustained his place as minister of our country. He is
from Connecticut, and received us with great kindness and
frankness. We then went to drive in the Prater, the most
famous drive in Europe, at this season, beautiful in its autum-
nal tints. It is but little frequented by the higher ranks.
In the people's quarter we found many entering and seeing
the antics of a Punch and Judy, and children riding in a
whirlligig.

As the children were with us we gave them also a ride, and
as it grew dark we returned stopping at some shops to make
a few purchases for the children. Tommy begins to stand
alone against the wall, and is as proud as a little peacock.

We have met several Hungarians on the steamer who
unite in saying that Kossuth is not a true man or patriot;
that he has always carefully avoided personal danger, into
which he has led others, and that he labors for his own glory
alone, all which I believe is true. *Verbum sat, etc.* I suppose he will soon be showing off in America.

16*th.* No letter yet, but I have sought to forget my disappointment in seeing sights with which Vienna 'is full. I
have seen to-day the coffers or rather bronze inclosures of
some four hundred years of Austrian Emperors and their
children. The Empress Marie Theresa has the loftiest tomb
of all. God in mercy bless and preserve you, adieu.

DRESDEN, *Oct.* 22*d.*

Having escaped the perils by which life and liberty are
so often and so innocently jeopardized in Austria, I positively
breathe more freely now that we are safely beyond its con-
fines. While beneath the shadow of the double-headed eagle,
which is but the type of the fabled Argus, I was positively
afraid to tell you how heartily I despised their entire system
of oppression. Since twelve o'clock to-day, we breathe Saxon

air, which, though bad enough, is safe, and I may venture,
under a seal, to say what I think. Since the last and most
absurd revolution, Austria has been one great camp, having
out posts at every practicable point, and no one is allowed to
pass without permission previously obtained. Soldiers singly
or in numbers quietly ride or walk through the streets by
day and night, and large bodies of troops are marching and
counter-marching in every direction. In all places of public
resort or amusement, they stand guard as if in a garrison.
At the railroad stations, especially, they are armed *cap-à-pie*.
Whilst so many men are withdrawn from the industrial
affairs, the women take their places as laborers, and more
women twice over are engaged in agriculture than men.
They are constantly engaged in ploughing, driving oxen, digging, scattering manure, and are in bodies working on the
roads. They carry away dirt in wheel-barrows with surprising agility, and dig as vigorously with pick, axe, and spade as
any of our Irishmen. They are also principal street cleaners.
They look happy and healthy; in general, more so than our
women of the same class, but are coarse, brown, and wrinkled.
The general stupidity of the people is remarkable, and, so
far as I can learn, they are encouraged by the higher classes
to go on just as their forefathers began, and discourage all
progress or change. A gentleman in Vienna told me that
there are thousands of men there who had learned their
trade in a certain way, and starved upon it, whereas, if they
would sometimes make the slighest alteration, they would
speedily grow rich, but being accustomed to one way, nothing could induce them to change it. Carpets are unknown,
at least unseen—blankets too—and a common sized decanter
of water and a sort of pie-dish with one towel, with perhaps
a large and elegant mirror and pretty frescoe paintings, a
narrow bed with covering never wide enough to cover you."

This, it must be remembered, was nearly forty years
ago. The great increase of travel and the exactions of
English and American travelers for their accustomed

comforts and necessities have made a vast change in the convenience of European travel. Before the great ingress of foreigners into this country, the code of propriety in regard to the use of tobacco was very different from that which now exists. The following extract from a letter will show not only the feeling of an individual, but the tone of public sentiment among Americans at that time :

"You enter an elegant salon and are stifled in a moment by clouds of tobacco smoke of men who call themselves gentlemen regaling themselves on this nauseous weed, regardless of the presence of ladies."

This would not astonish an American now, for in his own country private, as well as public, salons are invaded by the tobacco smokers ; alas, encouraged by the women.

"We were in Vienna five days and saw a number of pictures and sculptures, but here (Dresden) the collections are far finer. On Sunday we attended service at the royal chapel and at the Greek Church. At both the music is very fine. At the latter was of a character quite new to us—a sort of chant very different from any thing we have ever heard. Only think of our standing beside the coffin of Rudolph of Hapsburgh. We left Vienna on Monday, and passing over the field of Wagram, and soon after the battle-ground where Rudolph gained the victory which made him master of Bohemia, and along the frontier of Hungary and by Austerlitz, halting a while under the fearful walls of the Spielberg, we entered Bohemia, and arrived at eight o'clock at Prague. All of yesterday we drove about to see its lions, which are many, and to admire the wonderful beauty of its position and environs. It is, by far, in its locale the most gloriously beautiful city that we have seen ; not in itself, but in its environments and the judicious position of its principal edifices. The language is different from the German and decidedly oriental. We were able to give but one day to Prague. We arrived at Dresden to-day in time to set forth to see sights, and accomplished a good deal before dark. Our first visit was to the gallery of paintings, which is one of the best in Europe. The buildings here are quite inferior to Munich or Vienna, but their contents are greatly superior to the latter. The greatest work of Raphael, the Madonna di San Sisto, is here, and I am quite willing to call it an "immortal production." I am inquiring carefully the prices of copies, and devoutly hope to persuade our friends in Cincinnati to order some of the best here.

There is one of the San Sisto just being finished for the King of Denmark, as nearly as possible equal to the original, and the Emperor of Russia is getting copies of a great number. We have also been through the royal palace, etc.

23d. This has been a busy day. We have visited churches, and again the gallery and the Green Vaults, containing a collection of articles of *vertu* amounting in value by computation to £200,000!! To describe it would require a volume; but I shall bring for you the catalogue, to show you its contents. It is the finest collection of its kind in the world. The diamonds are magnificent. There is also the best collection of medieval armor in Europe, containing suits of every distinguished man for centuries. One of these is inlaid with gold and covered with *relievos* of great merit, representing the labors of Hercules, etc. The British collections are small compared to this. During three hundred years, the princes of Saxony have diligently enlarged and preserved this collection, and such is the reverence in which it has been held that neither Frederick of Prussia nor Napoleon allowed it to be touched or injured in any way. It is a treasure-house for art and genius. We drove out also to see the little monument erected by Alexander of Russia to commemorate the death of Moreau on the spot where he fell.

BERLIN, *Oct.*

On Friday night we reached Berlin, and passed all of yesterday in running about. The galleries here are quite inferior

to Dresden, though very extensive. The palace is gorgeous
beyond any precedent. Every door is gilded, and as much is
put on the walls as they can readily contain, with frescoes on
the ceilings. The most remarkable sight, however, of all is
the Egyptian collection, arranged by Dr. Lepsius to represent the temples from which the antiquities were brought.
Each room represents the interior of some temple—its columns
covered with hieroglyphics, and the sculptures and sarcophagi,
etc., brought from Egypt. I called on Mr. Barnard, our minister, an old acquaintance, who seemed very glad to see me.
His health is bad. To-morrow we set out for Paris, where I
devoutly pray I may find letters. We are all well.

PARIS, *November* 11*th.*

Since sending off my last letter, we have been so busily engaged in sight-seeing that we have nearly completed our pro-
gramme here. We have visited in turn the ancient parish
church of the Faubourg St. Germain, St. Sulpice, St. Etienne
du Mont—very old, heavy with age and historical events—
and the Sarbonne, so renowned in the Middle Ages, with its
beautiful monument of Cardinal Richlieu, and the famous
Port Royal, etc., full of reminiscences of Angelique Arnauld
and her illustrious family, whose ancient buildings are used
now as a maternity hospital—five thousand children born annually within its walls. To describe either of them would fill
my sheet, and I must wait to tell you what I can not write.
We also passed some hours yesterday in the gallery of the
Chamber of Deputies, or, as it is now called, the Assemblie
Nationale, having been furnished with tickets through the
kindness of Mr. Walsh. The confusion and entire absence
of order was such that to imagine such a scene one must see
it. The members could not be brought together until nearly
an hour past the appointed time for speaking, and the president, M. Dupin, vainly endeavored to induce them to be
seated by ringing again and again his *not* little bell, to which
they paid no attention whatever. As the speakers mounted
in turn the tribune, which resembles the reading-desk in front

of the pulpit, we could see them harangue, but not a word could we hear, although seated in the best position. Some intelligent women who sat near us expressed their displeasure to me in no measured terms, saying that each revolution made things worse; that men now neither feared nor respected any one, and the republic was a farce, proclaiming a liberty which had no real existence, and sustaining it at the point of the bayonet. The chamber is plainer than any thing I have seen, but I believe it is only temporary.

We left Paris at 8 o'clock on Thursday morning. Before leaving Paris, we went to a little cemetery, quite on the border of the city, to visit the simple tomb of La Fayette. It is attached to the Covuent of the Ladies of the Sacred Heart, and within a small space repose, perhaps, a larger number of the noblest families of France than in any other spot. Not even Père le Chaise can boast so many historical names of ancient renown. The *concierge* told us that many Americans visit it. One of La Fayette's daughters alone survives of his family. His grandson is a member of L'Assemblie Nationale— no great honor. After all, Paris did not equal my vast expectations. The people are evidently quick-witted and *spirituelle*, and the best workers we have found anywhere. Every thing is well done, and they are honest just as far as your bargain is accurately made; but it is impossible to feel any confidence in a people who have no fixed principle, and who are perpetually in a state of exaltation. It is singular, with all this capacity, there is so very little comfort, according to our ideas. The houses are elegantly decorated, but are cold, and the locks often out of order; the apartments are not well arranged; quantities of useless and cold ante-chambers, with small, ill-proportioned parlors and bed-rooms. In Dresden, I bought several pictures (copies), which I had neglected to mention: the Magdalen by Correggio, St. Cecilia of Carlo Dolce, both by Kallmeyer, who has furnished the Emperor Nicholas with some of his best pictures. I purchased them from himself, and hope they may induce others to order copies

of other pictures.   Kallmeyer is one of the board of directors
of the Dresden Gallery.   I shall be truly glad if the Cincinnati people will ask to have some copies for their gallery.   I
also purchased two porcelain pictures: Murillo's Fruit Sellers
and The Tribute Money, by Titian.   These are all valuable
pictures and perfect copies.

Whilst in Paris, Mrs. Peter busied herself in seeing
all that could be crowded into the short time she had
given herself to see this great capital, as she had determined to take Mrs. King and the children to Canterbury
to remain during the time she was pursuing her further
travels.

It had been her intention to go from Vienna down
the Danube with the whole party to Constantinople, and
after visiting Turkey and Greece, to go on by water to
Naples; but, on further consideration, it seemed too
much of an undertaking and a risk to the children, too
young to enjoy or profit by it.   Therefore, the determination was made to return to Canterbury; and after a
short sojourn in Paris, Mrs. Peter set forth with her
charge and reached the destined point safely.   All arrangements were made for a comfortable winter for Mrs.
King and her children, under the kindly care of Miss
Peter, and Mrs. Peter again set forth on her travels.

PART II.

DIJON, Nov., 1851.

I had a stormy passage over the Channel, and I was for the
first time sea sick.   I am now, however, quite recovered, and
am sitting in a nice room by a little wood fire in an old
fashioned chair, which doubtless had figured in some noble
residence.   In fact, I strongly suspect our hotel has been in
its day the residence of some dignitary.   Its noble *porte cochére*
and double courts; its thick walls almost bomb proof; its

long winding corridors; its rambling *escalieres* "up stairs and down stairs and in my lady's chamber," all seem to indicate an origin widely different from its present uses. I have had to-day some sensible bourgeois for my *compagnons de voyage*, and my day passed rather agreeably. I am very much struck with the vigorous activity of the French people, in which they seem greatly to excel the English. You never see among them the squalid misery and raggedness which especially the town order of English continually exhibit. I have been more struck with them in my late comparison of the English. It would seem that unless they can get just such employment as they choose and wages to suit, they will do nothing, while among the French one sees more good humor and versatility, and always decency of attire.

There is a good deal to see in Dijon. The tomb of Philip le Hardi and Jean-Sanspeur are the finest gothic structures of the kind in Europe, and some curious antiquities are also preserved. The churches, too, are fine, and in the cathedral, the sculptures are equal in execution, though not in numbers, to those in the Belgic cities. There is an old clock in one of the churches placed there by Philip le Hardi, which Froissart thought the most curious object in Europe in his day. The shops also show great advancement in the industrial as well as the fine arts, and there is also a school of design. This happened to be St. Cecilia's day, the Fête of the Musicians, and in the cathedral there has been a great celebration in music which of course I have heard. Yesterday en route from Paris a young woman entered the railway carriage carrying a baby a week old, bound up, as all French babies are, precisely after the fashion of a mummy. The parents it seems are shop-keepers', and the mother's time was too valuable to be spared in nursing, and the baby was therefore sent down into Burgundy, their place of origin, to be nursed. I give you this as a trait of manners which I thought obsolete. I left Dijon yesterday at 2 o'clock, and reached Chalons at 7, without any other adventure than the offer of a traveling companion who desired to have my company. I fear I seemed rather churlish, but it is not safe to take up such proposals lightly. The lady is an English spinster traveling with her maid, and I suspect possessed more money than head. In order to have a little quiet this afternoon, and expecting to attend an English service, I took the steamer at 6 A. M. (there is one nearly every hour) for Lyons. It was the prettiest and cleanest and best managed boat that I have ever seen any-where, and brought me down the Saone in six hours. On arriving I found the service is discontinued, and I pass the afternoon in solitude with my thoughts. The weather is cold and wet; there has been fine snow all day. I left England with flowers in full bloom in every garden. Since leaving Paris and advancing always further south, no vestige of a flower or green leaf is visible, all is like mid winter. The beautiful range of hills Cote d'or are lightly covered with snow with vineyards peeping out all over them.

Comfort and apparently happy industry constantly greet the eye. If we could judge the people in such a rapid transit, I should think the domestic and social virtues flourished to a degree that I had not suspected. Up to this moment I have not seen a single wretched looking vagabond in France, and the women, especially the old, have a cheerful, merry, active manner, which betokens happy hearts, very different from the woe-begone, look of the women of the rustic classes with us. I am quite perplexed at finding them so different from what I had preconceived. In manners Paris is no more France than Washington is America, nor in fact so much. The men I meet with are so far quite as attentive and polite as our Americans are to women, and they have an honest air about them which indicates right purposes, and a sort of plain common sense we do not find among the Germans. I am told I have passed through the finest part of France, as the name Cote d'or represents. I chat freely (thanks to my good knowledge of the language) with the people I meet, and they attribute their good condition both to the soil and to the equal fortune of the people. None very rich; none, but the worthless, poor. I do not pretend to offer these remarks as being worth more than the time which I have had for observation would entitle them.

From Lyons Mrs. Peter went to Avignon, and throughout this region she was diligent in her investigation of the Roman ruins. After arriving at Avignon she was escorted to the Hotel of the Palace National where she secured a good room and a *valet de place*.

This functionary soon appeared and proved very attentive and intelligent. With him I went to the grand old Palace of the Popes, the Cathedral, the Musée of Antiquities, Picture Galleries, etc. Among them the *refacciamento* of the tomb of Laura, who as you know lived and died here. Her proper tomb, with that of her family, was destroyed by the brigands of the revolution of '93. This being completed, and some souvenirs in the form of private purchases, I made haste to my rooms to finish my letter to R——. I must not forget to mention the cathedral as a combination of Roman, Byzantine, and Gothic architecture. Originally the front belonged to the Temple of Hercules. It was enlarged by the Greeks to form a Christian Church, and finally adorned and further enlarged by the Catholics. Several of the Popes are interred within. The Palace contains sad remembrances of the atrocities of the French Revolution. The whole is now occupied as a barrack for the three thousand troops who are necessary to maintain *Liberté, Egalitié, Fraternité*. Having finished my letter, I hurried down to dinner, and when at the *table d'hôte*, a seat having been reserved for me, judge of my surprise on seeing seated by me at the same table the lady who at Chalons had desired to be my traveling companion. She had joined some English people and was on her way to Marseilles, or wherever her kind star would lead her. She seemed so glad to see me, and I was glad to hear my own tongue, which is now almost strange in my ears, that I answered her questions with good will; and, as she seemed greatly to desire it, I consented that she should accompany me that morning to Vancluse.   Thither then we went, setting out at 6:30 o'clock.   It lies some fourteen miles east of Avignon, and the road passes over a pretty country planted in olives, which the people are just gathering, also grapes and madder, which is a great source of profit in the department at Vaucluse.

The fountain is really wonderful.   It lies at the base of a mountain of solid rock some five or six thousand feet high. The fountain is very deep, and at high water overflows and washes over the valley.   Now, at low water, it finds a subterranean outlet some fifty feet distant, and pours forth a copious river clear as. crystal into the Rhine at Avignon.   It is not possible to convey a correct idea of this wonderful phenomenon, and it is not surprising that to a poetical mind like Petrarch it possessed so high a charm.   We returned by the same route passing the country house of the well-known deputy Cremieuex, a Jew.   Having deposited the lady at the Hotel and paid my bill, I changed the horses which had taken us to Vaucluse and placed my trunk behind the carriage, I again set forth with my *cochére* of the morning to visit the *Pont de Gard*.   We reached the village as it grew dark, and I was not a little surprised to see my driver plunge suddenly into an arched passage as solid in its structure of groined arches as if intended to support a cathedral.   Here he requested me to descend, and forthwith conducted me through this crypt, which it appeared was a stable, to the other end where issued light indicating the existence of a household.   He then ushered me into a large kitchen, which contained some half dozen people engaged in various culinary affairs, and having asked a smiling, matronly dame if she could give me a little chamber with fire, she answered in the affirmative, and seizing a tallow candle conducted me along the brick floored entry, up the stone steps and along several narrow corridors, to a decent apartment with a red tiled floor, a good bed and muslin curtains.   I begged leave to stay by the kitchen fire until my room was warm, then descended again to sit by the spit on which was extended a savory looking pair of fowls. I suggested to have one of the chickens for my dinner, and as soon as my room was warm re-ascended to commence my letter, but was soon interrupted by the appearance of three bouncing damsels bringing, one a table cloth, another castors, knives and forks, a third something else. My dinner was soon on the little table, and the mistress having joined her maids, altogether, with an immense dog of the Pyrenees and two cats who had taken leave to offer the pleasure of their company for reasons best known to themselves, the whole posse manifested a strong desire to see me dine. I, however, managed to induce the bipeds to withdraw, and the others, perforce were obliged to follow, and I ate in quietness; and now I must say good night, and pray that God will preserve and bless each one of you.

MARSEILLES, 1851.

To-day has been rich in sight-seeing. I emerged from our little cabaret at Remonlue's, Department du Gard, about 7 this morning, and proceeded toward the Pont du Gard, one and a half mile distant. The whole aspect of the country is singularly arid, as if the soil had long been exhausted. The south of France, I find, is by no means a land of beauty and fertility. The country is covered with olive orchards which, at a distance, resemble apple orchards, but on approaching there is neither freshness nor grass, and the bluish green of their foliage soon wearies the eye. The soil is a mingling of sand and pebble, and the wonder is that any thing can vegetate. The hills are chiefly bare rocks, with a scanty vegetation in the fissures. Here, it is true, you can find the fig and the jessamine, the box and other trees and shrubs we are accustomed to think rare, but they are sadly inferior to our healthy and fresh vegetation in a region which refuses even the olive.

All solitary, in the broad waste, stands the magnificent structure I propose to visit. Eighteen centuries have failed to subvert a work which seems destined to last while the earth

9

endures. I will not occupy my remaining space by a description you can find in print. Seek, therefore, for an account of this venerable relic. I walked over and around it under a beautiful and bright morning sun, most rare during my experience on this continent, whose lead-colored skies grow wearisome, and then I passed on over miles of olive and doleful mulberry trees, stunted and misshaped from being constantly stripped of foliage for the silk worms, but nothing which we should denominate a tree has cheered my eye for some days. It is doubtless a want of forests and their shade that the country is so wasted. The villages are all built of the limestone of which the hills are formed, and look old enough to have been built and washed by the waters of the flood.

Thus I and my *cocher* reached Nismes about half-past 10 o'clock. Having deposited my luggage at the railroad depot, I set forth instanter on my quest after the antiquities which here, it appears, are quite equal to any in Italy. The Arène is said to be in better preservation than the Coliseum. It is wonderful, but the exquisite little temple called the Maison Carré is a gem in the most astonishing preservation. It is now, after fearful vicissitudes, in good hands and carefully looked after. All these, and several of minor interest, belong to the age of Augustus. I have prints of all, which I shall bring home, *Deo volente*. Leaving Nismes at 2:20 P. M., I reached here by railroad at half-past 7. I have to wait till 12 to-morrow to get my passport *viséd*, then on toward Nice, passing Sunday at Cannes. I get on without the least difficulty, the French are so polite, but I would gladly have one of you with me. God bless you all.

NICE, SARDINIA.

The day before yesterday I sent off to you from Marseilles a sort of general epistle, thinking you would all be anxious to hear from your solitary wanderer. I now avail myself of the first hour of repose to recommence my journal. It was annoying to me to be obliged to stop at Marseilles, a town of ill-fame, which contains absolutely nothing to interest a stranger, especially as I had thought to pass the Sunday here, where there are English services. I was obliged to console myself by thinking you would all remember me in your prayers, and passed the day in writing to several persons, to whom I ought to have written a month ago had I found time. I also accepted an invitation from some fellow-travelers to take a drive on the Prado, a pretty public place on the seashore, with some beautiful views. The American Consul is an old acquaintance from Philadelphia (Mr. Hodge), on whom I was obliged to call to *visée* my passport.

He appeared rejoiced to see me and invited me to dinner, which I willingly accepted. All this being accomplished, I went to bed and rose to set forth in the diligence for Nice. The day was beautiful, and the roads fine as are all the roads which I have seen in France. The Alps are constantly in view with their snow crowned summits. Just as we were about to start on our journey, a curious procession passed along the street. It was the first Sunday in Advent, and a number of male penitents were making a pilgrimage. They wore a sort of white cloak with a hood and mask. Their faces were entirely covered, though I suppose they saw their way through some imperceptible slit in the mask. We set forth on our route and met carts and men and women employed at their usual work. Within two hours we came to a village where a number of people were just returning from church, having a number of little girls dressed in white with veils and garlands on their heads, attended by boys of their own age each wearing a crown of thorns. In the evening, as we passed through other villages, we met processions of men marching after a drum, each bearing in his hand a paper lantern, some of them being tri-colored. This, they said, was a political association. I traveled all night and slept quite tolerably in my comfortable seat until about daylight. We passed Lord Brougham's pretty villa near Cannes, facing the sea. After leaving this village the road becomes beautiful,

indeed.   It is regularly planted with olive trees of large size,
and borders along the beautiful sea through plantations
where the orange and the olive seem to dispute the possession
of the land with the fig tree and vine.   Near Cannes,
Napoleon landed from Elba and passed his first night in one
of these olive gardens through which the road passes.   A
poor little column is raised at the place to commemorate the
event, and at a cabaret near by the traveler is invited to
enter and drink in honor of the Great Emperor.   It is astonishing to note every-where, especially in Germany and
Switzerland, where he did so much mischief, how tenderly the
memory of Napoleon is cherished.   Passing along this lovely
region by the light of a magnificent morning sun, with the
snowy heights of the Col de Tenda constantly in view, we
soon reached the Pont de Van, a little stream which separates
France and Sardinia—here our passports are examined by the
Sardinian authorities, who also had a right to search our luggage, but contented themselves with most of us by our affirma-
tion that we had no contraband goods.   We then came along
the beautiful bay on which Nice is situated, and arrived
about 11 o'clock.   When I had deposited my luggage in a
nice room at the Hotel des Etrangers, I indulged in a comfortable warm bath, and set forth for a walk up to the old
fortress.   Nice is a great resort for English people, many
making it a regular winter residence.   So far, owing to my
most useful knowledge of foreign language, I have not the
slightest difficulty in getting on.   This morning an Englishman (who, poor gentleman, had been obliged to depend upon
me to translate every word he had uttered since we left Marseilles) remarked that it was a great undertaking for me to
travel alone.   I replied it was a far greater one for him, and
he frankly admitted it.   Yet I do deeply feel the want of my
kindred, and yesterday and the day before, the 29th and 30th,
which always brings the last hours of our dear T. perpetually to my thoughts, I grieved that no sympathizing heart
was near to cheer my thoughts and talk of him.

GENOA, *Dec. 3d.*

The road along the Mediterranean from Nice to Genoa is renowned as the most beautiful in Europe. It passes around a constant succession of bays and headlands, these latter often crossed at a dizzy height, so that backward and forward the views are the loveliest imaginable, whilst the beautiful blue sea stretches away in the distance. The day was lovely, and wherever the clefts of the rock of which the mountains are composed admit, little patches of land are terraced so that we had a continuation of olives and oranges, and figs and grapes. Palm tree are not infrequent. We passed the little kingdom of Monaco and had our trunks examined. Did you ever before hear of this ancient thimble full of monarchy? Look just north-east of Nice for it. This road is called the Riviera and the Cornici road. We traveled by a brilliant moon all night, and passed this morning the village of Cogotette, where it is said Columbus was born. The claim is asserted in large letters on the front of a house where it is declared he first saw the light, and his portrait is also painted on the wall. Pursuing our way, we reached Genoa about one o'clock, and I lost no time in securing a *valet de place* to guide me about the town. I first ascended the highest cupola, Sante Maria di Carignan, and magnificent is the view there displayed. I saw the Doria palace, and a benevolent institution, which still retains the name of the founder, the unfortunate Fiesco. I visited all the beautiful public walks and other places of interest which I shall tell you of hereafter.

My room is high up, and overlooks the grand harbor full of vessels and of transcendent beauty. There is a bright moonlight, and as I look down upon the stately ships lying in rows in the symmetrical curve of the harbor, and the lofty snow-capped hills, I wonder if these people do not remember some times that their forefathers once contended with Venice for the mastery of the world, while they—degenerate—have allowed themselves to become the mere appendage of this third-rate, broken down Sardinian princedom.

Ever since we left France there is a singular falling off in the prosperous appearance of the peasantry. Beggars swarm around, and all looks at a standstill. This is the season for the annual conscription for the supply of the army of his Sardinian majesty, and as we wound around the mountains on the way from Nice, we met frequent large gangs of wretched looking creatures, not one in twenty decently clad, each party being attended by two or three in military dress. This conscription claims by lot—twenty out of every one hundred men of twenty years of age. I was preparing my sympathies for their hard fate, when I was told that nothing could be more advantageous to these ignorant peasants who, during the four years of service, learn to read and write and behave like men. The costume of the women in Genoa is quite remarkable, and I am bringing some prints to show you. The churches in Genoa appear to be all of Greek architecture, and to my taste too much crowded with ornament. The Church of the Annunciation startles you on entering with the prodigious quantity and splendor of its gilding, all in marble of different colors, red, black and white and variegated. The vaulted roof is wrought in panels inclosed in a blaze of gilding, and every possible spot is covered with gilding or painting in fresco. In the cathedral there is an inscription that Genoa was founded by a grandson of Noah, etc. This same church contains a chapel dedicated to John the Baptist, into which, out of spite to Herodias, no woman is allowed to enter except during one day in the year—a very useless sort of vengeance, however, since every cranny of the interior is visible and best seen from the front, which is open to all the world. It is strange to stand so familiarly at the hearthstones of the Dorias and Balbi and Durazzo, which are very kindly opened to the public every day. I passed through the breakfast-room of the Balbi just as they had finished at 11 A. M., and a moment after the marchesa, a pretty creature, ran in to recover a letter which had been left on the table. I cease to wonder that Italy is the school of art, for every thing here is picturesque. You

can scarcely see a common porter standing against a wall
waiting for work, but you are struck with the picturesqueness
of his attitude. The houses all look like palaces, and many
are eight or nine stories high, for, as somebody says, "Genoa
is a dreadfully up and down place;" and then there are houses
built in the valley by the side of streets, running along on
arches, which have more stories than I am willing to tell
you.

The style of architecture is positively Cyclopian, and seems
destined to last as long as time. The Palace Brignoli has the
finest collection of "old masters." I left Genoa yesterday by
the Malle post, and reached Milan to-day at 2, and before I
went even to look for a hotel, I flew as fast as a pair of horses
could carry me to the bankers to get my longed for letters;
and, heaven be thanked, I found one from Mr. Peter and one
from L., but there was none from you. All I heard from
are well, and Mr. Peter gives me great encouragement in my
solitary travels. I get along without any sort of difficulty,
but it is not good to be alone. As soon as I had read and re-
read my precious letters, and had taken refreshment, I set
forth to see the Duomo, close by, the most magnificent piece
of Gothic architecture in the world. It is all white marble,
highly finished, and if it were cleaner I should fall into ecsta-
cies about it; but dust, however venerable it may appear upon
masses of coarse stone, such as York and Canterbury Cathedrals, looks downright nasty when it begrimes and sticks to a
smooth white surface. But it is a shame for me to speak so
irreverently of this grand pile. The interior fully equals the
outside, and from its freedom from screens and partitions the
proportions are better felt. The floor, as is usual in Italy, is
entirely of marbled Mosaic of varied patterns, and the exquisitely arched ceiling is so exquisitely painted that you suppose
t to be a mass of fretted stonework throughout. I was really
sorry to be informed that it was not carved, it is so exceedingly beautiful. Its subterranean wonders I shall see to-
morrow.

I passed through Pavia this morning, and grieved that I could not pause, for among many interesting things it contains the tombs of St. Augustine and Boethius, but I could not stay, for I expected letters here. I shall have to stay three days to see the cities of Como and Monza, and then on to Venice. I shall get on to Florence as fast as I can, for until I get there I shall hear nothing further from you. God bless and protect you all.

MILAN, *December* 6, 1851.

The labors of the day over, I fancy I am not so far away from you when I can devote the evening to a recital for your amusement of the various objects which have occupied me. Imagine me then, after Italian ideas of comfort, seated (by special request) in the smallest and warmest room which the Grand Hotel de la Ville can afford. It is about twenty-two feet long, twelve wide and fifteen high with a tile floor covered by a thin cheap mat, such as is often seen at home. At one end is a fire-place some three feet deep, and on a pair of low irons lie some scraps of wood, which somewhat resemble fire, but emit no heat. If you were burning some light poplar shavings in the open air you would have as comfortable a fire as mine. I sit as near it as I can with my heaviest cloak on, and yet my hands are chilled and my breath like a little steam pipe. As a consolation, I look on elegant frescoes whenever my eyes are turned to the ceiling, and I have the honor of being quite in the neighborhood of Manzoni, and the grand Duomo is close by. Every thing here is enormously dear, and when I get safely to Florence, perhaps it may be safe to tell you why it is so. For the present, "the least said, soonest mended," *verbum sat*, etc. Having secured a *valet de place* last night, all was ready to begin my quest this morning at 8:30 o'clock. When the *fiacre* drove to the door, I ascended it. The first object en route was the farthest off, viz., the Arena, built by Napoleon for the exhibition of all sorts of games, *à la romain*. It is, in form at least, an imitation of the Arena at Nismes, but very inferior as to architecture. Like

the others it can be filled with water for regattas and in winter
for skating, and being an oval of seven hundred and eighty
feet in its greatest diameter, there is ample room. There are
seats within for thirty thousand persons. It is, of course, open
at the top. It adjoins the Champ de Mars, a large open
space on the opposite side of which is the most beautiful arch
I have yet seen, commenced by Napoleon on the marriage of
Eugene Beauharnais, who you will remember was viceroy
here. His palace still exists and is now occupied by Marshal
Radetsky. My next visit was to the ancient monastery of
Santa Maria della Grazia, to see the remains of the great
fresco of Leonardi da Vinci, "The Last Supper," which you
have seen engraved. In the changes of time, the convent,
like many old churches, had been converted into a barrack,
and the refectory had absolutely been used as a stable, and
this great work of genius was covered over like the other
walls with dirty white-wash. It is to this good Eugene
Beauharnais, that we owe its cleansing and preservation so
far as possible, but it is sadly dilapidated and produces almost
as much grief as pleasure to the beholder. It is wonderful
in its ruin. Next, we went to the splendid Church of San
Vittori al Corpo, remarkable as having been the scene of the
exclusion (see Gibbon) of the Emperor Theodosius, by St.
Ambrose, Bishop of Milan, in consequence of his cruelties at
Thessalonica. The richness of this church in frescoes of three
or four hundred years old, is remarkable. Next, I went to
the Church of St. Ambrose, founded by himself, A. D. 387,
rebuilt, 868. In the nave is a pillar some ten feet high, on
which is a serpent, which it is pretended is the same which
Moses was commanded to sit up in the wilderness to heal the
Israelites. The tomb of the saint is said to contain immense
wealth and will be open to the public to-morrow, his fête,
when I hope to get a view of it, also to hear some of the far-
famed Ambrosian chants. They showed me, I forgot to say,
in the Church of San Vittori, the most wonderful embroidery
(almost finer than painting), which they say was executed five

hundred years ago. Then I went to the church of St. Lorenzo, which was built of the remains of a temple of Bacchus, and rebuilt by San Carlo Borromeo, of the same materials. Before it is a long row of Corinthian columns of Roman construction. One of the old chapels still exists, built by Ataulphus, successor to Alaric, whose wife was Placidia, sister to the Emperor Honorius.

Hers and her husband's tomb still remain there. Next we went to the Academy of Arts and Sciences where there is an excellent collection of the pictures of the old masters, and where I wished I could have authority to order some for home. I then went with my valet to the railroad station for Monza to see there the iron crown and the relics of the renowned Queen Theodelinda, the *genia loci* of Monza. In fifteen or twenty minutes we were set down, and proceeded to the old church founded by the queen, who was an intimate friend of Gregory the Great, who presented the nail of the true cross which forms the interior circlet of the crown, this nail having been brought from Palestine by the Empress Helena. The relics of the queen, her crown, cross, fan, etc., all jeweled and exceedingly curious, are first shown, and then proceeding to a chapel with several priests in robes bearing frankincense, one of them mounted a stair to a little altar, while another threw about the censer and filled the air with odors making with the others all manner of genuflections on account of this relic of the true cross.

In the midst of this the casket was opened, and inclosed in a reliquary adorned with gold and gems, and covered with glass, hung the object of my visit. The dozen candles which they had previously lighted looked strange in the broad sunshine. One of the priests proceeded with great reverence to inform me of the history and legends with which, of course, I was previously acquainted. All this ceremony was for my sole benefit (for, except my valet, I was alone), and for the prefixed sum of five francs. I lingered long in the old, old historic church, and thought of how much pleasanter it would have been had you all been there, hoped you would come next summer, and came back by the railway; walked to the hotel, past the Lazaretto described in *I promessi sposi*, ate my dinner, wrote to you, and now to bed. God bless you all.

Some one has said "See Naples and die." For Naples write the Lake of Como, for if the earth possesses a living image of the beauty of Paradise, I can imagine nothing nearer to it.

In order to meet the trains and boat, I was obliged, with my valet, to set forth this morning at half-past six o'clock by candle light. We had an omnibus to the railway, and passing again through Monza, we reached Como (the city at the south end of the lake) at nine o'clock and went immediately on the little steamer Larisse. The day was one of the loveliest of the season. There was a goodly company of Italians on board, but no travelers, except myself. The surrounding mountains, the advanced guard, one may say, of the Swiss Alps, are all sprinkled on their crests with snow. A pond near the town was covered with boys sliding on the ice; others were busy scraping dust off of certain places well known, I dare say, to the little urchins, preparatory to a good slide for themselves. As we went along the lake the most beautiful images were constantly presented. In Italy it seems, as in Mexico, one must count upon position, not latitude, for temperature, for in sheltered spots or sunny nooks we saw roses, laurestinus, and oranges and olive gardens all along the shores. The first notable mansion we passed was that of Cerito, the *danseuse*, who married a Russian Prince, and makes her chief residence here. Then came the residence of Pasta, then of a very different notability, the residence of the Prince Belgioso, a magnificent mansion at Pliniana, this having been the place of birth of the younger Pliny and the family abode. Then came, after passing on either side beautiful villas and fine mansions, the villa of poor Gonfaloniere, so frightfully imprisoned at the Spielberg. This is one of the finest situations on this most beautiful of lakes, for not one that I had before seen is at all worthy of comparison. After remaining on board one and a half hours, and increasing our numbers by accessions from almost every village, who came to us in little boats they managed very dexterously, we reached the central point, Centenobia, and went ashore. Near this is the residence of a Russian princess, and I entered to see some fine sculptures of Canova and Thorwaldsen. We then crossed the lake in a gondola to Ballagio, and here I saw the most exquisite spot which could be found for the residence of mortal, I think.

A bold and lofty headland juts out into the lake covered with rocks and trees, and nearly surrounded by the two arms of the lake which it divides. It is probably eight hundred or a thousand feet above the lake, and so skillfully are the walks arranged that it is a complete labyrinth, presenting at each moment views the most varied, wild, picturesque and beautiful. In many places the rocks are perforated in different directions from the same point with tunnels that you seem to be looking through tubes, at the end of which are the most enchanting objects. There are precipices in certain places from the summit directly down to the water, and in these ever-changing and magically wrought paths at one moment you are surrounded by rocks which threaten to fall upon you, at the next you are surrounded by a luxuriance of flowers so disposed that they seem to have planted themselves; and proceeding you find yourself, on turning an angle of shrubbery, in a gentle, quiet forest, with birds singing around, and all nature in repose. I was positively so agitated by a sort of instinctive delight at these sudden and rapid changes that I was nearly feverish. Every thing is harmonious, and seems as if wrought by nature only—it is the perfection of art. All this is the possession of the Duke of Sabelloni. It was really necessary to calm the nerves in order to walk some three-fourths of a mile to the adjoining grounds of the Melzi family. This *villa* is a pretty,

quiet place, a charming country residence fitted up with a
taste which seems to belong only to Italy, and here comfort is
combined with it. I returned to Como only in time to take a
hasty view of the cathedral, of white marble, polished within
and without, and containing a great number of beautiful
sculptures, among which are statues of the two Plinys, father
and son, under which are placed some ancient inscriptions belonging to their family that were found in the earth during
the Middle Ages. I arrived in Milan to see the noble Duomo
in the bright full moonlight, and to pass by the prison in
which Gonfalonieri and his fellows were confined. It is a
comfort to me to feel that you at home look daily upon the
same sun and moon which lightens my path.

VENICE, *November* 10, 1851.

The news of the revolution at Paris produced a good deal
of trepidation at Milan, which was evident from the number
of soldiery who mingled with the people in every possible
place, in undress, but all wearing swords and small arms.
The great festival of St. Ambrose was much impaired by it.
The tomb was not opened from fears of its safety in case of an
emeute. I attended a small service there and a great one at the
Duomo, when I heard by a full choir the famous Ambrosian
chanting, which is so nearly like our own that I fancy we have
a feeble imitation of it. All the services and vestments, too,
differ in many particulars from the Roman ritual; there is
more simplicity. Of course I did not fail to mount to the top
of the Duomo, which is the most remarkable part of the won-
drous architecture. I visited also the grand theater of La
Scala, which is not yet open for representations, these usually
commencing the day after Christmas. The *custode* took me
upon the stage, which is enormous, also into several of the
boxes, which are the property of different wealthy families,
and are elegantly fitted up with sofas and mirrors, the walls
being covered with rich damask. Each box is also provided
with a dressing-room at its back on the opposite side of the

corridor. There are six galleries, which may give you some idea of its height.

I left Milan on Monday, traveling all night through a flat country with numerous rice-fields, and mulberry orchards, and corn-fields, and vineyards, and next morning, as we passed along the Lago de Garda, we again found the olive. We stopped some hours at Verona, and I improved the opportunity to visit the vast remains of the Roman amphitheater, the tombs of the family of La Scala and the descendants of Dante, the house and tombs of the Capuletti and Juliet, and some remarkable churches which the Middle Ages have left to this now wretched and dirty old town. From Verona to Venice is a railway, and about seven in the evening we reached the latter place, and, getting into a gondola, I was rowed to an ancient palace, which is now the Hotel de l'Europe, where, after dinner, I was too fatigued to write, and went to bed. This morning at 8½ I was out again with a *valet de place*, and, being very near, I went at once to the Piazza del Marco, where is the old church and the Doge's Palace and the prison, which lies along the canal, that alone separates them. Between these is the small bridge which prisoners must pass in going from their cells to the court-rooms, and which the Venetians have called the Bridge of Sighs. The two famous columns stand near the water's edge, in front of the palace, and the whole scene is in its way extraordinary. I have not yet entered the palace, reserving this for to-morrow. The church more resembles our ideas of a mosque than of a church, and it is filled with pictures of mosaics and sculptures. I have visited a large number of grand and beautiful and remarkable churches to-day, which contain untold treasures of art, in pictures of the old masters, in ornaments of historic value, and bas-reliefs and statues. The most touching was the monument of the unhappy Doge Foscari, which was executed by his grandson, a son of the unfortunate, whom his father sentenced to die.

There is also a noble monument to Canova in the same

church, and one of Titian. It is impossible to convey to you
an idea of the grandeur and richness of some of these monuments. In our country we are so deficient that we can
scarcely believe such erections possible unless we see them;
and it surprises me that of so many who have traveled, and
who must have seen them, no one has ever attempted to imitate
any but the very worst and meanest models. The silence
here is very striking. I understand there is not a single carriage in Venice; in fact, there is no way for passing. The
streets are canals having cross-alleys from four to perhaps six
feet wide to unite them. The houses rise immediately out of
the water, and have at the sides only room enough to effect a
landing. The gondolas are the only carriages, not even a
hand-barrow is to be seen—there is no clatter of wheels nor
ring of hoofs. I suspect the silence has misled thoughtless
people into the idea of the deserted condition of Venice.
The contrary is the fact. I find it a very busy place.

The famous Rialto is divided into three parts (in the width),
from having a sort of street in the middle, formed of two
rows of as thrifty looking shops, as you will find in your town
market streets. The canal is wide. I mounted to the top of
the Campanile of St. Mark this afternoon to see the sun set,
and the scene was exquisite. The city and its canals lay
around. The great Church of St. Marco, with its five mosque-
like towers, and the Palace of the Doge and the Piazza (an
open square surrounded by fine buildings, the palace and the
church forming one side) were all reposing below, while across
the lagoon the whole surface was made brilliant by the re-
flected rays of the sun.

The tide was low; canals meander in every direction; a
noble Austrian steamer was close in shore; the steamer was
coming in with its passengers from Trieste; little boats were
moving rapidly hither and thither, while numerous vessels
from foreign lands were lying about without order as they
chanced to anchor. Here and there were islands but little
raised above the water, yet covered with houses, and always

one or more churches lifted their tall spires toward the skies. You will readily believe that the view was inexpressibly beautiful, yet I have no sympathies with Venice in her present debasement. Every-where, pointing to their finest works of art, they will say (without pain or shame): "This made a visit to Paris, or Napoleon carried this away with him," etc., and it seems that during his short reign he accomplished more for the well-being of the community than had been done in hundreds of years before.

To-morrow I expect to set out for Florence *via* Padua and Bologna and Ferrara. Before this reaches you, you will know far more about the present state of Europe than I. I do not see a newspaper for days together, and, having no society whatever, I have few means of learning any thing. I am under the impression that the present revolution in France will not go far. I saw enough of the French to perceive their extreme reluctance to wake up another revolution, and I think they would infinitely prefer the chances of peace under Louis Napoleon (though he is not their first choice) than to take the risk of another revolution.

I fear you may get tired of my long letters. My health is excellent. I have grown hardy to a degree of which I was never before conscious. I have walked to-day certainly not less than fifteen miles, and yet I can not say I am tired, and I am kept so unceasingly employed that I have no time to think of my solitude.

VENICE.

I set forth this morning, at 8½ o'clock, with my valet, and went first to the Church of St. Marco. It is of vast size, and even the porticos, extending along three sides, are covered with frescoes and mosaics. Every spot within and about it is historical. Some of the marble pillars and sculptures are from Jerusalem; some from Santa Sophia, at Constantinople, from whence the famous horses also were brought. Only imagine the labor expended when the entire vaulted ceiling and large part of the walls are covered with mosaics, of which there are probably not more than twenty pieces of over one-half an inch square. I must refer you to the printed accounts, which probably fall far short of the reality. Some of the pictures in mosaic are as large as life, consisting of numerous figures and very fine. The floor is also laid in fine mosaic throughout. Then I went to the Palace of the Doges, which adjoins it, and then, ascending the Giant's Staircase, where poor Foscari fainted in descending, and between the pillars of the vestibule where the unfortunate Faliero was decapitated, I entered by the golden staircase, and passed through a quiet suite of historical apartments, meeting here and there other of the lions' mouths so dreaded in medieval times—each *salle* covered with paintings by old masters, though seldom of great merit. In the great council chamber the doges are all ranged in portraits, two and two, but Faliero's place, as you know, is covered with black. It required more than an hour simply to pass through this great palace, and then I went to the prisons. I entered many of the cells. The political prisons are at the lowest depth, and there I entered the small chamber used for execution for political offenses, real or supposed, which rendered the Venetian republic infamous for all time. In these deserted scenes of crimes, without a name atrocious enough to express them, I could scarcely avoid the hope that the perpetrators, who had escaped this world's judgment, might find no mercy in the next. Never in my life did I feel so vindictive.

From there, of course, I passed to the Bridge of Sighs; and then, very pleasantly changing the scene, I took a gondola and proceeded some three or four miles along the grand canal, which exhibits a continuous row of palaces rising from the water. The grandest of them is that of the Duchess de Berri, and, as she is now absent, I obtained permission to see the palace, which formerly belonged to the family Londano, of ducal honors, who have left in it many very ancient memorials, to which the duchess has added what she brought from France; and it is the finest within as well as without of any

10

in Venice.　We passed in turn nearly every historic name of
the ancient republic.　I was surprised to find that many of
the families still survive and occupy their palaces.　The Count
de Chambord has a palace not far from his mother; Lord
Byron's residence is also pointed out, and that of the Countess
Guiccioli; and Taglioni, the danseuse, lives in one of the
most striking of them.　The weather since I have been in
Italy is always fine, and the sail (or row) along the canal was
really enchanting.　At the limit of my voyage was the Palace
of Maffini, which has the finest private collection of pictures in
Venice, and which is open on Thursdays.　The paintings
here, however, are not to compare with the collections in
Munich nor Dresden, or even at Vienna, but the churches are
rich beyond description in sculptures.　I had still time enough
to cross the Lagoon to an island to see the Church of San
Georgio Maggiore, which is grand.　In its neighborhood, ships
are scattered in the bright sunlight here and there.　Little
boats glided silently in every direction.　Several large ones,
picturesquely formed, were filled with Austrian troops, who
were changing their position, and in the background were the
domes of San Marco and the famous columns—one surmounted by the winged lion of St. Mark, the other by St.
Theodore—and behind them a succession of domes and pin-
nacles, and, away to the right, the public gardens; but there
is no time to describe the smallest part of this enchanting
scene.

I left Venice at three and reached Padua at four, and proceeded while the daylight lasted to see, first, the great hall of
the Palais de Justice, the largest in Europe, where Titus Livius
is absolutely entombed in state, with every historic evidence
that his remains are really here!!　But what is still more
singular is the tomb of Antenor who, it has always been said
by the Romans, was the founder of Padua.　The tomb is, of
course, of unknown age.　The Church of St. Anthony was
my next object.　After all the magnificence I have already
seen in churches, I confess I was astonished at this, and also

to find it in so small a place. The chapel of St. Anthony is entirely surrounded by magnificent sculptures in high bas-relief, which give the history of his life and miracles. God bless you.

Mrs. Peter passed on through Bologna, where she dined on the famous sausages, and found the people in expectation of the advent of Garibaldi at the head of an army of Americans to liberate Italy. She expected her home letters at Florence, and could not linger on the road, though attracted by many objects of interest she was reluctant to pass by.

FLORENCE.

Leaving Bologna yesterday morning at five o'clock, we passed over a pretty country in so bright a moonlight that very little of the landscape was lost. Saturday seems the universal market day, and although it was so early the road was, for miles, filled with little carts conveying all manner of things for sale, chiefly, however, brushwood, which is the common fuel of the land, where I fancy few but the rich are warm from November till April. The land was less flat, for, since leaving Genoa and the Alps, I have scarcely crossed a hill. Within a few miles of Bologna the Apennines begin to appear. They are higher than I thought, and covered with snow. Beggars, as usual, pursued us all along the way, but it is a comfort to have better horses. I reached Florence last night at eleven in a fog so thick we could scarcely see the wheel horses. I have a fine room and hot water, and was soon made very comfortable. In fact I am just now in the enjoyment of a degree of warmth to which I have long been a stranger. My room is well carpeted, and the fire throws out abundant heat. As soon as I could get my breakfast, I went to the banker's who, thank heaven, keeps his rooms open for the delivery of letters, and I was soon devouring favors of the 13th of November. There was also a most comfortable note from L., assuring me that she and the children were well. I then went to the English church, where the services were well performed and much to my mind; and then longing to see some one who would know us and speak my own language, I called on Powers, who seemed really glad to see me. He is as simple and natural an American as if he had left home a month ago. I am glad to find he has no intention to remain here, and that it is always his intention to go home as soon as he is able; but he says he must now remain because he is in the way of finding employment which, at home, he fears might be more than uncertain. How I wish I were rich enough to ask a work from him. As I looked around I thought I could see the peculiar excellence in the delicate outlines and refined beauty of finish which are remarkable, and, I think, superior to any sculptures I have seen anywhere. I wish there were circumstances around him to awaken his native faculties, or that he had had early means to imbue his mind with images and ideas for heroic and imaginative composition. In these he is immeasurably surpassed by Schwanthaler who, I must believe, is really the great productive sculptor of the age— greatly superior to Canova and Thorwaldsen, whose *chefs d'oeuvres* I have seen. These have been fortunate rather than great. Schwanthaler is positively sublime. Yet the delicate, gentle sweetness of Powers' execution is not to be found in the conceptions of Schwanthaler, whose genius seems to have been too grand, too rapid in its development, too mighty in its purposes to submit to the refined excellence of the chisel of our countryman. If Powers' ideas were but as prolific as his taste is pure and chaste, he would, indeed, be the first sculptor of our race. He invited me cordially to see him, and I shall go to his studio as often as I have time. I am glad you have seen good Bishop Otey. I have no idea of going to Palestine, and, it may be, I shall not go to Constantinople if I find there is any particular risk. I feel now that my life is valuable, for much of the well-being of dear L. and the children depends upon its prolongation, so far as I can see, and I am trying to gather both health and new ideas for the work which is before me in the education of our darling little boys. This afternoon I went to the service at the magnificent cathedral near by, whose dome is thought to be finer than St. Peter's, and afterward to Santa Croce, but it was shut. To-morrow night I hope to tell you all about it.

Monday.—Up betimes. I was at Santa Croce before eight o'clock. In front is an oblong square, graveled, and in this space some Austrian troops were drilling. The church is large, but no one thinks of it but as the casket which contains the tombs of Michael Angelo, a worthy monument of Dante, Machiavelli, Galileo, Alfieri, Feliciana, etc. All these I studied, book in hand, at leisure, for I had resolved, for this day at least, to take no valet with me, whose presence would have been an insufferable annoyance. The church is crowded with sepulchral monuments, and among them is a chapel belonging to the Joseph Bonaparte family, with some pretty sculptures; there are also numerous frescoes. 'From this thought-inspiring spot I went to the vast Duomo, which I ascended to the top, from whence I had a most beautiful view of the environs. The interior of the dome represents the Inferno and Purgatorio of Dante, with Paradiso at the top. All being examined, I then went to the Medicean Church of San Lorenzo, where is the burial-place of the family, rich in monuments of sculpture and painting; and here, on the tomb of Julian de Medici, are the world-renowned statues of Day and Night, but I was not so much impressed by them as I expected to be. Perhaps I am not prepared to form a correct judgment. I saw casts taken of them some years ago in Boston, and I think you also must have seen them. The Chapel of the Medici is entirely covered (and it is large enough for a moderate sized church) with agates, jasper, chalcedony, lapis lazuli, florentine, mosaics, etc., yet the effect is not good. The frescoes at the top are beautiful.

From there I went to the old Palace of the Medici, which contains many magnificent rooms and many articles of vertu which formerly adorned their home. On the way, I stopped at the Baptistry of the Duomo, where all the children born in Florence are baptized, and saw a troop of little aspirants, just born, accompanied by their smiling friends. Most of the babies had an outer covering of silk, embroidered in gold. I have also walked about the town to see the shops and work people, and, although entirely alone, I had no difficulty whatever. I often think of Mariotti, now that I am making use of the language which he taught me, and which seems to come back at my call. The small shops here seem to be kept in the streets entirely, and I can not conceive how they manage in bad weather. The public places around the churches and markets are crowded to such a degree with tables and hand-barrows—these latter in perpetual motion, and all covered with goods—that carriages get through with difficulty. Each peddler, as he moves on, screams or shouts the value or excellence of his commodities, and you may imagine what bedlams these places are. The women go sailing about in tuscan flats—i. e., like men's hats, but of enormous size, such as were formerly brought to America. These have no wire, and flap about with the wind or motion of the wearer; a small black band and bow of ribbon round the crown is the only decoration, and always they are worn like an umbrella, or the whole front flapped up by the accident of the moment. These women have the usual checked handkerchief on the shoulders, and fastened down under an apron, which is of bright colored patterns.

Passing around the corner of a church to-day, I saw a sort of semi-circular barrier, some four feet wide, from which issued a sort of screechy chant. I rose on tiptoe to look within, and there sat a son of Crispin diligently employed at his last, while he employed his voice in calling passengers to avail themselves of his incomparable abilities. You can hardly imagine how convenient it is for me to be able to speak Italian, which I find I can do quite beyond my expectations. It comes to me whenever I want it.

Tuesday.—To-day has been fully occupied since half past eight in seeing the Gallerie Imperiale and the Pitti Palace. This immense collection of sculptures, pictures, gems, antiques, etc., is justly considered the rarest and the most varied in the world. It was collected chiefly by the Medici in the days of their splendor, and it contains study enough for a life-time. The Venus de Medici is one of its treasures, and I passed half an hour at her side, and left her with a conviction that she was not half so beautiful as several of the creations of Powers. After the closing of the galleries, I again called to see Powers, who gave me a hearty welcome, and we sat together in his studio by the iron stove, chatting, I am afraid for nearly an hour, comparing opinions. I did not tell him how superior I thought his busts were to all I had seen, for he is so ingenuous that he would have thought it flattery; but I was glad to find that my opinions of the chef d'oeuvres that I had just seen accorded with his. At the same gallery were several sculptures of Michael Angelo. Few of his works are entirely finished. The group of poor Niobe and her children affected me deeply—fifteen figures in all. It is vain to attempt any description of this magnificent collection.

I will bring home a catalogue for you. If the Cincinnati people had any idea of how beautiful a collection they might make for four or five thousand dollars, they would make haste to collect such a sum, in order to enjoy the result. There is a copy of the "Fates," by Michael Angelo, for $40, which I think I shall get; the three figures are finely grouped. The one at right of the spectator spins the thread like an old crone. The next looks kindly; the third holds in her hands the fatal scissors, which, by a slight movement, are prepared to sever the thread which comes from the distaff, but she hesitates, and looks to her sister for counsel, and both desire to delay the dreaded moment. You may imagine how fine is the effect of such an expression. Nothing is extravagant or exaggerated—all is natural. There are some beautiful Raphaels. Most of them have been engraved. Whether it is that

artists are afraid of Michael Angelo I know not, but he is
rarely copied. I could not finish seeing all to-day; I shall
be here to-morrow.   There was no fire, and at the end of
three hours I felt chilled, so that it was prudent to warm
myself, which I did, by walking to the Pitti Palace.   This is
an old Florentine residence, now that of the reigning duke.
There are pictures, only, arranged in noble apartments.   Here
are the originals of the " Madonna della Seggio," which you
have seen so often, the " Ecce Homo," the " Judith and
Holofernes," and many others you have heard of.   Those elegant and spacious salons have each a little stove, which di-
minishes the cold, and seat so that there is less fatigue.

It is a sad grief to me to see all these things alone, for, although there are others always present, it seems to be an established rule, which the English have made, and which the
Americans have been foolish enough to adopt, that every
body is to avoid every body.   If I had a party with me I
should break through this abominable practice without hesitation, but, being alone, I should only render myself suspected
of a desire to join myself to some of them.   I find myself
coldly repelled.   I therefore am silent and reserved.   At
table I sit next to a very intelligent German consul, who has
been in America, and once a day I have a little chat.   My
health is excellent, and my travels decidedly agree with me,
though I suffer from want of fire.   The other day as we entered Ferrara I saw several cart-loads of ice, *four or five inches*
thick, and very transparent.   I am still under the shadows of
the double-headed eagle of Austria.   The people of this country hear little of what is going on in France.

I am too little informed to give you any opinion.   Travelers
say Louis Napoleon has gone too far, and he may wake up
some morning and find himself without a head.   It is not
common for ladies to travel alone, neither is it to me agreeable to be without my family, as you will readily suppose,
but I have found no obstacles whatever in my way; therefore,

if my letters do not come regularly do not be anxious. May God bless and preserve us all until we meet.

I could not write as usual last night, for reasons to be mentioned below. I set out as usual alone after breakfast in my room at half-past eight, and proceeded to the Gallerie Reale to see the apartments I had not had time to visit before, viz., the antiquities—many of them Etruscan—the gems, inscriptions, etc., all of which are well worth far more study than I could give. I did not fail to make another visit to the sculptures and paintings of highest rank that I had seen before. From them I went to see the Ducal manufacture of the celebrated Florentine mosaics, where visitors are allowed to see the laborers at work, and to examine the various collections of stones prepared for composing the elegant productions which are fabricated there. Tables of all sizes are made, and friezes and ornaments of every description for household use, but I saw more for personal decoration. Then I went to the remarkable library founded by the Medici at the fall of Constantinople, which contains only manuscripts, the whole building and arrangements having been ordered and designed by Michael Angelo, under whose care the previous collections were reduced to order and symmetry. There are MSS. from the fourth and fifth centuries downward, and among them is a copy of the "Pandects of Justinian," found at Amalfi, in fresh and beautiful manuscript, and all sorts of the most rare and curious things written by the most eminent men of each successive age. Passing over several objects of lesser interest, I set forth by way of finishing the day. I drove some two miles beyond the city walls.

The afternoon was beautiful as so far I have always found the weather in Italy, and the drives are crowded with carriages. Two very magnificent and well-appointed equipages were there of the Grand Duke's, each having four horses, and there seemed to be a sort of display, rather too evident among the carriages generally. The Arno lies along the east side, and the banks are devoted to walking. These grounds are called the Casein, through which is a walk and drive of two miles or more beyond the city walls. The grounds are more than half a mile wide, and are well planted with large trees and shrubbery, which nearly separates the different roads from each other. On the west lie the beautiful Appenines, a peak now and then rising from behind covered with snow, whilst all below reposed peacefully under the setting sun, dotted with pretty country houses and villages, with the fair city between. It was a lovely sight, and not to be forgotten. I reached our hotel in time for dinner at half-past five o'clock, and soon after dinner I had the pleasure of seeing Mr. Powers, who came with his wife to pass the evening with me. She is a nice person, very ladylike and intelligent. Powers thinks well, and has read much; has a strong moral tone of thought with, as you may suppose, great delicacy of sentiment. After being deprived for so long a time of every thing like social intercourse, I enjoyed the evening very much. I visited again the Duomo and other places on my way to the house of Michael Angelo, which is open to visitors one day in the week. It is still in possession of his family, but the present is the last of his race, and at his death the name will be extinct. Great pains have been taken to preserve every thing as he left it, and the house within is unaltered. Many relics which the family used are carefully preserved and all in the best condition. I also saw (outside) the houses of Dante, Boccacio, Guiciardini and Machiavelli. All have inscriptions marking each house as having been the residence of one or the other.

The beautiful gardens of the Ducal Palace were next in course, and then the Museum of Natural History, in which the imitations in wax of vegetable fibers and human anatomy are the finest I ever saw; and it is the first time I have ever had an opportunity to examine an anatomical museum, for it is among the stupid follies of our countrymen to exclude women as much as possible from all that may really tend to strengthen their intellects. *Addio.*

Friday.—I went this morning first to the Academicia to examine the collection of old paintings chronologically arranged. It is remarkable to find how delicate was the perception of the beauty of the human features, both in form and expression, before any thing was understood of perspective and of the mode of expressing motion. All these pictures preceded the discovery of the mixing colors in oil, and are done in distemper, *i. e.*, colors mixed with water and thickened with white of egg or some similar preparation. The brilliancy and clearness of these colors is greater than any of modern date. I then went to visit the galleries of the Corsini family—some ten or fifteen rooms full—and then to see still other churches containing magnificent frescoes and sculptures till half-past twelve o'clock, when, jumping into a little carriage, I drove out to Fiesole, an Etruscan city, the original Florence, and older than Rome. It lies on the top of a hill some three miles out of town, and was formerly surrounded by a Cyclopean wall, of which there are ample remains to excite our wonder. There are also fragments of an amphitheater, columns, sculptures, an altar to Bacchus, etc. The views are exquisite all along the road, and from the summit I found there, as every-where, a man who rushed up to the carriage as soon as it stopped to offer his services to guide me. As I was examining one of the finest parts of the wall and in full view of the country residence of Galileo, I was joined by two young men, one of whom proved to be a son of Mr. R. G. Shaw, of Boston. It is rarely that I meet with Americans, and I can not imagine what has become of them. Mr. Shaw told me that Mr. Story and Mr. James Lowell are again in Rome. Fiesole has, of course, churches and convents well worthy of attention. It was nearly dark when I returned to my hotel, and soon after Mr. Powers came by appointment to convey me to his house to pass the evening. There was no one else, and I had a very pleasant evening chatting with Mr. Powers, who is very agreeable, and, I should think, one of the purest-minded men to be found. He insisted on seeing

me home, although I had ordered a servant to come for me.
It is now late.   God bless you.

Saturday.—At seven this morning I was in a railway carriage for Pisa, where we arrived in two hours, and I was escorted from the station into the town by a mixed rabblement
you never could have imagined would have environed your
mother.   There were few passengers, and an immense number
of carriages waiting to receive them.   The station is out of
the town, and a carriage may be required for half a mile or
a mile to go to the different quarters.   The hackmen, seeing
little chance of getting a fare, rushed upon me with a sort of
fury, actually touching my clothes to gain attention ; a dozen
voices screemed in my ears at once, " Signore duo pauli," duo
Pauli i mezzo;" " Mezzo" paul, paul i mezzo; " Signore ligna
niente," while as many others are hurling " il Duomo, il Campanile," and as many others, the halt and the hungry, " Signore Per Dio de meos fama," etc.   Once and again, I shook
them off, and ran desperately forward, but they pursued in
full chase, until, at length, seeing no way of escape, I jumped
into the foremost of the carriages, which had kept pace with
me, the driver holding up his whip the while, and crying,
" mezzo pauli," and commanding him to drive fast, the most
of the vagabonds were compelled to disperse to avoid being
run over.   Though not given to laughter of late, it was impossible to resist the ludicrous effect of the part which I was
forced to play, and for some minutes, I was so convulsed with
laughing that I could not get voice enough to tell them to
leave me.   It is wonderful, in a town of such moderate pretensions, to see such artistic excellence as the Cathedral and
its adjuncts, the Baptistry, the Campanile (leaning tower),
and the Campo Santo, in which the richness of the materials
employed seem to vie with the almost superhuman talent
which has wrought them into shapes of beauty.   All are
constructed of white marble, outside and within ; precious
stones are combined with an unsparing hand.   The Campo
Santo contains frescoes so wonderful that it is necessary to see

to believe. Our countrymen who come here with money seem to have no conception of the artistic beauty they might make their own. Do stir up the Cincinnati people to send for some copies of painting and sculpture. Either Powers or Kellogg will act with a hearty right good will, and, as our vessels of war are always willing to take home works of art free of cost, they could be acquired cheaper than you could imagine.

Sunday.—On waiting in the vestibule of the church this morning, I had the pleasure to meet my old acquaintance, Mrs. Allen, and her family, of Providence. We sat together, and she made me a visit on my return, after which I came to take leave of Mr. and Mrs. Powers. I found Mr. Kellogg there. He came over, soon after my return to the hotel, to bring me a letter which he had written to introduce me to Mr. Cass, and was very kind in offering to aid me if I needed his services. If you meet his brother in Cincinnati, pray mention to him that I have spoken of his brother's kindness.

ROME.

I reached here last night at eleven o'clock, and have been to Tortoni's to inquire for letters, but, alas! alas! there are none. I have been to see Mr. Case. He is very kind, and has assisted me to find lodging. I think I may stay a month here, if you are all well, and I can be content so long; but, without any of you, my time drags wearily, and my only refuge is work and study, by which I hope to improve.

ROME, *Jan.* 1, 1852.

During all my travels I have found myself bound to occupy my time to its utmost possibility toward the accomplishment of the objects for which I have incurred so much labor and so much expense, and, what is still dearer to me, the separation from the society of all who are dear to me. To-day, for the first time, I indulge myself in shutting out sights, remaining in my apartments. I have been to the English church, where there were services, prayers, and com-

munion. Have dismissed my servant until five o'clock, and
hope to pass the intervening hours without interruption com-
muning with you. I hope you have received my journal
regnlarly, for I have had no time to write any thing besides,
and the only record you will have of my tour will be found
in it. There has been no time for the expression of thoughts
and feelings. I have only set down facts or observations
which I thought might interest you, hasty as they were.
My stay here allows me leisure, and, after much long continued labor, it was time to rest awhile. I hardly know how
I have been able to endure so much without injury to my
health, which seems proof against every thing, though, as
usual, I am scarcely sensible of having any real appetite for
food.

I mentioned in a former letter that William Story and James
Lowell were here with their wives, and also Mrs. Crawford,
formerly Miss Ward, all of whom are disposed to be exceedingly kind to me. Mr. Peet and his party have resolved to
remain longer, and will probably remain as long as I do.
There is also a party of Philadelphia people, whom I knew
in a *benevolent* way at home, who have lodgings just opposite
mine, and thus I have society enough, and they are all rather
agreeable people. I dine with this latter party every day,
paying my proportion toward the dinner, which is sent from
a restaurant. Mr. Peet has invited me to dine with them this
evening, and, although it is a painful exertion for me to go
out to-day, I thought it best not to refuse. I shall go. To-
morrow evening I am to pass quietly with Mr. and Mrs.
James Lowell. The Storys will, I suppose, be there also;
they all have apartments in the same house. It is singular
to us accustomed to occupy an entire house to find how
many families can find accommodations here under the same
roof. I can not yet discover the plans of the houses, or,
rather, of the palaces. Except a very few of the finest
princely abodes, the entrance is on a level, or slightly elevated above the street, through a great coach-house looking

door, which leads into an entry paved with bricks. Within this entry is a little side room for the porter, and shops of every description occupy the ground floor. At the further end is a flight of rough stone steps, which appear never to have been washed since the remote period at which the house was built. Sometimes they are swept; oftener they are left to the petticoats of the unfortunate females, where long skirts perform this office. Arrived at each successive floor, or piano, as it is called, you pass through one, two, or three small antechambers, floored with rough bricks, sometimes having a narrow breadth of carpet to walk on, until, finally, you are ushered into a suite of rooms, one opening into another, and affording no other means of egress than the one door at which you have entered. In looking for lodgings, I found one apartment, numbering eleven rooms, with still but one outer door. It seems useless, however, to occupy your time with descriptions of Rome. Lady Morgan has long since given such graphic pictures, and Fanny Kemble's sketches are true to the life. Apartments are most commonly used by strangers who wish to be out of the noise of hotels, and they are also more economical.

This morning I enjoyed the precious comfort of receiving your letter of the 4th of December. I have also had comforting letters from L., who, I trust, is getting on at Canterbury, but in her solitude she must be very sad. The last two days have been devoted to the Museum of the Vatican and capital. The ancient statuary, especially in the Vatican, is well arranged. I wish poor Mary W. were with me. I am persuaded that her malady has grown to its present extremity solely from the want of due prevention. Two years ago I should have reveled in scenes which I now regard only as studies, and with her temperament I can easily imagine her enjoyment. What would I not give if you were here? For the present, I suppose all expectations of European warfare are at an end. I should be so glad if you could make an excursion to Europe before you go to housekeeping. In three

months you could see more than you can imagine of England,
Scotland, Belgium, the Rhine, Switzerland, and Italy, and
home by Germany and France. You would find yourself
advanced by some years in judgment and knowledge. If we
all live, I look forward with certainty to settling down beside
you with our little boys just as soon as I can—and, of course,
to be as near as possible in town or country as is best. The
Lowells have postponed their invitation for a day or two.
James gave me a charming letter to read from Maria Fay,
who is now in England with her brother Richard and family,
who have taken an old country mansion, near Shrewsbury,
for a year.

Maria's descriptions of their daily life are among the most
entertaining that I have ever read. The Storys and Lowells
desire me to say how glad they should be to see you both.
Yesterday was a melancholy day for me, the birthday of our
dear, dear T., the first for many years which was not spent in
writing to him. In order to avoid company (for all my
thoughts were in the past), I walked about the city and
among the ruins all day with my servant. I think of leaving
here for Naples, in about two weeks. Kindest love to M.
God bless you both.

ROME, Jan. 9, 1852.

I have just had the comfort of receiving your's and M.'s letter of the 11th of December, by the same mail which brings
me one from L., the 28th, and one from Mr. Peter, of the
15th. It is an inexpressible comfort to me to know you are
all well. I write every week regularly, and I have just sent
off a budget in time to reach the next Cunard steamer. I
know you must all be anxious to hear regularly from me, and
I never fail to write, in fact, I am often afraid my intermin-
able epistles will weary you all, and I leave out a great many
incidents which I should like to relate, for that reason. The
day after my last letter was the Epiphany, on the morning of
which I went to a Greek church, opened only once a year, on
this day. The services were very imposing, differing in many

respects from the Romish, and I like them better. In the afternoon, we went to the ancient Basilica of Ara Coeli, where the ceremonies are in honor of a miracle-working bambino (baby of wood), which is usually kept in its own chapel, in the midst of representations of rocks, shepherds, angels in the back ground, while in front it is attended by the Virgin in an elegant dress, St. Joseph being present, and also splendidly dressed. The bambino is covered with jewels which, on this occasion, were unusually splendid. The country people come from the Abruzzi, and even from Calabria every year to attend this service, and also to make an honest penny to pay their expenses, if you may judge by the appearance of thrifty traffic, in which many hundreds of them are engaged on the 135 marble steps, wide enough for half a dozen coaches abreast, by which the church is reached, for it is on the Capitoline Hill. The immense area of this old church was filled by people of all ranks, chiefly from the country; and soldiers, elegantly equipped, lined the approaches to the altar, not so much, however, to guard as to adorn. From behind the altar at stated times, issued by two and two, hundreds of capuchins (to whom the church and bambino belong), each bearing a lighted torch nearly as tall as himself, and thus, finally, the prayers being ended, the bambino was conveyed by the endless procession, borne in the arms of the glittering high priest, round and round the inside of the church, with music and incense, and then out to the top of the steps to be exhibited to the thousands without, accompanied by loud sounds of the largest trumpet I ever saw, and then up the center of the church to the altar, where it was placed in a golden niche in the midst of clouds of incense and deafening music. In the evening, by the light of the brilliant moon, we visited the Coliseum, and the ruins of the ancient Forum around the capital.

On Wednesday, I visited the studios of a number of the most eminent foreign sculptors. I looked into some shops which have pictures to sell. Yesterday we (i. e., the Peets

11

and myself) set forth on an excursion to Tivoli, which seems
to have been the chosen summer retreat of the Romans of the
Augustan age. The excavations at Adrian's villa, two miles
nearer Rome, have afforded the most perfect sculptures which
are left of ancient times: the Apollo Belvidere, the Gladia-
tor, etc. There is scarcely a collection in Europe which is
not possessed of one or more of its *chefs d'oeuvres*—so full and
so rich it was—but now it presents only a mass of hardly dis-
tinguishable ruins of some miles in circumference. We
wandered among them two or three hours, and then mounted
the hill to Tivoli, which is surrounded by a most agreeable
and unusual verdure. The olive groves are very extensive,
and beyond is a fine oak forest, though it is of no great extent.
Here is still pointed out the ruins of the fine villa of
Mæcenas. All these villas should be written palaces. The
enormous ruined arches of the house of Varus (who lost his
legions in Germany), the house of Catullus, of Horace, etc.
Amongst these rises in the midst of the prettiest gardens I
have seen, the villa of d'Este, owned by the Duke of Modena.
The falls of the Anio have a wonderful variety and grandeur
in their beauty which, of course, is greatly heightened by the
ancient association around them. Just above is the beautiful
ruin of the temple of the Sybil. The Sabine hills are in full
view, with Soracte behind. The Volscian and Latian hills
bound another part of the landscape, and the vast plain of
the melancholy Campagna de Roma is on the other side, with
the dome of St. Peter's in the horizon.

We slept at Tivoli, and after a donkey ride of some hours
to see the caverns and grottoes of the neighborhood, we returned to Rome, stopping awhile at one of the old Basilicas
outside the walls (San Lorenzo), where there is a curious
opening into the Catacombs. Just after I entered my apartments, which my good Pietro had made warm and cheerful
for my return, I had the consolation of receiving your last
letter. Yesterday was passed in going over the great palace of the Pope in the Quirinal, where the conclaves are

held, and which is the summer residence of the Pope, full
of fine pictures and tapestries all in modest and excellent
taste. We also saw the statue of Moses, by M. Angelo, and
the Rospigliosi Palace, where is the original of the Hours
fresco by Guido, and many other fine paintings. Then to
the Protestant Cemetery, where poor Shelley and many more
are entombed, and then to a magnificent church, St. Paolo,
fuore le Mura, which, still in progress, bids fair to rival St.
Peter's. In the evening I went by invitation to take tea with
Mr. Cass, who is always very attentive to me. This morning
I went to church, and at two o'clock to the Propaganda, where
there were addresses delivered by students in some twenty or
thirty different languages. It was a very interesting scene.
Among the speakers were three negroes, besides Egyptians,
Ethiopians, Burmans, Chinese, etc., all speaking in their own
tongues. Of course the European languages were all represented. You can hardly believe how well I can speak Italian.
It comes to me like a well laid up store which had been forgotten but found in good order just at the right time. But every
good has its opposite, and I am worried in my sight-seeing by
hangers-on who have been too lazy to study, and think their
ignorance a sufficient claim to give them right to demand
translation at every turn.

In two days, provided I have no bad news from home, I
shall go to Naples, and expect there to meet a lady who wishes
to go with me to Athens and Constantinople. Every day I
have a divided mind, which inclines me forthwith to turn
back at the same time that yours and Mr. Peter's letters urge
me onward. I try to please you rather than myself. Do
write often to poor L., who must be sad and lonely. It is
bad enough for me, who am constantly in motion, but it must
require in her a sort of heroism to sustain herself as she now
is. I wish she were with me. I have been strongly tempted
to write to her to join me at Naples, which she might do without danger to the children, by Marseilles and by sea. I shall
get on as fast as possible, but it seems a duty now that I

should leave nothing undone. Rome is, however, so vast that a year diligently employed would hardly suffice. The architecture, modern as well as ancient, of Italy astonishes me by its vastness, and the people present many good traits. You find no meanness, and one would think that under a better government they might be as noble in mind as they are graceful and beautiful in person. I am beginning to have a very kindly feeling for them. May God bless you all.

There is something very touching in the tenderness of Mrs. Peter to her widowed daughter, the wife of her son whose death she so deeply mourned. It was altogether wisest and best for the children that the plan of settling them for the winter at Canterbury was adopted. They were there with the son and daughter of Mr. Peter, whose kind, sympathetic interest was not to be doubted, and, as the result proved, was satisfactory and beneficial in every way to Mrs. King and her little boys; but Mrs. Peter's deep motherly heart was not satisfied that she had left them, and it was only by earnest entreaty that she was persuaded to carry out a plan, which, if she had failed to accomplish, she could never have ceased to regret. Her own conviction in after life was that the divine Hand had led her on, for it was on this visit to Jerusalem she became interested in the teachings of the Catholic Church as set forth by the Roman missionaries at Jerusalem. Her convictions from that time led her into investigations which resulted finally in her entrance into that branch of Christ's Church which gave to the closing years of her life so much happiness and consolation.

ROME, *January* 18, 1852.

I am depressed in spirit to-day, from not having received my expected letter from you, which, of late, has come to me

from Thursday to Saturday of each week. I devoutly hope
it will come before I have closed this. The past week has
been so busily occupied by day, and in the evening also, that
I have had no time to write as usual the events of each day.
I have visited in turn churches and villas, and paintings and
sculptures, and two days have been passed in an excursion to
Frascati and its environs, including Tusculum, Grotto, Fer-
rata, Marino, Alba Longa, the Lake of Albano and town,
the Castle Gandolfo (summer residence of the popes), etc.
I was accompanied by a lady and gentleman whom I have
met often since I have been here, who shared the expenses of
the excursion. Carriage hire is cheaper than with us, being
about $3.75 per diem. Frascati lies on the side of one of the
Albanian hills, and is a favorite resort of Roman families during the summer months, when every house is full of lodgers.
The last of the Stuarts, the Cardinal of York, was bishop of
the diocese, and died there, as well as his brother, Charles
Edward, but both are buried beneath St. Peter's. This town
is on the site of the ancient Tusculum, where the ruins of
Cicero's house still exist, as well as an amphitheater and theater—all, however, in utter ruins, except the seats of the latter. It is to me at all times a mournful pilgrimage to these
desecrated relics of the past, and about Rome they are so utterly neglected as to make the view positively painful. The
whole country is covered with debris, of which there exists
not even a tradition to mark their original uses. A sepulchre
of Lucullus is shown, another of Ascanius, another of the
Horatiæ and Curatiæ; mounds of earth, beneath which
masses of Cyclopean walls are half seen; portions of ruined
towns are strewed over the fields by the roadside. The
great aqueduct, which formerly supplied Rome with water,
stretches its gigantic and broken arches over the Campagna. Often the road passes along the excavated rocks of
ancient catacombs, and all seems to belong more to the dead
than to the living, since no dwelling-house is visible in this
region of malaria.

Yesterday was the day of the Roman Calendar, devoted to St. Anthony, whose benevolence, it seems, was turned to the inferior animals, and is now honored as the patron of the quadrupeds and fishes, having once delivered from a jutting crag an address to the latter so edifying that they all held their heads above water, and were moved to tears by his eloquence. During these degenerate days, the fishes seem to have fallen into disrepute, and horses, and asses, and mules monopolize the favors of the saint. We have seen, at various times during the last month, three, six, even eight pairs of horses attached to the same carriage, and drive headlong through the streets, practising, we are told, for the solemnity of St. Anthony's blessing. At Frascati the festival was celebrated with great *eclat*. A priest stood in full canonicals at the top of the six steps leading to the platform before the church. At his side a boy also in costume was placed, holding a silver vessel of holy water. Behind, in their gay costumes, in which scarlet always prevailed, were grouped numbers of peasant women and children, interspersed with men, wearing, as usual, their cloaks thrown over their left shoulder, and steeple-crowned hats, breeches, and stockings. Beggars, of course, were numerous. The open square in front was also full of people, chiefly men, and across the place was driven a constant succession of horses and mules, some harnessed to carriages of various descriptions, some ridden, and some driven in flocks. As each passed, the old clergyman threw from the silver sprinkler which he held in his hand some drops of holy water, none of which by any chance could reach the objects of his benediction, but all seemed perfectly content with his good intentions, and handed forward one or more large bougies of wax tied with gay ribbons, which were placed in the care of an assistant, whose arms speedily became loaded by these offerings. Sometimes a handsome carriage drove up with a flag or a standard for St. Anthony, all of which was joyfully carried into the church. All this time, I had been standing by the side of the old priest, and enjoying

a friendly chat with him. He commenced by asking me if I
were English. I, of course, replied I was an American from
Philadelphia, whereupon the worthy man added that we all
spoke Spanish in America. I disclaimed this accusation very
promptly, but I more than suspect that he gave no credence
to my statement that English was our language. The old
man was unlettered, but apparently amiable, and much beloved in his flock. You will readily believe how difficult it
is for me to preserve any real cheerfulness or even composure
during these sad anniversaries of our bereavement. I have
my diary of last year with me, but the days are too deeply
graven on my memory to read it. It was a year yesterday
since I sent off the dispatch to inquire after our dear T.,
and, on the arrival of your answer, set off in the night train
to be with him. Perhaps the restraint which I am obliged to
assume in the presence of strangers may be beneficial, but my
loneliness in my sorrow is oppressive. I so often waken in
the night with a sudden pang of memory which brings all
back as vividly as in the first days. Poor L.! I fear she
needs our consolations. She tries to write cheerfully, but I
know she must need my sympathy. What a change this year
has wrought for us. After a rain, the sun again shines
brightly; the weather is that of the finest of our April. At
Frascati, roses and daisies were in full bloom on the hillsides
and in the gardens, which are surrounded by walls. Here in
Rome they have not ceased to bloom during the coldest
weather—when there was ice all day in the streets. Every-
where the orange and lemon trees with ripe fruit, and yet
there were several days about Christmas quite as cold as is
usual with us.

The Allens, of Providence, are here, and I shall have the
pleasure of their association in Naples. I first saw Mrs. Allen
when you were a baby of five weeks old—a fat red little
thing, with large features and always asleep—the best baby
in the world. She was young then, but now looks like an old
woman, yet good and amiable, and her husband equally so.

There is another anniversary of buried hopes, the birth-day
of my dear little Mary, who, had she lived, would have been
thirty years old, and your dear friend and sister, and it is
only that my long years of untold suffering have been covered
over by unceasing effort to appear cheerful, that I am not
in the eyes of others what I feel myself to be, yet every one
tells me how happy I am! It would seem that I can produce
cheerfulness in others which has no place in my own feelings.
I have made up a party of Americans to go with me on a
drive to see many interesting things, which I hope will force
my thoughts into other channels. I am also invited to join
a party to Ostia in a day or two, and I must be as busy as possible, for I find a single hour which is not occupied by present
things tells painfully on my spirits. May God preserve you
all in health and safety. I have suffered so much that I am
always fearing the worst.

ROME, *Jan.* 21, 1852.

I set forth yesterday morning with a party of Phila-
delphians to pass the day among the ruins. We first went
to see the Cloaca Maxima, the temples of the Vestal Virgins;
and of Fortuna Viriles, and the house of Rienza, all lying near
together. From them to the Pyramid Cestus and the English
burying-ground, and, examining them, we passed on to the
magnificent Church of St. Paolo *fuore e mura*, and two miles
further to San Paolo *di tri fontane*, which I had not before
seen. Here are built in a solitary spot on the Campagna,
far from any house, three small churches within a few yards
of each other. These commemorate the spot where St. Paul
was beheaded. One of them is built (it is said) on the very
spot, and it contains, on the same legendary evidence, the
marble block on which he was decapitated, which stands on
a line with these fountains which instantly gushed forth at
the three spots from which his head rebounded. On each is
erected an altar having in front a marble head to represent
the miracle. Another of these little churches contains in a
subterranean apartment the bones of the many (so they say)

of the martyrs of the Diocletian persecution. Our cicerone was a feeble, sickly looking girl of thirteen or fourteen, attended by an equally pale little sister of six. I asked her if she had suffered from malaria. Ah, my lady, have I not? and when I asked her why they did not go elsewhere, the poor little thing replied with a faint smile, where can we go? It is dreadful to see a whole population fade before this insidious and fatal disease, which seems creeping on like a leprosy, year by year, until it seems to threaten the existence of the entire city. From this gloomy spot we proceeded to the fountain of Egeria and the neighboring groves, all beautiful, and thence to the Church of St. Sebastian, this being the saint. Our object was to pass through it to the Catacombs, but we were arrested by the apparition of some three or four omnibuses, from whence issued, like a flock of pigeons, a large number of religieuses in holiday attire, i. e., white muslin veils and capes over their black dresses, quite fancifully put on, all having very pretty ear rings, and apparently on a general pilgrimage in honor of St. Sebastian. I asked them of their order, etc., and they told me they were Trasteverini, i. e., from a certain quarter on the other side of the Tiber, where it is said the Roman race remain less mixed than elsewhere, and rather warlike in habits. Willing to please them, I observed to two or three as they passed on toward the church, that I had always heard of the Trasteverini as a very handsome race, and I now saw that they were so, whereupon they bridled up and received the compliment 'with as much pleasure as if belonging to a court circle.

Returning to the city through a narrow lane we met the Pope, who is accustomed to walk out in fine weather. He was preceded by two guardsmen on horseback, and two on foot, and was attended on each side by a cardinal. He wore a long robe of white woolen cloth, with a belt of the same material, and a broad-brimmed scarlet hat, and shoes. Our carriage stopped, of course, until he passed, and we arose at his approach and bowed. We were rewarded by a kindly smile from the really benevolent face of this good man, who at the same time gave us signs of his benediction. He was followed by two dark crimson carriages, of large size, drawn by four immense black horses, attended by some half dozen out-riders.

A part of to-day has been occupied in going over the Castle of St. Angelo, from turret to foundation-stone, under the guidance of a French officer. It is a great pity that the French can not have the civil administration in their hands as well as the military. The Pope can not do as he wishes, and if they, possessing the power to enforce these laws, could carry out his measures, there might be some hope of Italian regeneration. I have bought some fine prints and bronzes. One of the latter is a statuette of Michael Angelo's "Moses," one of the finest sculptures of the Middle Ages. These, with the picture of the "Fates," which I mentioned to you, I requested Mr. Kellogg to forward immediately. I am afraid to enter more expensively into these things ; it is better to abstain than to embarrass oneself. I hope the pictures from Dresden have arrived safely in New York. Order them all to be sent to you in Cincinnati. They will afford you much pleasure, and more to me if they are yours.

Expecting so soon to leave Rome, and regretting that I could not be presented to the Pope, I mentioned it in conversing with a Scottish gentleman a few days since—Mr. McPherson—my disappointment that Mr. Cass had not been able to gratify me. Mr. McP. at once offered to apply to an eminent cardinal, who is his friend, and the result was an immediate acquiescence to my request. The audience was fixed for three o'clock to-day, His Holiness receiving ladies only on Sundays. After attending the usual divine service at our embassy at eleven o'clock, I set forth with Mr. McPherson at half-past two o'clock for the Vatican. We were ushered onward, in the midst of Swiss guards, in their parti-colored dresses, and serving gentlemen in crimson, up the long staircase, through the rooms containing the cartoons, the frescoes, and the transfiguration of Raphael, until reaching one carpeted, and a brazier in the center, I found some dozen persons, chiefly ladies, wearing like myself black dresses and veils. The Russian ambassadress, with her husband, formed one party, the wife of the French Chargé had another. There were several other persons apparently unattached. We waited some fifteen minutes, when a signal was made to go somewhere, and by the advice of Mr. McPherson and Captain Malcolm (brother of the Russian ambassadress) I joined the party of that lady. After passing through several ante-chambers, we reached a folding-door, which was suddenly thrown open. This was the entrance of a room of some thirty or forty feet long, at the further end of which sat the Pope, near a sort of desk—the room being destitute of any other furniture, and covered with a plain green carpet. His Holiness wore a long white worsted robe, or gown, of cloth, with a belt of the same material. Round his neck was a clerical band, and a gold chain was suspended, having a gold cross of the same material tucked into his belt. His hands were bare, with one or two seal rings upon his fingers, and he wore red slippers having a small cross embroidered on the foot. He rose smilingly as we entered, and each lady bowed low at the door. One of them, a German princess, born Wallenstein, fell upon her knees and bowed her head. On approaching His Holiness, he extended his hand for each to kiss, but the devout lady persisted in kissing his foot, which, as the worthy man was standing, was, I dare say, decidedly inconvenient to him, but he took it in good part, and managed as well as he could. He at once entered into an animated conversation with the Russian Ambassador, who stood next him, and in a clear tone, which was easy to understand by any one who even imperfectly knew Italian.

After a few minutes conversation, the gentlemen were introduced, and, hearing the name of Malcolm, he asked if it were not Scottish. When the ambassadress replied that it

was the name of a distinguished Scotch family, he then inquired if Scotland had not two millions of inhabitants. The
lady did not know, and asked her brother, who knew no more
than herself; whereupon, to relieve the growing embarrass-
ment, I informed the lady there was not less than *four* millions, and she, recovering herself, gave the desired information
at once. After some further remarks, which I have forgotten, we received the offered benediction, kissed the hand (the
German princess persisting in kissing the foot), and retired,
not backing out, but walking out very properly. On coming
into the anteroom, the gentleman in purple inquired if I had
had any conversation with his holiness. I replied in the neg-
ative, and he intimated that I was expected to have had a
special audience. I therefore returned to the waiting-room
until I was called by my new friend in purple, who, I was informed, was of the family of the Prince Hohenlohe, and who
detained me in conversation in French some ten minutes,
during which he inquired whether I preferred to address the
Pope in French or Italian. I preferred the former; whereupon, he said that the Saint Pere could speak with me in that
language. At length, the little bell rang, the doors opened,
and, preceded by my friend in purple, who whispered, I suppose, that I had been introduced before by mistake, and that
I spoke French, and then withdrew. I was left alone with
the " head of the church." I saw by his smiling eye that he
recognized me as having been on the same spot half an hour
before; and, as I approached again to kiss the proffered hand,
said that I could not regret a mistake which had procured me
the honor of a second audience with our so venerated, etc. He
smiled kindly, and said he was glad to see me, and asked if I
was alone in Rome. I replied I was with friends who were to
remain longer than myself, who would have the honor of
being presented by our own Minister; that I had feared to
have been obliged to leave Rome without an opportunity to
pay my homage, and that I was greatly indebted to his kindness, through Monsignor Talbot, in having my request so

promptly acceded to, etc. His holiness then remarked that he had heard of my works of charity and mercy, and blessed me for it. He then spoke of several of the Romish dignitaries in America, especially of Doctor Purcell, of Cincinnati, and mentioned one after the other of the churches he had founded. He then gave me his blessing. I kissed the proffered hand, he rang the little bell, the doors opened, and, on passing through, I made another low bow, and the door was shut. I had purchased some chaplets to be blessed, as is the custom; and, on my coming out, they were sent in to receive the usual benediction. One of them is intended for M——, of course.

Monday, 26th.—Thankful for any thing that takes me away from myself during these days that so vividly bring back the scenes of last year, which I find myself, when alone, perpetually living over again, with all their bitter memories, I was not sorry to be obliged to pass the evening with one or two Americans, who had invited Gibson, the first of English sculptors, to meet me. He has a great fund of conversation about his early days, thirty-five years ago. I found some relief to sad thoughts in listening. This morning early I was awakened by martial music, and, on inquiring the cause, learned that it was occasioned by carrying to the place of execution, at the Porte del Popolo, quite near by, a soldier condemned to be shot for murdering a fellow soldier to get his money. This poor wretch has perhaps a mother to break her heart for him.

I shall leave this positively for Naples on Friday or Satururday—as soon as I receive my letter of this week from you. I wish the excitement was over about Kossuth. After all I have heard of him from good authority, it is impossible to have a good opinion of him. As for Louis Napoleon, I incline to think he is doing the best he can for France, which needs a strong hand, and he shows, as yet, no disposition to be cruel. God bless and protect you all.

ROME, *January* 30, 1852.

One subject alone occupies us both to-day, my beloved child, and its return will continue as long as we may live to be consecrated to the same memories of the loved and lost— but as we trust, lost only for a while. The lapse of a year has had but little effect in subduing my sorrow, and time has gained for me nothing but the power of restraining the outward manifestation of what is ever present in my thoughts. I find this restraint very painful to me, yet among entire strangers I have no right to obtrude my private griefs, and the constant interruptions to which I am necessarily subjected, deny me even the privilege of weeping alone. I am growing exceedingly anxious to rejoin some of my family, and devoutly trust that L. may have the courage to accept my proposition to join me at Naples, and return to England with me. You will hear of the decision almost as soon as I shall, for the mail creeps along in eleven days from England. I have only waited for the mail day to pass to set out for Naples, for I had not the courage to be among new faces, and here I have grown accustomed to see a circle of very kind and pleasing people, chiefly Americans, who, if I had been disposed would have drawn me into a round of society which, even under other circumstances, I could hardly have enjoyed. The Storys and the Lowells have been very kind to me, and I have found some English people who are very humane and amiable. I have seen as much of this grand old city as my time would admit, but I think no one should remain less than six months, and then, even if well employed every day, it will still be found that the great part is unexplored. Sunday evening I was interrupted, and it being known that I was about to go away, the calls for leave-taking, and preparations for removal, together with the last sight seeings have taken up my time, and indeed I have been glad to be forced to constant occupation. To-morrow morning I am to set out in the diligence for Naples—sleep at Terracina and arrive about four Tuesday, P. M. I earnestly hope to find letters already there. The Allens, of Providence, I mentioned are in Naples, My health is good, notwithstanding the depression of my spirits, which I can not shake off. I trust in Heaven that you are all well. I am sorry to send you so empty a letter, but one comes in after another, and I can write no, more. God bless you all.

P. S.—I think I mentioned in my last letter that I had bought no pictures, only some bronze statuettes and valuable prints of Middle Age artists.

NAPLES, *February* 4, 1852.

I left Rome on Monday morning, the second inst., at seven o'clock, mounted on the top of the diligence, passed over the pretty hill road about Albano and Arricia, and through the melancholy Campagna, and the Tontine marshes to Terracina, where I slept until four P. M., and then by a fine moonlight we entered the Neapolitan territory, where I was not slow to perceive a better cultivation, but a population so covered with rags patched in every color, and variegated still more by the poor dirty skin which peeped forth, that one wonders that they do not adopt at once the time-honored costume of the fig leaf. Poor souls! they seem to try their best to look picturesque, if they can not be comfortable. We met at early dawn scores of them trooping toward their daily task, for which they receive from five to eight cents per day. The country is very pretty, and every-where covered by crops of wheat, or beans, or flax, with vast orchards of olives, and trees planted like orchards to support the grape vines, which hang in festoons from tree to tree. Near Gaeta we passed the high tomb of Cicero, raised by his freedman on the spot on which he was murdered. The scenery of the bay and mountains in this vicinity is beautiful beyond description, and the bright sky was in harmony with the landscape. Passing at each moment some spot of poetic or historic fame, and purchasing at Capua some half dozen nice oranges, just plucked from the trees, which seem borne down by their loads of fruit, we came on to Naples, and about seven o'clock I entered the

Hotel Victoria, where I was kindly welcomed by the Allens, who only awaited my arrival to set out for Pæstum. They leave here for Rome in a few days. I had promised my Philadelphia friends (the Pughs) to look for lodgings for them, and I employed the morning, after leaving the banker's, in looking for apartments, and I have succeeded in securing some for them and for myself, in a boarding house, a rare thing in Europe, kept by an English woman in the pleasantest part of the city, overlooking the magnificent bay, with Vesuvius beyond.

Sunday Evening, February 8th.—The Allens and I set out early on Thursday for Pæstum, some fifty-two miles distant. Twelve miles on the way lie the remains of Pompeii, and having passed through Patrica and by Herculaneum, we stopped at the first excavations, and for four hours we walked along the disinterred streets and houses of this once rich and populous city. You have read so many descriptions of it that it would be useless for me to attempt any, especially as it is impossible to convey any just idea without having seen these most curious and touching records of the every-day life of those who two thousand years ago felt and thought, perhaps, nearly as we do now. Almost every utensil of their domestic life has its counterpart among us. Ours, it is true, are less gracefully fashioned, but less different than I dreamed of; but they indulged in an elegance of household decoration which only the few rich at present can attempt. From Pompeii we proceeded some twelve miles further to Salerno, the capital of Calabria, and beautifully situated on the bay of the same name. Here we slept, lulled by the moan of the waves which dashed ceaselessly against the shore within a few feet of our window. After an early breakfast we set out for Pæstum, twenty-six miles distant, over a level country, well cultivated in wheat, grapes, oranges, etc. The Apennines lay as usual at some miles from the sea, and our road followed, for the most part, the curve of the Bay of Salerno, at the southern extremity of which, in a solitary tract of country,

stand the giant skeletons of three magnificent doric temples,
built of a yellow petrified substance so durable that, though
it seems composed of only canes and reeds and all kinds of
small rubbish, it has endured more than three thousand years
with less injury from time than others of five hundred years.
They are the oldest structures in Europe, yet their beautiful
proportions prove them to be the work of a people advanced
to a higher degree of art than was ever attained by any but
the Greeks. It seems that malaria has done more to destroy
them than neglect, for to this day few constitutions can sustain the deadly influences of this spot, and those who cultivate
the fields take refuge at night in the neighboring mountains.
Some poor, sickly-looking creatures, with ghostly faces and
swelled abdomens, came to beg alms, and but that the fields,
covered with growing wheat, gave a cheerful aspect to the
place, nothing could have exceeded its loneliness. The ruins,
however, are in good keeping—worn, indeed, but not bedrag-
gled as they are in Rome, and looking as if three thousand
years hence they might be as firm as now. We ate our cold
duck in the Temple of Ceres, and, wandering along the old
walls of the city, eighteen feet thick, and composed of huge
blocks of the same petrified masses as the columns of the temples, we entered our carriage to return to sleep at Salerno.
These shores are the scene of the wanderings of Ulysses, and
so graphic are the verses of Homer that many of his descriptions are true to the life to-day.

Yesterday we came by Castellemara, where we ascended a
mountain to take a view, and reached Naples about six, where
I had the great comfort of finding a letter from L. I trust
her next will tell me that she will join me. I am troubled
to hear that our dear little R. has been ill. How painful
it is to be so widely separated. If she does not come, I
think I must hasten my return to England. There was also
a letter from our bankers, inclosing a remittance. You
always send these remittances in good season, my dear child,
so that I am relieved from anxiety so far as you can aid me.

12

Naples deserves all that has been said of its beauty of situation, for I do not think the world can find its parallel. But what a contrast in its population. In the street they seem a sort of mongrel race, and painfully inferior in their aspect to the noble forms and symmetrical physiognomy of Rome. As yet I am entirely uncertain whether I can get to Athens. I do not like to go alone, and I have not yet received the letter from Miss Howard which I expected. In any event, I suppose I must be here two weeks, and if I should not hear of any suitable companion, I shall relinquish my plan. To-morrow we go to Vesuvius.

NAPLES, *February* 9, 1852.

I have seen Vesuvius and clambered half way down the crater, until the ashes being too hot to walk upon admonished me to penetrate no further. At eight o'clock this morning we set forth in a carriage five miles to Portici. Here we mounted mules, and under the care of a guide proceeded zigzag up the sides of the mountain to the Hermitage, which, until the last three months, could be easily reached in a carriage, but the rains of November rendered the road impracticable, and the repairs are not yet completed.

To the house called the Hermitage we picked our way across masses of lava and scoria, which lie in heaps as far as the eye can reach, across the level of the old crater, which must be traversed in order to reach the point of ascent of the new crater which rises almost perpendicularly from one side of the debris of the old. At the foot of this, some eight miles from Portici, we left our mules and commenced the toilsome ascent, which requires about an hour and a quarter. Finding that the loose scoria and cinders slipped under my feet at each step, I was glad to accept the assistance of one of the men who followed us; these have a leathern strap fastened to their shoulders, with a loop hanging down behind; and by holding fast to the loop, and treading in the footsteps of the man, one is saved from falling and much assisted in getting upward. At length, without much fatigue—for I am now so accustomed to scaling heights that nothing seems to weary me—I reached the summit, from numerous fissures in which steam of a sulphur-ous odor pours unceasingly; it is sometimes quite stifling, and so thick as entirely to obscure the view. The wind, however, which is always fresh at this elevation, by sudden puffs blows away the vapors from time to time, so that by waiting a few minutes a perfect view may be had of the whole. The sur-face of the ground, which is entirely composed of cinders and stones thrown up at the close of the last eruption in 1850, is covered with yellow sulphur, so hot in many places that eggs are taken up by the guides and cooked for the refresh-ment of the visitor, merely by covering them for a few mo-ments in the cinders. The views of Naples, of the bay and the islands, are exquisite and of immense extent. I walked about and gathered relics as usual, and then we ate our cold chicken and descended, as you may suppose, much more rapidly than we went up; the descent upon mules was also more agreeable. The declining sun lent a new beauty to the landscape, and about its setting we reached our lodg-ings, content with the day.

Friday.—This is the first all-day rain that I have seen in this beautiful Italy, and I have availed myself of it to restore some of my tattered habiliments to decent condition. Since my last notes I have again passed some hours in the Museo Borbonico, which possesses the rare treasures of Herculaneum and Pompeii, which are not remarkable as adding much to high art, but wonderful as revealing to us, after eighteen cen-turies, the habits of their possessors. Some of these I men-tioned in my last letter. Since then I have visited another department, which contains a number of bodies taken from the marble tombs which still adorn the roads of entrance to the excavated city. These, though blackened, are more perfect in their preservation than any I have seen from Egypt, and the nobler form of the heads and the more intel-lectual expression, which yet remains impressed upon their features, render them intensely interesting to me. They are just what we see among the highest types at home; and interesting as it was to examine them, I felt that violence was done to their delicacy in being thus exposed to the vulgar gaze. This never before struck me in looking at a mummy, but these were veritable ladies and gentlemen of refinement, as may be traced in every lineament. In this same museum are two of the finest sculptures of antiquity; viz., the Farnese Hercules and the Toro Farnese, or group of Dirce, which the King of Naples inherits from his ancestress, the heiress of the Farnese family and wealth, which have thus been transferred from Rome to Naples. I have also visited three of the royal palaces; that in the city has more comfort in it than any royal palace I have seen, being beautifully carpeted and elegantly furnished. It is remarkable that the palaces of the second-rate kings are often finer than the first; for we observed the same thing at Munich, Dresden, and Berlin, while England and Austria are quite behind.

Friday, 13th.—Returning to-day from a visit to Portici and Herculaneum, I had the precious comfort to find your letter had just arrived. Yesterday I received one from L., who declines to join me here, to my great regret, for Italy is so wonderfully rich in every thing which can interest a cultivated mind, that I can not bear that she should be so near and yet lose it all. I shall now see Naples as fast as I can, and sail for Malta, hoping to find good company for Athens, and, if possible, for Constantinople.

I rejoice that the demagogue Kossuth is soon likely to find his level, and I doubly trust that our people may be preserved from the insane idea of intervention in European affairs. I am entirely persuaded that nothing can be now more dangerous for any part of Europe than a sudden change to what they call a free government, which in reality would be another name for anarchy, and in attempting to assist their purposes we should but aid them to cast off all government, and at the same time we should injure ourselves.

My travels in Italy have afforded me as much enjoyment as

I am capable of receiving now. I had not the least conception of its all-pervading beauty, and as little comprehension
of the immense treasures of art that it contains. The people, too, seem far better than I had expected. I met with
none of the brutality of the English, nor the stupidity of the
Germans, nor the polite selfishness of the French. They exhibit quick perceptions and kindly feelings. We see no
turbulence, and a general willingness to oblige, even if they
are not paid. Begging seems to be a thing of course, but
if you refuse there is no insolence, and one is rarely defrauded.
You will be surprised when I tell you that never, since I left
home, have I been so comfortable as in this boarding-house,
where room, bed, and table are all good; and in looking out
of my window, the most beautiful view on earth meets my
eye. The whole bay is spread before me. If you and M.
were here how much you would enjoy it! It is a thousand
pities that Mr. Peter could not come, for there are many
English families here, and the consul (whose family have
been very friendly) is as staunch a Whig as himself. You can
scarcely believe how little time I get to write. I accomplish
more in less time than other travelers, because I occupy every
moment in seeing and studying. My knowledge of languages
saves me much expense in guides, interpreters, etc., and gains
me far more facility in knowing the people.

NAPLES, *Feb.* 14*th.*

After carrying my letters to the banker yesterday, I went
with the Pughs from church to church for some hours. Among
the cathedrals dedicated to the patron saint of Naples, St.
Gennaro is one of the richest in Europe. It is in itself a
fine church, full of frescoes, and paintings, and sculptures,
especially in bronze; but its chief wealth lies in the amphora,
which contains the blood caught by a Neapolitan lady as it
flowed from the head of the saint when he carried it under
his arm to Naples after he had suffered martyrdom by decapitation at Pozzuoli! ! In the various recesses of this church

are forty-seven statues in silver, chiefly half lengths, but of the size of life, of the most honored among the company of saints and martyrs. Besides these there are candelabra and large bouquets of flowers three or four feet high, also of solid silver, finely wrought, which are used on those great annual festivals, when the blood of the saint is seen by the admiring thousands to liquefy—both here and in Pozzuoli, where some is preserved. This precious blood is kept in a sort of small closet inclosed by silver doors, which are never unlocked except by an order from the king through a cardinal, on these festival days. But the really beautiful ornament is a massive front of the altar, some six feet long and four wide, over which is a representation of the procession which brought the relics of the saint from Pozzuoli, where they had laid for many hundreds of years. The cardinal is introduced in his robes on horseback, bearing before him a sarcophagus supposed to have contained the relics. Under his horse's feet lies prostrate a man who in his overthrow has scattered several books on the ground. This impersonates—Hurry. Pestilence also falls prostrate before these miraculous relics, and War and Famine, all full-length allegorical figures, are seen hastening away. Religion and Charity sit on either side, in the exercise of their functions, while the king and a goodly array of courtiers come to welcome the happy arrival. All this is wrought in solid silver, exquisitely finished; and the figures are not in relief, but complete, and placed on the ground work of the piece, which is also silver. It was executed in the Cinque Cento, as it is called, i. e., the fifteenth century, or the prime of modern art.

From the church we went again to the Museum to see the Pompeiian collections, and entered the chamber of the most precious. These consist of gold ornaments, cameos, etc., which are beautifully wrought. There are also eggs, and bread, and beans, and glass vessels, and all sorts of things in daily use among ourselves—or, rather, among their descendants. From there we took a carriage, and drove some three or four miles

to the Campo Santo, beautifully situated on a hill overlooking
the town. This is literally " a city of the dead," most of the
monuments being inclosed in small chapels arranged in hollow
squares. There is also a garden beautifully planted, in which
while I was there a poor little girl of eight years old
was laid to rest. I wandered through the place led by
a gentle and kindly Capuchin monk, whom I should really
like to know better. Taking a friendly leave of him, I again
entered my little carriage, and, accompanied only by my *cocher*,
a Neapolitan boy of fifteen, I drove some miles to the Catacombs, or ancient burial place of three thousand years ago.
These are arched-ways of large size, three stories high, which
are cut literally into the mountain, and subdivided into chambers of various sizes and forms, some being adorned with
mosaics, and many with frescoes of no great merit. They are
so large that their extent is not known. This afternoon I
wished to go to the French service, which is held at the Prussian embassy, and to my surprise as well as delight I found
there the pastor who founded the Order of Deaconesses in
Paris, who had been invited to give some information to the
audience about that institution. His whole manner was calculated to win friends, and after service I approached him to
tell him that I was from America, and perhaps had interested
myself more than any other woman in that country for the
advancement of the principles which he advocated. He took
my address, and was apparently much gratified that I had
spoken with him, and in a day or two I hope to see him. To-
morrow, if the day be fair, we shall make a journey to Capri.

Thursday, 19th.—Since writing the last sentence, I have had
no moment to resume my pen. We set out for Capri on the
weekly steamer, and reached the island in about three hours.
One of ours would have made the voyage in half the time.
The great curiosity of the island is the Grotto Azurra, a sort
of cavern, low and small at the entrance, but long enough for
a small boat, and hollowed into a lofty arch within, the walls
of which are all of a bright ultramarine blue, from the re-

flection of the hue of the water, which is the most brilliant
blue imaginable.   It seems precisely the color you see in the
druggist shops, while the water is really transparent as crystal.
This being done, we landed, and, mounting on mules, rode to the
top of one of the two mountains of which Capri is formed, where
we found, as usual, a chapel and an old, but very civil and kind
Capuchin to welcome us.   From this giddy height of 3,500
feet above the water, we looked down upon the neigbboring
ruins of the Palace of Tiberius, and the precipice from
which he caused criminals to be thrown, and also upon the
Bay of Salerno, at the further extremity of which are the
solitary temples of Paestum.   The Bay of Naples lay at our
feet on the other side.   We descended with some dozen other
travelers who had come with us in the boat, among whom
were several American gentlemen on their way to Egypt,
Palestine, and Constantinople.

   Tuesday.—The day after we went to Baiæ, the seat of ease
and luxury of the Romans in the later days of the republic and
the early empire.   Here lived Cicero, and Pompey, and Augustus, and Lucullus, and truly it must have been an earthly
paradise; the map will show you the locality, but nothing
short of the reality can convey to you the incomparable
beauty, even in its lonely and dishonored ruin.   The whole
coast for miles is covered with confused masses of rubbish
and Roman walls, which have in clear outline the uses for
which they were created.   Tradition, occasionally confirmed
by historical data, gives a celebrated name to this or that
fragment of a temple, or palace, or villa, or bath.   In the
immediate neighborhood are the lakes of Acheron and Avernus, the Styx and the Elysian fields, and the haunts of the
Sybils.   We passed the entire day in examining the varied
remains, of which the baths are the best preserved, and frescoes and bas-reliefs are still visible.   This whole neighborhood seems to be based upon extinct volcanoes, and near
Baiæ from the ancient times the hot stream issuing from

crevices has been used by invalids. It is so hot that eggs are cooked in a few minutes.

Wednesday.—Mrs. May, of Philadelphia, and her daughter, are passing the winter here, and having an invitation from her to accompany them to Caserta, the residence of the King of Naples, I set out at half past seven, A. M., to take them up on the way to the railroad. They had for their escort an officer of the royal guard, who had offered his services, and a most perfect cicerone he proved to be. At the railway we were joined by a cousin of L., Mr. Yarnell, who is professor of mathematics on board of the Independence, which, to my great comfort, lies constantly in the harbor. He had called on me hoping to find L., and was disappointed to learn she was not with me. He is a right good fellow, and I like him. Under the guidance of the very elegant officer of the royal guard, we visited, to our great pleasure, the immense and beautiful gardens of this magnificent residence, a pretty villa some three miles off, to which is attached a manufacture of silk, where the richest brocades and velvets are made, the palace, one of the very finest in Europe, and finally the ampitheater of the ancient Capua, which is a beautiful ruin, and returned about seven o'clock in the evening content with the day. This morning we set forth again early for Pozzuoli, near which is the famous temple of Jupiter Serapis, which has seen rare vicissitudes—first overrun by a volcano, next by the sea, and finally by ashes from a neighboring crater. From thence we went to the ancient Cuma, now a mass of ruins, with traces still distinct of the temple of Apollo, and the grotto of the Sybil, and looking down upon the Lake of Avernus. We visited the numerous ruins scattered all over the country, especially the Amphitheater, but having been entirely overrun by lava and cinders has been well preserved. Excavations have been made of the greater portion, and the walls are as fresh as if just built. This arena is nearly as large as the Coliseum. It is related in the Acts that St. Paul landed near this place, at Pozzuoli, and the place is still shown. We also visited a sort of city of tombs, all in ruins, the Grotto del Cane, etc., and Solfetare, a lava crater in which is heard a loud sound of boiling steam. All the earth around is covered with sulphur—the sand is so hot that the hand in many places can not endure the touch, and hot steam issues from many different crevices. On our return, about six o'clock, I found Mr. Yarnell awaiting me. He tells me that the party for Egypt consisted of a Presbyterian clergyman, etc., who will have great pleasure in taking charge of me if I wish to go, and that the steamer for Malta sails on Monday. Mr. Morris, our *chargé*, will give me letters, and it seems I may make this tour if I choose. On the way to Malta I shall be able to see of what stuff the party are composed, and judge if it be expedient to join them. Having finished my sight-seeing on Thursday evening, I proceeded on Friday to look about for something to take home, and to my surprise I found that good copies of works of art were to be had cheaper here than elsewhere. Mr. Yarnell kindly offers to take charge of any purchases I may make, and see them safe on board the Independence, which will carry them to New York free of charge, and I have accordingly launched forth as boldly as I thought I could venture. I have purchased a marble statue of Flora, half the size of life, a copy of a holy family from Sasseferate, do. by Raphael, Masaniello, a little original, very good large vase enamel pralta, Guache pictures and statuettes, Toro Farnese, prints, small vases and antiques, of which I can not give you the value until I have time on shipboard to make up my accounts. The opportunity is too good to be lost, and I trust you will be able to make all right without inconvenience. I have made these purchases in accordance with your requests and my own judgment. I think I have not made a mistake. I have drawn on our banker for a part, the remainder can be paid when the Independence reaches New York, which will be soon, as they constantly look for orders to return home. The Flora is a copy of what is considered the most beautiful draped figure

of antiquity.   Within some three months we must remit the
whole amount to our minister here, Mr. Morris, of Philadelphia, who has been exceedingly kind to me, and Mr.
Yarnell has been a great comfort and help.   As I do not
know exactly yet about the Egyptian tour, I can not estimate
my future wants.   I shall get back to England as fast as I
can, after seeing and learning as much as I can.   Italy has
afforded me real enjoyment, and if I had not ties and duties
which call me elsewhere, I should linger here merely from my
love for the land of beauty and of art.   As it is I have not
lost a day, no, not an hour.   Every moment is busily occupied.
I am grieving every day that I am seeing so much in which
you and M. can not participate; and it is especially vexatious
to me that L., who is so near, and might so easily have been
with me, is alone at Canterbury.   I am sadly disappointed
that she did not accept my offer.   It is easier traveling in
Italy than anywhere else, and we could have got along better
with the children than elsewhere; but the stupid people who
blinded us by their foolish counsels made so much difficulty
that it seemed impossible.

PART III.

Oriental Letters.

At Sea Off Cutaine, Sicily. }
Ash Wednesday, February 25, 1852. }

The steamer was detained a day at Civita Vecchia by high
winds, and I was in consequence detained a day longer at
Naples, which luckily afforded me an opportunity to be present at the celebration of Washington's birthday, on the evening of the 23d, at the house of our *chargé* (Mr. Morris),
where were assembled all the Americans in Naples, including
the officers of the Independence and the ambassadors from
the different European courts, officers of the British navy and
other English visitors, and officers of the Neapolitan army,
besides a number of ladies and gentlemen, priests, etc., of the
city, in their various costumes.   Everybody who is anybody

lives in a palazzo at Naples (our boarding-house was one), and therefore you must not suspect our worthy representative of extravagance when I say that the large entrance (the *porte cochère*) of his palazzo was magnificently illuminated with colored lamps all around the wide arch, while the name of Washington appeared also in brilliant colors at the top; and as the palazzo is separated from the bay only by the street, which runs along its entire and beautiful semicircle, the illumination was seen far and wide.   The stairs had living plants in pots arranged along the sides, and the suits of apartments were beautifully lighted up.   In one of them a table was prettily arranged for such light refreshments as the better taste of this part of the world demands—ices, jellies, and confections—and when any of the company were so inclined, they helped themselves to what they wished.   Mr. Thurlow Weed, the editor of the paper your Cousin Rufus assisted, was there, but I observed no other American notabilities; there was a band, and dancing of course, but there were so many rooms opened that this in no way affected those of quiet taste.   L.'s cousin, Mr. Yarnell, seemed highly to enjoy the dance—I, of course, passed the evening in quiet chat. Among others I was introduced to a most gentlemanly and enlightened ecclesiastic, who I hope some day to see in America.

I can never be sufficiently thankful for my knowledge of so many modern languages, which has enabled me to converse with the people of all the nations of Europe without let or hindrance; and especially in Italy I have found the immense advantage which I derive from it.   If added to this I had the time and fortune, which so many ignorant and idle people enjoy, how much use I could make of my time and travel! (The boat is rolling at such a rate that it is difficult to write.) I came on board this steamer (French) at two o'clock yesterday afternoon, and find Mr. Haskell, a clerical professor of the Baptist Seminary at ˙Newton, Massachusetts, a most gen-

tlemanly and agreeable man, traveling for his health. The
three other members of the party, the same I mentioned in my last letter, seem common-place, and are,
like nearly all American young men, rather *cubbish.* Mr.
H. is, I suppose, about forty-eight or fifty years of age,
and has a wife and children at home. He seems very desirous
I should join the party for Egypt and Palestine, and if I hear
at Malta it is safe and easy, and does not require too much
time, I will go. My chief reluctance is on L's. account, who,
I fear, will weary of passing another month alone, for I suppose it will require from three to six weeks longer. This
morning as I emerged from my cabin, the first object that met
my eye, quite near us, was the island volcano of Stromboli,
which had been emiting flames all night. In about four
hours afterward we passed between the long famed Scylla and
Charybdis, without, however, falling foul of either; and a
little while after we entered the harbor of Messina, and going
on shore walked about the harbor for several hours. It has
been raining ever since, and I have been below reading,
until everybody has gone to bed, and fearing I may not have
time to write from Malta, I avail' myself of the quiet saloon
This being the mail-boat, I had the great satisfaction to receive
the joint letter of the 15th, and M's. of the 23d, by the same
mail, together with one from Mr. Peter dated 12th of January. I was truly grateful to receive them before setting
forth on another journey. This will be my last expedition;
and being concluded I shall set my face homeward, feeling
that I have done as much as I could possibly accomplish.
What a comfort it will be to sit down among you all again;
and yet I see no immediate prospect of coming to Cincinnati,
and to live so far from you as Philadelphia seems little better
than to be on this side of the Atlantic. I have all along
hoped that you could join us here for a few months, and see
something of Europe, so as to spare the pain of another separation. If this could be done, I would willingly remain
abroad next summer.

MALTA, *February 26th.*

We reached this island and entered the venerable port of Valetta about ten o'clock this morning, and expecting to get off in the evening, after bringing our luggage to the hotel I set forth in a carriage, with Mr. Haskell, for St. Paul's Bay, where the apostle landed, on the opposite side of the island, twelve miles. We visited on the way the beautiful house and grounds of the Governor, and Civita Vecchia, where Publius lived, who entertained St. Paul during his stay here. Quite near the place are extensive Catacombs, which were ancient and extensive burial-places. The island is highly cultivated, and sustains a dense population; and the views are beautiful in all directions. Here, for the first time, I find a language I can not speak—the Arabic, much corrupted, being the language of the common people. On returning, I went to the Cathedral, which is beautifully paved with the armorial bearings in Florentine mosaic of the numerous Grand Masters of the Order of the Knights of St. John, who have commanded here—the last died in 1797. The church is magnificent.

The population is a mixed multitude from every land under the sun—the Moor being predominant. We sail to-morrow for Alexandria and Cairo. If I find it easy, and not occupying too much time, I may go into Palestine; but I am reluctant to leave L. so long, and this thought hurries me homeward. I shall write to you by the return steamer, from Alexandria, where I expect to pass two or three days, and then two days at Cairo, and so to see the Pyramids, Memphis, etc., and then if I do not go to Palestine I shall sail from Alexandria to Athens and Constantinople, and then to England. I shall keep you all as well informed as possible of my movements; but if you do not hear from me regularly, do not be uneasy, for the mail must be irregular in the East, and I shall not expose myself to danger.

Friday, 27th.—We are to sail this morning in the French steamer for Alexandria, and so on to Cairo and the Pyramids, which will occupy about a fortnight, and then on either overland to Jerusalem or turn about for Greece. It pains me to hear of so many deaths of those we know. Will God in his mercy spare me awhile from other bereavements? Heaven bless you all!

AT SEA, OFF THE BARBARY COAST, *Feb.* 29, 1852.

My letter from Malta will have prepared you for my distant travels. The weather, so far, is the finest possible, the steamer excellent, and the company small, an immense advantage, without which all others are of little avail at sea. Having nothing else to describe, it may amuse you to hear of our passengers. In the cabin, which is beautifully furnished, are Mr. and Mrs. Parker, and their son, the first a brother of Mr. Peter Parker, whom you know. The lady is exceedingly fashionable, and in bad health. There is also a French lady who came with us from Naples, who is going to Jerusalem with two Frenchmen, her *compagnons de voyage*. On deck we constantly see an Arab in Turkish dress, who seems to feel himself of some consequence, but who constantly eats (on deck) out of a white wash-basin, with a sort of a wooden spoon, while he sits like a tailor. There is also a Capuchin, as dirty as usual, who moves about with more freedom than is agreeable to some of us, who take a religious care always to get to the windward of him, a movement of which he seems to entertain no suspicion. I happen to be almost the only passenger who speaks Italian—all but the Americans being French, with the exception above named—and the poor Capuchin, apparently of a very social disposition, naturally likes to have a little chat, and oftener than is at all desirable to me. He tells me he is going to Jerusalem to convey alms to his brethren there, who, being mendicants by their vows, can expect to obtain but little in a Mohammedan country. The Arab is on his way to Mecca, as he informs us, for Italian being the language of the Levant, the possession of it enables me to make acquaintance with all sorts of people, and you

may imagine how often I thank poor Maccaroni, as you used
to call him, for having imparted to me a language now so useful.   Our steamer, the Osiris, is excellent, clean, and well
managed, though, perhaps, slower than one of ours would be,
but in other respects it is nowise inferior.

Monday evening, March 1st.   At an early hour to-morrow
morning we expect to reach the shore of Africa, and about nine
o'clock to-morrow night to land at Alexandria.   Our voyage
has been without incident, and tranquil in every respect.   I
have availed myself of my leisure on Saturday and to-day,
the very first I have had since I left home, to repair my dilapidated garments, and all are now whole.   Yesterday being
Sunday, I was less occupied, and found my thoughts turning
more painfully homeward than I was willing to admit, and
the day wore heavily.   I think a great deal of our dear L.,
lest she should feel lonely and disappointed at my delayed
return, and shall lose no time in hastening through.

                    ALEXANDRIA, EGYPT, *March* 2.
We landed this morning at this far-famed port, and were
instantly surrounded by a mixed multitude of Arabs, negroes
and Franks, chattering, clashing, fighting for our baggage,
and tumbling over each other, hoping to secure their pay.   At
last, through much tribulation, we contrived to get ourselves
and baggage in boats, and so on to the custom-house, where,
on the payment of a *douceur*, we were suffered to escape to
our hotel, which we found good and comfortable—but what a
motley crew fills the street!   Camels with every imaginable
load, from lime and wood to women and children ; Turks in
elegant costumes mingled with European officers; Arab women, with their white veils, like masks, and Moorish women,
with black petticoats over their heads; negroes, black as
ebony ; Abyssinians ; Nubians, tattoed like our indians;
Italians, French and English, all in one mass, under a bright
and burning sun, and you may, perhaps, form some faint idea
of the living crowd which moves before me from morning till

night. I have been driving about all day, to Pompey's Pillar and Cleopatra's Needle, and the Pharos and Catacombs, and the Pasha's palace, etc., and have found here, to her great apparent delight, the English lady who wished to make this tour with me. She has forthwith joined my party, and with the dragoman Mr. Odenheimer employed, and who gives him a high character, we are to set forth to-morrow morning for Cairo, to stay some eight days, to see the Pyramids, and Memphis, and all that region, and then on through the desert to Gaza and Jerusalem. I am right glad to have a lady in the party, and I know you will feel more contented. There seems to be no danger whatever of any kind, and I hope to arrive in early time for the "Passover" at Jerusalem. I am writing with all the gentlemen of the party in my room, who are chattering away making their bargain with the dragoman, and referring to me at every moment, and yet, as my letter must be closed, I must write on. I hope to give you a fuller account from Cairo.

On the Nile, March 4th.—Seeing that I have the whole day before me, and having found a corner of a sort of sofa on the deck of the steamer which suits my purpose, I have got out my writing-case to attempt a description of the novel scenes around. Our boat has just stopped at one of the Arab villages for milk, and instantly the bank is lined with a ragged regiment, clad down to the knees in every imaginable form of draggled garments in the shape of gowns, or chemises, or mantles. All the slim legs are bare. The heads are generally covered with dirty white in the shape of a turban for the men, while the women wear a dirty black or dark blue cotton shawl, which covers their face and form to the waist or knee. It is market day in the village, and about half-past seven o'clock A. M. Camels with loads, and donkeys, buffaloes, and cows are led along the shore all in single file, for in this and many other things the Arabs wonderfully resemble our Indians, even in the color of their skin. Trees are uncommon, but behind this village there rises a very pretty grove, the palm, of

13

course, predominating. In front—this village being evidently
of a superior character—are quite extensive though rudely
constructed yards for the manufacture of sun-burnt bricks,
for which the clayey soil of the bank seems to be particularly
adapted. The soil is mixed with straw, and the bricks are
formed with the hand. I hear that when sent down to Alexandria they are previously subjected to some incomplete action
of fire to harden them, but the scarcity of fuel must prevent
the possibility of burning them as ours are done. These
Arab villages are all constructed of them, and then plastered
over with mud—roof and all of the same material, with holes
for doors and smoke, and having flat roofs generally, only six
or nine feet high, they look rather like the dens of beasts than
the dwellings of human beings. They nevertheless swarm
with humanity. Our steamer is about equal to third rate on
the Ohio, and as my bed was uncomfortable, I rose early to
see the sun rise on the Nile, and whatever else there might be
to be seen. It was curious to see the natives issuing forth all
along the bank to wash themselves in the river, sometimes entirely undressing and plunging into the water; then emerging
they put on their garments (seldom more than a sort of long
shirt, covered by a dark woolen mantle) all wet. Towels, I
suppose, are unknown. The river is, in itself, as nearly as
possible, another Mississippi. The palm trees, thinly scattered, substitute the cottonwood forests, and for mud villages
neat plantations, and the resemblance is complete, but the
scenery beyond is strangely different. Here and there we
have a tract of sandy desert.

CAIRO.

We reached the Egyptian capital about six P. M. Three
hours before we obtained our first view of the pyramids, looking very like the drawings we see of them, only more pointed.
As you approach Cairo the aspect of the country improves,
and even some pretty dwellings are visible within a few miles
of the city. There is an immense work, called the *barrage* of
the Nile, a few miles below, to drive up the water in low sea-

sons, which, for magnitude, exceeds any thing of the sort in
Europe. It is the work of a French engineer.

We did not see an individual, except in the boat, who wore
the European dress, from Alexandria to this place, and the
Arabs are generally at the lowest stage of misery and degra-
dation. Since leaving Scotland (the Highlands) I have not
seen such wretched habitations. We find here a good hotel,
with all the ordinary comforts of Europe. The servants, except the head waiters, are Arabs, who speak English, and the
cuisine (I have just dined) much better than we generally
meet with at home. We arrived too late to see much of the
city, which I reserve for my next letter.

I find parties are leaving here every day for Jerusalem by
Gaza and El Arish and Hebron, and I have resolved to take
that route. The only disadvantage will be that as there is no
post-office on the way, I can not write to you so regularly as
usual while on the way. Eleven days to Gaza, three at Gaza
for quarantine, and three more to Jerusalem. I shall write,
but I can not send away what I write until we reach the latter
place. Do not, I repeat, suffer yourselves to be anxious, for
the desert seems to be the safest place possible. After seeing
Jerusalem and the Dead Sea, etc., I shall go on to Constantinople and Athens, and so on to L.

Friday, March 6th.—This has been a memorable day in
sight-seeing, and I have kept my letter open until my return
this evening to give you the latest account of my doings.
Mounted on a nice little donkey, and attended, with the rest
of the party, by a dashing Coptic dragoman in Turkish dress,
we visited to-day the Isle of Roda—the Nilometer. Attended
a service in a remarkable ancient mosque, and another in a
Coptic church, this (Friday) being the Sunday of the Moslems,
and then a strange fanatical service of the Dancing Dervishes,
and thence to the tomb of the family of Mahomet Ali, and
then to the graves—highly decorated—of the Mamelukes, so
cruelly murdered; and then to the citadel, a magnificent new
mosque lined with alabaster, and immense pillars to match;

and then to the tomb and mosque of Sultan Hassan, one thousand years old; and then to our hotel to dine with nearly two hundred passengers just arrived from India by the overland route. No part of my travels has been so strange as this—entirely different. Do not be anxious. I shall leave a letter here when I set forth on the desert. There is no danger whatever in the journey. God bless you all, my dear ones.

CAIRO, EGYPT, *March 6th.*

As I recede from you all, you seem to grow nearer and dearer to my heart. What longings do I not feel at each moment to penetrate the fearful distance that separates us, and relieve the anxiety that oppresses me, lest some misfortune should have happened! I have, nevertheless, been as industrious here as elsewhere, resolving to make the best of my time; and the world here is so wonderfully strange to me that my only difficulty is to know how to choose among the many objects that press upon my attention. I have now the great comfort of having a lady for my *compagnon de voyage,* which, after my long solitude, is very agreeable. I mentioned in my last that Miss Howard would accompany me, and she accordingly followed me two days after our departure from Alexandria. I find her an exceedingly agreeable companion; but the men of the party are not to be boasted of. We are to leave here on the 15th, and for Miss H. and myself a sort of palanquin is provided, which is placed on the back of a strong camel, and which, being covered with an awning, with curtains at the sides, forms a very comfortable conveyance. It is well lined with cushions, so that we can sit or lie down at pleasure. We made a trial of it this morning, and found it very comfortable. We have a tent for sleeping, which is furnished with a carpet, and quite comfortable cot beds, so that we can expect to make our journey over the desert with ease and safety, so far as is possible. In eleven days we expect to reach Gaza, and after three days of quarantine, to arrive in Jerusalem about the 1st of April, in time for the Passover;

and then, after a brief visit to the Dead Sea, we shall go to Beyrout and on to Constantinople, until when, I fear I shall have no letters from you, for I fear to lose them if I order them to be forwarded to Jerusalem.

I find Egypt more barbaric than I expected. We had heard so much of the vigor of Mahomet Ali, that I thought to have seen some approaches toward European civilization among the people; but there seems to be none at all. I find they are but little advanced beyond our Indians. It is true they practice many of the ruder species of handicraft, and even gold embroidery on their saddles, but their dress is miserable, and they are filthy to a disgusting degree. On Sunday morning I went to a Coptic church. I have now seen several—all have compartments; viz., interior, or holy place, for the officiating priests, a court for the men, divided by a screen, and aisles for the women—a place which is further back, and also shut off by another screen of open wood-work. The patriarch of the Copts was present; the services had but little resemblance to Christian worship, and I do not suppose it is much, if at all, better than Mahometan. Each turbaned fellow, as he entered, went up to the patriarch as he sat (like a tailor) squatting down, knelt, touching the floor with his forehead; then rising, he kissed a small cross which the old man held, and passing on squatted down with the others. We also witnessed the baptism of a child by immersion, after a long "pow-wow."

On Monday, we set forth again on donkeys, to ride three miles to the great Pyramids, You may suppose how strong I am, when I say I mounted to the top of Cheops without fatigue. I had the assistance, it is true, of three Arabs, but many of the stones are as high as my breast, and must be climbed perpendicularly. There are many fine tombs around the base, beautifully sculptured in hieroglyphics, of which much of the coloring still remains. The Sphynx sits alone in silent majesty, covered up to the chest in sand. I also entered the Pyramids; but you can see descriptions of them in books. You can readily imagine my contemplations in view of these stupendous remains of the past. The Arabs present formed a strange contrast to the ancient civilization, and it was curious to hear such barbarians speak very tolerable Italian.

On Wednesday we rode out to the petrified wood, a singular phenomenon, and also to see the tombs of the Caliphs, which are of fine Saracenic architecture; and in the evening I was glad to accept an invitation to take tea with good Mrs. Lieder, the English wife of the missionary here. I found there Lady Harriet Kavanagh, and Mr. Murray was expected, but did not come. His wife, Miss Wadsworth, of Geneva, N. Y., died, as you must have heard, in December.

On Thursday, attended by a dragoman of the consulate and a government janissary, having a permit, we visited several mosques, which can only be seen where Christians are thus attended. There is no real beauty in any of them, though the proportions are sometimes pleasing from their vastness, but the designs are generally very poor and the coloring bad. On Friday we set forth to see the Pyramids of Lanara and the site near them of the ancient Memphis. The distance was some twenty miles over a charming rural landscape. We met frequent herds of cattle and goats and sheep, apparently coming to market, and long strings of camels, heavily loaded, as usual. The country is nearly all cultivated, and herds of cattle browsed here and there on the meadows, attended by their Arab herdsmen.

There is also much wheat nearly ripe, and barley and beans, On our return, we rode through some miles of palm forest, the slight shade of the tree interposing no obstacle to the growth of the rich grain that covered the soil. The culture is rude, and we saw many Arabs engaged in the fields; but the Nile annually deposits its rich alluvium, and the soil produces with little aid. I crept into the subterranean opening and entered into the larger of the pyramids. I also entered some magnificently sculptured catacombs. We lunched in one of them, and returned to Cairo about seven o'clock.

through unlighted streets, except where the lamps sent forth a feeble blaze. Yesterday, again attended by a janissary, we visited the palace of the Pasha and the citadel. I have not yet been able to see a harem, and as we set out for Syria to-morrow (I am writing on Sunday afternoon, 14th) I shall not have an opportunity here. Mr. Lieder has lived here some sixteen years, and tells me of many interesting things, which I hope some of these days to repeat to you. My next letter must be from Jerusalem—not less than seventeen days hence. Do not, I repeat, be anxious about me. There is less danger in this journey than others, notwithstanding the false alarms of good Bishop Otey. There is no plague to be heard of, and the sheik, or Arab chief of this district, is made answerable for our safety under penalty of being hung, so you may rest assured he will not suffer any one to attack us. We have four men in our party, each mounted on a camel. Our drago-man has three servants, and each camel has a driver. We have three tents, besides others for the servants, and for Miss Howard and myself there is the camel and palanquin already mentioned. We have also several camels loaded with provis-ions, all of which must be furnished here, for we travel pre-cisely as the patriarchs did. It was curious enough that the first lesson this morning related to the sale of Joseph by his brethren, and the episode of Potiphar's wife. To listen to this history I have so often heard at home, here on the very spot where the events occurred, gave a strange interest to the subject.

We suppose that here we are on the border of the land of Goshen.

I hope to reach L. by the first of May, and to return home as soon after as possible. I can not yet say how I may return from Constantinople. I prefer the Danube if it be not too slow. A Rev. Mr. Spencer of New York was here last year, and returning, wrote a book entitled "The East"— sketches of travel in Egypt and the Holy Land. I thought it worth reading, and advise you to get it by all means.

Monday morning.—All is ready. They are loading the camels—in a little while we are off to the desert, though not on Arab steeds, as the song says. May God be with us all and soon bring us together again.

HELIOPOLIS, March 15th.

I am now able to diversify my history by giving you some details of life in the tent. After dispatching my letter, or rather depositing it with the landlord to await the next steamer a week hence, I went over this morning to take leave of good Mrs. Lieder. She gave me the kindest letters of introduction in Jerusalem, Damascus, and Beyrout; and, returning to luncheon, we afterward set out, about three o'clock P. M., with our camels, for this spot, where our first encampment was to be made. The servants, tents, and cook had preceded us some two or three hours, so that on arrival about five o'clock we found our tents pitched, the beds made, and baggage in order. The cook had been not less busy, as the steaming sauce-pans abundantly proved, and within half an hour we were seated before a very neatly served dinner. We were some seven or eight miles distant from Cairo, the minaret of which could be seen along the horizon in the beautiful sunset. Of the ancient Heliopolis scarcely a vestige remained, save one tall monument of Egyptian granite, which I described in a former letter. The place, however, abounds in beautiful gardens, and the obelisk arises among them to mingle its white-pointed top with the rosy hues of the evening sky. All around us, between our encampment and the gardens is the deep, dry sand of the desert, while the magnificent sky above sparkled with the richest splendors, as the large stars came forth to view. We have three tents for our party, and one for the kitchen; seventeen camels, tethered, either lie chewing the cud, or limping around the tents. Two horses and two donkeys make up the complement of our retinue. Each camel, besides, has a driver, and the dragoman has three servants to supply our wants. I must confess that the outset promises more comfort than I had at all

anticipated. Miss Howard and I share a tent of some twelve
or fourteen feet in diameter. It is round, with a pole in the
middle, to support the roof, which is some ten feet high. The
tent is lined throughout with alternate red and yellow, and
prettily decorated. The earth floor is covered with mats and
carpets. Our beds are good, and are placed in nice little
fold-up bedsteads, and I am writing on a table quite firmly
supported like our dinner trays. We have also a curtain
to hang across before we undress, and we are also the possessors
of a wash-basin, etc., each, of tin, with pitchers to match. The
coops of unfortunate chickens which attend us give assurance
that we shall not starve. Oranges and vegetables are abundantly supplied. But I must go to bed. God bless you all.

Tuesday evening.—We rose about six, and breakfasted in
the open air, while our tents were struck, and packed. By
half-past eight, all were again on the way, and we moved
slowly along, sometimes over a sandy desert, sometimes through
Arab villages, which are always near a forest of palms, sometimes along extensive fields of wheat nearly ready for the
harvest. At one we paused near a tomb to rest the camels,
and to take some refreshment, and then continued our journey till five, when we again encamped near an Arab village,
and, after washing off the dust of the day, I seat myself to
tell you of its uneventful current.

Wednesday evening.—To-day has been cool and pleasant,
light clouds having overshadowed the sun, and a slight haze
has obscured his too brilliant rays. We were awakened at six
o'clock, for it requires two hours and a half for our troop
(you will remember they are all, except our dragoman, Arabs)
to get their breakfast, strike the tents, and pack the camels.
Our breakfast was served as soon as we were ready. We had
very good Mocha coffee, with milk and butter from the neighboring Arab village, with fried chickens and omelette and
bread, brought from Cairo, made of American flour, the
Egyptian being so badly prepared that it is not used by Europeans. Breakfast being over, Miss Howard and I strolled

to a decayed tomb, at a little distance, which was prettily situated under a fine sycamore, the solitary occupant of this part of the desert. From this, the camels not being quite ready, we walked a little further on, where we saw some natives at work in constructing a well, for the Nile water percolates the soil for a great distance, and water fit for irrigation is procured at a short depth, and is raised by means of a wheel surrounded with earthern pots, which, on rising to the surface, turn and empty themselves—the whole being moved by oxen. Here we were offered coffee in small cups, which we were obliged to taste, of course. At length, all being ready, we mounted our palanquin and continued on our way.

In two hours we passed the ruins of Balbec, an ancient city, in which Onias, the High Priest, was permitted to build a temple in imitation of that at Jerusalem; but this, as well as the city which surrounded it, has disappeared. Nothing is seen but unsightly mounds, on which an Arab mud-walled village stands. We passed alternately over trackless sands, now and then an oasis, to which the water of the Nile had been conveyed through canals. At one place, the camel which carried our wine tripped and fell, but to our great comfort nothing was broken. At another point another unfortunate fell into a ditch, but after she was unloaded she was got out unhurt. At two o'clock we paused to eat a little cold chicken, etc., when a party of magnificent-looking Arabs, mounted on large and fine horses passed, and soon after we overtook a small caravan of Copts going to Jerusalem, who accompanied us, and who have made their encampment just beside us this evening. It is singularly interesting to see the various parties engaged, each in their own way. The Copt party are conveying two gentlemen (Copts), whose quaint little tent was soon spread, and the ground being covered with a Persian carpet, the turbaned gentry soon seated themselves, reclining on some very pretty cushions. If they stay with us to-morrow, I shall decidedly try to make their nearer acquaintance. Meanwhile, their servants having dug a longish hole in the ground, have made up a little fire and set a kettle over it, while they sit smoking as they watch it. Our cuisine is conducted on a much larger scale. It possesses a tent of considerable dimensions, and boxes of various forms and descriptions are ranged around it. In front is a little portable kitchen, having compartments for four little charcoal fires, on each of which is placed a steaming copper sauce-pan. In a tent opposite is laid out a table for six persons, the number of our party, and active preparations are in progress for the coming repast. At a short distance on the other side, to the leeward of the baggage, is another fire, made up of camels' dung, and such fragments of the dry and thorny grasses of the desert as the sands scarcely afford, and around this stand some half-dozen nearly naked Arabs, holding up their miserable garments without scruple, so that nothing shall hinder the fire from imparting to them all its warmth. They are chattering as usual, like parrots, and with a vehemence that, among other people, would soon lead to blows, but it is only their way. The camels are strolling on the desert picking up what they can find, where there is as much vegetation as is usually found on a sea beach. Yet this scanty fare is all they will receive. I have given you a full account of to-day, since I suppose each day will be like its predecessor, and I need not occupy so much of your time again. I am far less tired than you could imagine, and it is such a comfort to chat a little with you, as evening comes on.

Friday.—We made a long day yesterday, so that it was nearly dark when our tents were made up, and I could not write. Having arrived the night before in the neighborhood of a village, notorious for its thieving propensities, a strong watch was set, for which it appeared there was much need, for about four o'clock a gang was seen approaching, and were only driven away by repeated discharges of pistols. A stray camel also ran foul of our tent, in the night, and horribly alarmed my companion. We passed, yesterday morning, the mounds of Ancient Goshen, and reached

Salahieh about 5½ P. M.   Here travelers lay in supplies of
water and other provisions for four or five days, to El Arish.
Once an episcopal city, it is now a mud-built village of
Arabs, who soon hastened to us with chickens, eggs, etc.,
and gazed curiously at our equipage.   Just by is an encampment of one thousand Egyptian soldiers, whose tents look
very pretty on the desert.   We left there the last palm trees,
and have had a desert way to the sea coast.   We are near the
spot where Pompey was betrayed and murdered.   We have
got on to-day without incident or fatigue.   The weather is
mild, but windy.   We paused last night (Sunday) at Beer,
which signifies the middle well, having traveled all day
through the desert, unenlivened by a single habitation.   In
the afternoon we passed a number of sand hills, which, in all
but color, resemble snow-drifts.   No incident marked the day,
and we were right glad to see the grove of palms, the first
we had seen since Salahieh, under which is the ancient well
of bitterish water, which gives name to the spot.   Our Arab
camel-drivers seem to be above the necessity of eating or
sleeping, consuming, in the midst of their great fatigue (at
least we esteem it so) nothing but the coarsest bread, baked
at night, under the ashes, and dates, and chattering all night,
like so many magpies, so that they really disturb my always
light slumbers.

At dinner, last evening, it was proposed to rest to-day
(Sunday), but the puppies, in the dress of three young men,
who are with us, declared their resolution to proceed, and so
we have traveled all day.

We had a little rain this morning, which the dragoman at-
tributed to Divine discipline.   I would willingly have rested,
on account of the camels, yet I readily console myself, I may
come to you a day sooner.   We stopped for luncheon at twelve,
on a spot now called Gallia, an ancient Roman outpost,
whither Pompey directed his steps, where he was murdered,
and where his remains were burnt by his freedmen.   I trust
you all remembered your wanderer in your prayers to-day.

My thoughts and prayers have been continually with you all.
May God bless and protect each of you! This is Mr. Peter's
birth-day.

Monday Evening.—All day we have moved on steadily, except three-quarters of an hour, at one o'clock, to lunch.
About ten, we met some men with fine horses in charge for
the Pasha of Egypt, from Damascus. These are the first
objects we have met for three days. At three we came up
with an Arab shepherd and his flock of sheep—a lamb of
which (poor little thing) was purchased for us to eat to-morrow, our provisions having become low. I have just returned
from a walk with Miss Howard, while our tent was in preparation. We have passed yesterday and to-day incessantly
over ridges of sand hills with basin-like valleys between, partly
and scantily covered with a bushy kind of broom, and some
other plant, resembling to the eye lavender, but hard and
thorny. Although the earth is one wide waste of fine sand,
yet these plants continue to find sustenance, and in turn furnish it to the poor camels. Besides these, there are every-
where springing up out of this dry sand the prettiest little
flowers possible, many of them the stunted miniatures of finer
plants that we have at home, but their diminutive size renders
them often more beautiful; and here they bloom and literally
waste their "sweetness on the desert air." Our walk led us
to a high sand-hill, just behind our encampment, from which
a long stretch of the Mediterranean is visible; and in the distance were seen three little vessels on their way, I suppose, to
Jaffa. The view is surpassingly beautiful. We are perform-
ing the journey with very little fatigue, and I can readily
imagine, with an agreeable party and good spirits, it would
form one of the green spots in a traveler's memory. As we
sit in our lofty palanquin, we find never-failing amusement
in the characters and observing the antics of our Arab guides,
who are increased by the retinue of the party I have already
mentioned as having joined us, and with whom, as they speak
no language but the Arabic, in which, unluckily, I am quite

deficient, we can only exchange friendly salutations by signs.
How our guides contrive to find their way among these trackless wastes I can not conceive—the road may generally, however, be traced by the snow-white bones of camels that line it,
and which so often remind me of that touching print of the
camel dying in the desert, which our dear, dear T. so often
admired.

EL ARISH, Wednesday, March 24th.

If you will look upon the map, near the south-east extremity of the Mediterranean, you will find the name of the
Egyptian fortress and Arab village near which I write. Since
my last, two days since, we have continued, with measured
steps, to traverse the desert up and down the drifted hills,
resembling more and more, except their tawny color, the
snow-drifts that we sometimes see at home, when the bushes
are half covered, and sometimes the trees are buried up some
ten or twelve feet. Some of these hills must be at least one
hundred feet high. To-day we have seen date trees again in
several places; but here again is only a wide, rolling plain of
sand, without even a shrub, for miles. We have been to see
an old Greek fortress, which was built in 1258, by the Turks,
out of the remains of unknown Egyptian antiquity. Napoleon
destroyed the tower, since which it has never recovered itself.
Our Arab camel drivers all belong here, and it is an interesting sight to see their friends all coming out to meet them,
having been warned of our approach by one of their number,
who yesterday took leave to desert us. We have now finished the first stage of our progress without fatigue or danger.

GAZA, SUNDAY EVENING, March 28th.

We left El Arish in a tempest of wind and sand—here
called a kampsin, or simoon, as we term it. It was difficult to
proceed, but, as it was at our backs, we struggled on, half
blinded by the sand, which penetrated even our trunks, locked
up as they were. We soon crossed the dry bed of "the
river of Egypt," and, toiling on, we reached the spot destined

for our encampment for the night, in a heavy rain, which we found far more tolerable than the sand. Thanks to the comfort of our palanquin, neither I nor my companion were at all wet, and we escaped without cold. Next day, Friday, we reached a prettily situated village, surrounded by gardens, and almond and pomegranate trees, hedged in by enormous prickly pears. Here our quarantine of five days commenced, and we were joined by a dashing Arab, with gun and pistols, on horseback, whose duty it was to see that we were not to touch any living thing. We were permitted to encamp in an old Moslem cemetery, and we were immediately surrounded by a throng of Arab men and boys, together with the functionaries who have to guard us. It was amusing to see them driving their bargain with our dragoman, who was obliged to purchase supplies for us. For instance, if a lamb or chicken were to be bought, our man could on no account be allowed to touch them, to examine their condition, and if once they were received into our (supposed) infected atmosphere, they could not be returned, and the owner took good care we should have little cause for satisfaction.

It is curious to see how really greedy of gain these barbarians are, and how thoroughly they understand how to avail themselves of all circumstances in their favor. As we approached, we found large troops of women at the further end of the cemetery huddled on the ground around certain graves, and uttering a slow measure, or sort of wail, or plaintive cry. This is the custom on Friday, which is the Moslem Sunday, but I saw many of them engaged in the same way the next morning at sunrise. The poor women of Egypt are treated as if belonging to an inferior place in the scale of being, and I have secured obedience from our camel-drivers only by assuming a threatening and authoritative tone, such as you would laugh to hear. We reached this city, renowned by the exploit of Sampson, yesterday, Saturday afternoon, about two P. M., escorted by an Arab soldier, who took care to drive away from our path every wandering sheep or eccentric calf

which showed any disposition to look at us. Even the little
birds were carefully scared away, lest we should infect them
with plague, though nothing is more certain than our good
health and the freedom of all Egypt from any pestilential
malady. We, viz., Miss Howard and myself, were so fortunate as to find two upper rooms vacant, of which we took immediate possession, and from which we have the most enchanting views of the beautiful environs. On one side Gaza, with
its tall minarets and mud-colored houses, and on the other
Mt. Sampson, prettily wooded, while extensive green fields,
with camels, and asses, and cattle, and sheep, quietly grazing,
form an agreeable contrast to the neighboring gardens, which
reach away to a graceful little hill, on the summit of which
rises the tomb of a celebrated sheik. Three Russian princes
and an English gentleman are our companions in captivity,
besides a quantity of Arabs, tawny or black, who have a
quarter apart. If I had some of you with me, how soothing
I should find the tranquil scene, our first experience of Syria.

ASHDOD, TUESDAY EVENING, 30th.

I was employed all yesterday in refitting for our continued
journey. About four o'clock the doctor came, and placing us
in a row our tongues were examined, and we were fumigated
with sulphur, after which we were pronounced fit to proceed.
We were early on foot this morning, and commenced the day
by looking about the neighboring town. Gaza is still a city of
some commercial importance as a frontier of Syria, and possesses some half dozen substantial stone houses, with several
quite respectable mosques. The houses of the six or eight
thousand inhabitants are, as usual, of one story, with flat roofs,
covered with plaster or mud. The neighboring country is quite
well cultivated, and abounds in wheat—much of which is ex-
ported—figs, oranges, pomegranates, and date trees. Many of
the fields are inclosed in grand-looking hedges of prickly pear,
filled up with jessamines. The country is most beautiful.
Mid-day we halted at the five rivers of Ascalon, and partook

of our luncheon beneath the shade of a ruined palace. The mounds of the ancient structure rise over a large space, but are chiefly covered by trees and shrubberies which the peasants have very tastefully planted. This place (Ashdod) contains hardly any traces of former splendor, and has sunk into a mere mud-walled Arab village. You will find in the scripture history that the Ark of the Covenant was brought here after the death of Eli. I had no idea of the fertility and beauty of the region, nor of the much better character of the population than that I had left in Egypt; the contrast is striking. Still the Mussulman is in the ascendant here as there, and the "better half" of creation are in the most degraded condition you can conceive. It is fearful to think what a Nemesis the spirit of woman becomes when she is thus inhumanly trodden down, and how her injuries are avenged upon the whole structure of society which thus oppresses her. As I write there is a perfect hurricane simoon blowing. It is nine o'clock P. M., and yet the air is as hot as an oven, and threatens to blow down our tents. The kitchen (tent) is already leveled to the ground, but as dinner is over, "cooky" replies to my sympathetic inquiries, "*un piccola cosa*"—only a tumbler is broken. Our dragoman is giving heavy blows to the stakes which secure our tent, and so I write on fearlessly.

RAMLA, *April 1st.*

I do not forget that this is my dear little Willie's birthday. I trust the little darling is well as when I heard last, but it is a long time, and I tremble when I think of what may have been while I am so unconscious of evil. May God protect us all. I have suffered so fearfully that I am always apprehensive rather than hopeful. I try to think, however, of the present, for it is worse than useless to anticipate evils which I devoutly trust may never come. We left Ashdod early, and reached Jaffa only in time to take a run through the bazaars and principal alleys, called streets; yet the approach, through miles of gardens exhaling the most exquisite perfumes, and

14

the lofty position above the sea of the ancient city, induced me to expect better things. We reached it through a long avenue of sycamore trees not yet in leaf. The gardens are hedged with enormous prickly pears, and contain the richest profusion of orange and lemon trees, apricots, pomegranates, and figs and apples and plums. The orange trees, as usual, are loaded with flowers, which filled the air with richest perfume. Our tents are pitched on high ground near the sea. When I went down to the gate of entrance the court outside was crowded with people selling fruits and vegetables. The gateway was filled with loungers smoking, and as it grew dark I passed a large café containing—seated around the quadrangle—some forty or fifty turbaned smokers, while a man read to them in a loud voice, and apparently to their great satisfaction, from the "Arabian Nights." I stood to observe them for some time without hindrance. This morning Miss H. and I made a visit to the English consul, who took us to the place pointed out by all tradition as the house of "Simon, the tanner." This afternoon we passed Lydda, where St. Peter lived when called to raise up Tabitha. Ramla is said to be the ancient Arimathea. It is a clean looking town, which is a remarkable circumstance in Syria, and the gardens are filled with tobacco. As I was writing the above, Miss H. entered to call me to see the beautiful view, and we proceeded to the top of the hill back of our tents, which is covered by an old Moslem cemetery. The sun was setting, and seated on a tombstone I gazed with delighted vision on the scene. Below us were our encampments in front of a broad tank of the olden times, full of water; just beyond, separated from us by hedges of prickly pear, rose a line of beautiful gardens containing all the fruits of Jaffa, and further on lay the pretty town, with its minarets and date trees rising here and there in picturesque groups, all gilded by the setting sun, which glanced from the dome-like housetops as they rose higher and higher on the slight elevation upon which the town is built. Far away to the right are fields of wheat and cultivated lands stretching over the plains as far as the eye could reach, with groups of trees scattered over them, while horses and asses and camels browsed leisurely. Here and there were strings of loaded camels gliding along the roads, and cattle returning to their homes. At our backs lay "the hill country of Judea," and, as we turned, a long line of gentle hills, with villages resting here and there on their sides, met our view; and to complete the scene, a great forest of olives filled up the left side of this truly oriental and most beautiful landscape, to which an additional charm was lent by the tinkling of the bells of the returning herds, voices of children at play, and all that combination which renders the scene of the distant city so soothing to the pensive mind. The whole earth is covered with flowers wherever the plough has allowed them to escape, and they are the most delicate and beautiful you can imagine. We left our camels at Jaffa, and to-day we are on horseback. I must not forget to remind you that Lydda is the birthplace of St. George (of England), and his tomb is also said to be there, but is unknown.

JERUSALEM, *Palm Sunday, April 4th.*

We left our encampment, near the picturesque Ramla, on Friday morning at six o'clock. Our tent was near the highway to Jerusalem, which comes from Beyrout and Jaffa, the only two points by which travelers enter Palestine from the sea. The moon shone bright, and I could not sleep for the gentle tinkling of little bells which announced the constant passing of pilgrims on their way to the great festival. I rose at almost every hour of the night to gaze at the novel spectacle. Nearly all were mounted on horses or asses, and every costume in the world seemed to be represented as the procession moved along the narrow path in what we call "Indian file." The horses' necks are generally decorated with little bells, which I mentioned, and their sound is decidedly musical. A few miles from Ramla we entered the hill country, and we continued, quite to the gates of the city, to wind over stony

and sometimes precipitous paths. We reached the gates about
five P. M., and, having engaged lodging in advance, we soon
took possession of our apartments. We (Miss Howard and
myself) were equally happy that there was no room for our
disagreeable companions over the desert, and we are now fairly
rid of their presence. You will imagine my gratification, half
an hour afterward, on going to dinner, to find my old friend,
Mr. Lucius Duncan, of New Orleans, together with several
other very gentlemanly Americans, among them Baker, an
artist from Cincinnati, and Ewing from Tennessee. We set
forth yesterday morning, early, to see the Holy City, and visited in turn the Holy Sepulcher, with all its intensely interesting associations—Calvary, adjoining the Via Dolorosa, the
Church of the Flagellation, the Coptic Convent, Abyssinean do.
(anciently the Palace of the Templars), House of the Pharisee,
Bethesda—and many other places of deep interest; and then at
three P.M., attended services of the Greek, Latin, Armenian, and
Coptic Chapels at the Sepulcher, and closed the day by witnessing, by invitation, the celebration of the Passover in the family of a Jewish rabbi, who had been to America, and was
glad to see us. The paschal lamb has ceased with the temple worship, and hence the whole is now only commemoration ;
the feast consisting of bitter herbs and wine, and a dish of
mingled raisins and dates; yet the service was very remarkable, and was not finished till after ten o'clock.

This morning we went at five o'clock to witness the Blessing of the Palms by the Patriarch of the Latin Church. The
Latins and the Greeks share the possession of the Holy Sepulcher, and the latter had held service about 2 P. M., leaving
the Holy Sepulcher to the others. You can read the description, doubtless, in some book near at hand. We had good
places, adjoining the *religieuses*, among whom was a nice little
French lady I had met at Naples. Miss Howard and myself
advanced with others, and, kissing the hand of the Patriarch,
received each a palm branch, and, joining the procession, we
walked three times round the Sepulcher, and once around the

place where it is said the Savior's body was prepared for the grave. The crowd was immense—certainly not less than ten thousand pilgrims filled the immense area of the churches and quadrangle, and from China to America there were pilgrims. It was a touching thought to contrast the dreadful scenes of Calvary, 1,800 years ago, with the triumphs of the present, when all nations and kingdoms and people had come together to adore the crucified One. Doubtless there is much superstition, but I can not envy the caviller who disbelieves and rejects all, because certain parts are rendered doubtful. We afterward attended service in the magnificent Greek Church, and saw the very richest display of dresses, etc., I have ever seen. Returning to a late breakfast, we then went to the English service, in a very pretty church on Mt. Zion. Here we found a strange assembly. Bedouin Arabs, in their wild garb and hawk's eye, were mingled with Armenians, and Syrians, in their various costumes, with the usual number of English residents and visitors, but there was no crowd. From here we proceeded to visit my French lady friend, Madame Lemoine, at the Convent of St. Joseph. She introduced me to the very accomplished lady superior, who in turn presented me to several clerical dignitaries, who called on her; and, finally, accompanied by Mde. Lemoine, we called to pay a visit to the Patriarch, whom we found a high-bred and most agreeable gentleman from Genoa. We remained nearly an hour in friendly chat (French), and were served with coffee and sweatmeats in the Oriental fashion. On our way to our hotel, we called on Mrs. Barclay, wife of the Baptist missionary, who has been very kind to us. She is a friend of the Rives family, and very pleasing. To-morrow we go to Jericho, next day to the Jordan, where the baptism is celebrated, and some ten or twelve thousand pilgrims will bathe in the river.

We shall remain here until Easter Monday, and then to Bethlehem, and afterward northward to Nazareth, and Damascus, and Balbec. I grieve to find I shall again be detained longer than I thought. The steamer only leaves Beyrout once a fortnight, and as we can not arrive in time for the next, we shall be obliged to wait till the eleventh of May. I grieve for this, as I am almost frantic with anxiety to hear from you all. God grant you may be well. If I had known that this tour would have required so much time, I would not have attempted it; but my information was inaccurate. If no one suffers by my absence, certainly I could never regret having made it, for no part of my travels has been more fruitful of knowledge; but I pine for fear some evil may have happened, and I fear that my dear L. suffers from solitude, or desire to change her place. I shall now be able, I hope, to write with more regularity. I shall proceed homeward as fast as I can possibly make my journey. Again, God bless you all.

PLAIN OF JERICHO, *April* 6, 1852.

We left Jerusalem about half-past seven o'clock yesterday morning, among the train of thousands of pilgrims, to come down here, some six hours ride, to celebrate the anniversary of the Savior's baptism in the Jordan. This place is the nearest point where so large an encampment can be made, and it is two hours distant from the Israelites ford, as it is called— for the baptism is said to have taken place at that point where the children of Israel, under Joshua, crossed over on dry ground, and left stones in the bed of the river to mark the spots at which the priest stood as they bore the ark of the covenant. For a description of this singular festival read Lynch's Expedition, pp. 260–62. It was to me a most touching sight, and it would have been difficult to conduct a ceremony in which so many thousands were engaged, from every nation under the sun, in a more becoming manner. One poor man, by venturing too far up the rapid current, came near drowning, and I, as well as hundreds of others, was terribly frightened by his danger; but he was happily rescued, and the whole passed off happily. I sought a sheltered cove and bathed also, without hindrance. The stream is narrow, but beautifully wooded on one side. So as to be in time, we set forth at three o'clock, and passing the host of pilgrims and their military escort, we reached the bank before they arrived. All being completed, we then proceeded two hours farther to the Dead Sea, and having gazed long at it, and at Pisgah behind it, we returned to our encampment, and proceeded to the fountain of Elisha (see 2d Kings, eleventh chap., 19th v.), a beautiful spot. As I write in the afternoon, the city of tents lies spread out before me; for, being Franks of distinction, we have the privilege of occupying one end of the ground. There is a detachment of some five hundred troops, with the Governor of Jerusalem at their head, to guard the pilgrims from the thievish Bedouins, who are constantly in wait for prey. They all wear the European dress, and though clean have rather a slouchy gait. Our tent is next to that of Mr. Duncan, and we ride together, which is very pleasant to me, so far from home.

April 7th.—The ride to Jerusalem is hot, and we joined the army of pilgrims, only keeping a little in the rear, at three o'clock, A. M., and retracing our steps over the stony and precipitous hills, where there is scarcely a vestige of road, we came on to Bethany, and turned aside to visit the tomb of Lazarus, the only one in the village, and undoubtedly the same which is mentioned in Scripture. It is two stories deep, but not large, and the descent is difficult from the condition of the stone steps cut in the solid rock. Near this is the place where the Apostles finally separated. Leaving this, we passed over the hills, from the top of which there is a full view of the Dead Sea, and the Mountains of Moab behind it, and passed on a mile to the Mount of Olives, the highest point near Jerusalem, from the top of which also there is the finest view of the Dead Sea, and its grand historic mountain range— from which, you recollect, Moses was permitted to view the promised land, the goodly inheritance of his people—so that at all times the people of the city are reminded of the wonderful means by which they had possessed it, and of the subversion of

the cities of the plain.   I say nothing of all the feelings excited
by these objects, to which from infancy we have attached a feeling of holy interest, for if I attempted it I should have no words
for any thing else, and I therefore leave this part of my subject
until with God's blessing we shall be brought together again.
On the spot on the Mount of Olives, which tradition has
assigned as the place of our Lord's ascension, a chapel was
built in early times, and within it is shown an impression
made by his feet on the stone where he last stood.   All this
is now in the possession of the Turks, who exhibit it to Christians!   On the roof is a cupola or lookout, which commands
the best view of the city, so good that one can almost count
the houses.

From this point we witnessed the entrance of an immense
body of pilgrims, some five thousand, in every fashion, on
camels, horses, asses, and escorted by the governor and his
troops.   This is the great sight of the year, and the women,
Christian and Mussulman, of the city and adjacent parts, are
accustomed to line either side of the winding and hilly path
for a long distance in order to witness it.   They always wear
a mantle, a sort of white cotton sheet, which envelopes their
whole persons, head and all, a small part of the upper face
excepted; and it was a pretty sight from an eminence to see
them in their fluttering white garments.   I confess I was
weary after all this exertion, especially as a hard-trotting
horse had fallen to my lot; but I have no time to lose, and
after a wretched breakfast in our poor inn, set forth and visited in turn the garden of Gethsemane, and all the traditionary places near it; viz., where the three apostles slept while
He prayed, and where Judas greeted Him with his traitor
kiss; and then to the house of Caiaphas, at a considerable distance; Pilate's house, now the Church of the Flagellation; and
the Via Dolorosa, as it is called, until it reaches Calvary.
On Wednesday morning, on horses, we visited the more distant places around the city; and beginning with the Valley of
Jehoshaphat, near Gethsemane, we visited the tombs of Ab-

salom, Zachariah, etc.—for the hills all around are riddled
with sepulchers, hewn in the solid limestone—and on to the
village of Siloam, the Virgin's Pool and the pool of Siloam, and
the Potter's Field and the so-called tomb of David, under the
same roof which contains the apartment where the Last Supper
was eaten (near which is the grave of poor Costigan, the first
explorer of the Dead Sea). I also witnessed an Armenian
funeral. On Thursday, I went to " the washing of the feet,"
by the Greek Bishop. The Church of the Holy Sepulcher
is entered through a long open court or quadrangle, and the
vast building is surrounded on all sides by convents (Greek,
Latin, and Coptic). Every possible point at which lodgment
could be effected was covered by pilgrims, clad, as usual, in
all the costumes of the world; few of them, however, were
European, except the Greeks, and Russians are most
numerous. Near the center of the quadrangle was elevated
a platform, and on this the ceremony was performed by the
bishop, assisted by the clergy, in magnificent robes. Those
of the former, however, were removed, and a coarse towel
girded about him before commencing the operation—this being finished within an hour, we took horses and rode out the
environs, beginning with the Grotto of Jeremiah, a vast excavation, subdivided into various apartments, where he is said
to have written the Lamentations. It is a short distance
without the city, of which it commands a fine view. From
this place we proceeded to the place on the Mount of Olives,
where our Lord is said to have wept over Jerusalem, thence
downward to the Catacombs, called the Grotto of the Prophets,
onward to the tomb of Absalom, of Jehoshaphat, Zachariah,
etc. ; and passing the village of Siloam, we drank of the water
of the fountain of the Virgin, which is connected with its more
renowned neighbor of Siloam ; and then proceeding along the
Valley of Hinnom, past the tree where Isaiah is said to have
been sawn asunder, up over the Potter's field and across the
valley to the tomb of David, the room where the Last Supper
was instituted, the house of Caiaphas, etc. On Good Friday

I was nearly all day in the Church of the Holy Sepulcher; and in the afternoon, while attending the Latin service, and all were on their knees, we were astonished by the shouts of the rabble, who entered pell-mell. These were the Greeks, whose manners are more barbarous than any here, not excepting the Arabs themselves. Every year this atrocity, this sacrilege, is perpetrated in this holy place. We were all hurried forth, and the area around the sepulcher was surrendered to these wild wretches, who chased each other in multitudes, clapping their hands and shouted, mounting on each other's shoulders in the most frantic manner. It seems the barbarous outrage commenced time out of mind, in order to insult the Jews by shouts of Christian triumph at the expected resurrection and the supposed humiliation of the Jews thereat; but in their frantic saturnalia, lives are often lost by suffocation or bloodshed,

At 7 in the evening, the crucifixion was to be commemorated in the Latin Chapel, which stands a little apart, and the Pasha was solicited to send a detatchment of Turkish soldiers to guard the Christian rites. As the ceremony is remarkable, I passed through the crowd to reach it as the procession was formed, and gained a place immediately behind the patriarch. A crucifix, nearly as large as life, was borne by a priest, who was followed by others having incense. Several of the dignified clergy followed in magnificent black robes; behind them followed the patriarch, whose seat was conveyed immediately behind him (a tabouret covered with black). Next him followed the French consul, the crowd of priests, and more respectable spectators, each (myself with the rest) carrying in the hand a wax candle. As soon as the nucleus of the procession was thus formed, all except the patriarch (*and myself!*) stood to hear the first of the series of sermons prepared for this occasion. I owed my seat to the politeness of the French consul, who is chief lay dignitary upon these occasions, and who politely insisted that I, and not he, should occupy it. The sermon being concluded (in Italian), we moved on to the next station on the corridor. Here we listened to another sermon (in German); at the next station one in Greek; at the next, one in English; and then mounting the stairs to the Calvary, one in French was delivered. After the sermon, the body was removed from the cross, and laid in a white sheet, while the cross continued to retain its place. We then descended the stairs, all movement being impeded by the crowd, and reached the stone on which the body (traditionally) was prepared for burial. Here a sermon in Arabic was delivered, and the body was anointed by the hands of the patriarch, and then we all moved to the sepulcher, within which it was conveyed by the patriarch and his assisting priests. This done, a closing sermon was delivered in Spanish. You will wish to know what I thought of all this, and I cordially avow that all feelings of repugnance had vanished, and for the moment I was as good a Catholic as the best. The service was conducted with a soberness and apparently true sympathy that disarmed criticism, and the historic realities which surrounded us were enough to warm the most philosophical of stoics. Two pilgrims were stifled in the crowd, and died. On Saturday morning, by invitation from our Jewish friend, we attended the closing scenes of the passover. There are about ten thousand Jews in the city, and being all resident in the same quarter, their synagogues are all united, from being in a measure, all under the same roof. The women are apart, as usual, but their galleries are better than in the old European synagogues. The service consisted in chanting, in Hebrew, by the men, and processions around the place. Our friend, at the close, accompanied us to an obscure corner of the temple wall, where some layers of immense stone still remain of the old temple. At this place the Jews assemble on Friday afternoons and Saturday mornings, to wail, as it is called, and the liturgy which they recite in Hebrew, as translated, is touching in the highest degree. Some of the stones above referred to are twenty-two to twenty-nine feet long, and about five feet thick. After breakfast we went to the top of the Governor's house (formerly Pilate's) which borders on and overlooks the Mosque of Omar—which neither Jew nor Christian is permitted to enter, and from thence to the Holy Sepulcher, to witness the production of the Greek fire. The whole is to prove that when our Lord had expired on the cross, the light of the world was extinguished. A miracle is wrought every year within the sepulcher, and fire is sent from heaven as a type and forerunner of the resurrection of the morrow. The kindness of the Latin patriarch secured me a safe seat in a gallery, from which I had a good view of the scene. The same gross outrages were perpetrated as yesterday, although the entire quadrangle was filled with Turkish soldiers with bayonets fixed.

At length, after howling and yelling and dancing, the mob proceeded (all within the church and inclosure around the sepulcher) to fighting, whereupon the soldiery was called in and peace was restored. At length, at half-past two P. M., fire was put forth from a window of the sepulcher, and then a new scene commenced. The multitude passed furiously toward the light with wax candles, with which they had provided themselves, and each strove to light his own rather than his neighbor's; and when lighted, each bearer holding aloft his light, often composed of many candles, until the whole area presented the spectacle of thousands of torches swaying furiously against each other. It is astonishing that a scene of general conflagration did not ensue; but, gradually, they either burnt out or were extinguished, and the Armenians, with numerous and splendid banners, filled the place so indecently occupied a half hour before. I was already tired, but a service was still to be heard in the magnificent chapel of the Armenian Convent, and thither I went.

Sunday, 11th.—I have endeavored to make this a day of rest, yet I went to church this morning and this afternoon, and took a pleasant walk outside the walls with Mr. Duncan.

Monday, 12th.—To-day we have been to Bethlehem and to the traditional place of our Savior's birth, with many other spots consecrated by monkish legends. We paused on the way at Rachel's tomb, lately repaired by Sir Moses Montefiore. The country about Bethlehem is finely cultivated, and the terraced gardens are filled with olive, mulberry, pomegranate and fig trees; the vine also abounds. The whole country is covered with broken limestone, yet the soil is productive. A Yankee has fixed himself near Bethlehem, partly, I suppose, from fanaticism, and chiefly, I do not doubt, to mend his fortunes, and he has already planted numerous trees. Bethlehem is a considerable and thrifty village.

Tuesday.—I have employed to-day in finishing the sights of Jerusalem, and in leave-taking of the acquaintances I have made, and drank tea at the British consul's (Mr. Finn), who is a valuable man, and his wife is a superior person. There is a circle of excellent society here.

Tuesday Evening.—I write again from our tent near Bethel, the scene of Jacob's dream. We left Jerusalem at one o'clock, but at nine Mrs. Finn called to accompany me to several of the schools and charitable institutions maintained by the English and Prussian missions. We also visited an excellently managed institution of German Protestant deaconesses, who are doing a great deal of good here. We then went out to visit the old Convent of the Holy Cross, which possesses some fine mosaic pavements and other curiosities. We issued from the city by the Damascus gate, near the tomb of the kings, and passing over a stony path through a country literally covered with broken stones, yet which is more or less productive, we reached the grave of Samuel, and then Bethel. How strange it is to find myself amid scenes which, from childhood, occupied my thoughts.

Thursday.—We passed last night near a village of modern date, surrounded by vast and new plantations of olive, fig, and pomegranate trees. Every inch which was not preoccupied by rocks or broken stones was carefully tilled, and it was consoling in the midst of the vast desolation to find awakening energies on the borders of Ephraim. We turned aside to

visit the now wasted and lonely Shiloh, the first resting-place
of the Ark of the Covenant after the entrance into the land
of promise. A ruined church, and an old mosque equally in
ruins, attest the equal reverence of Christian and Moslem.
The height overlooks the most beautiful and extensive valley
that we have seen since we have entered the hill country, and
as memories of the true-hearted Joshua, the feeble Eli, of
Hannah and her great son Samuel, to whom all these scenes
had been so familiar, I felt myself in the dreamland, and it
was difficult to recall my attention to the realities of the present. I had my Bible with me, and as my horse is gentle I
employed myself, as we followed our dragoman over the rocky
path, in reading those portions of the Scripture history which
are connected with this holy but now desolated and desecrated
place. The hitherto wild and rugged country became now
softened in its features, and we rode along through the green
valleys covered with young wheat and frequent olive groves
until we began to discern the distant minarets of Nablous, the
ancient Shechem, or Sychar, when, turning aside toward a
mound of ruins, we dismounted to seek among them the remains of the well at which our Lord revealed those wonderful
truths to the Samaritan woman which are now, to us, as
familiar as household words. Mt. Gerizim stood in the fore-
ground of the landscape, and Ebal on the right—the hills of
blessing and cursing. And as I sat on a stone and read, "The
time cometh, and now is, when the true worshipers shall worship the Father in spirit and in truth," and that the ends of
the earth from which I had come had learned the full comprehension of this grand revelation, while a veil remains over
the hearts of those who ought best to have known it, both my
heart and eyes grew too full for indulgence. A little further
on we visited Joseph's tomb, which is constantly kept in preservation; but before reaching it we met a small party of Jews
who had been to visit it, and it was touching to see the effort
they had made to show respect to their great ancestor in a little
lamp made of an excavated orange rind filled with oil, and

having a little lighted taper within. Since entering Egypt,
my reverence for the good and great Joseph has been much
increased, though I never could read his history in the Bible
aloud with a steady voice, and for the first time in my travels,
as a mark of reverence, I wrote my name on his tomb.

Friday.—Several other tents were successively pitched near
us last night, and among them that of the four Russian
princes, who were our companions in the quarantine at Gaza.
Our first excursion this morning was to the lofty summit of the
neighboring Mount Gerizim, where are the ruins of the ancient
Samaritan temple, and its city, which covers a vast extent of
ground, commands a magnificent prospect. The sea is clearly
visible, and the pretty oriental town of Nablous at its foot offers
an enchanting view. Descending, we passed through the principal streets, which are about eight feet wide, quite pretty shops
on either side, with sidewalks, and streams of water in the
center of nearly every street. Some are arched over like tunnels, with houses built upon them, all of course of stone, which
abounds. In better days, a Christian church was built at
the traditional place of Jacob's residence, where Joseph was
carried away, but this as well as a much finer one in the town,
is converted into a neglected mosque. It seems that a congregation of about sixty Samaritans still remains, and we also
visited their little place of worship, but I suspect they are
little better than Mahommedans whom I am beginning to
think (at least their accursed religion), the vilest on earth.
It is hardly possible to imagine how brutal their treatment is
of their women. Our Indians are tender and merciful in
comparison.

Saturday.—I have just returned from a high place near our
tent, where I have seen the rays of the setting sun flit across
the great plains of Esdraelon, while they still rested for a while
on the mountain of Giboa on the right. An Arab village,
tolerably built, lies on the hill-side opposite with its mosque
and flaming minaret, and gardens of figs and pomegranates,
and forests of all kinds, cover the valley. Several other parties

of travelers, natives I think, have spread their tents or equipages here and there on the open ground, and cattle and sheep and goats, with tinkling bells, areslowly winding their way across the plains followed by turbaned Moslems.   As I sit at our tent door, the view is nearly closed on one side by a high hedge of prickly pear.   At a little distance on the right is a Moslem cemetery, with its usual complement of ill-made oven-like tombs, with a rude imitation of the turban at the head of each, and an olive grove at the back of the whole.   It is a beautiful oriental scene, but the abominable faith which gives tone to all leaves me only regrets that this goodly heritage should be so unworthily bestowed.   A beautiful but solitary clump of palm trees, which rises opposite, behind a bridge, seem to respond to my sentiment, and to bewail the desecration of this scene of loveliness, which they scan from their lofty tops.

Monday, 19th.—Left the pretty Djennin early, and passing over the beautiful plain of Esdraelon, covered with exquisite and delicate flowers, we reached at four o'clock the ancient Rabbah—where poor Uriah, the Hittite, met his unworthy fate, by the contrivance of that man of contradictions, King David.   It is near the southern extremity of the plain, of which it apparently commands one of the entrances, and being somewhat elevated it overlooks it.   It must have been a strong place.   Part of the ancient wall still remains, guarded by a very broad and deep ditch.   All are now converted to the base uses of a miserable Arab village.   Mount Tabor was our next object of view.   It rises from the plain, at least a thousand, or perhaps fifteen hundred feet, like an enormous mound—as regularly formed as any of our ancient remains. It appears a very little flattened at the top.   Leaving this consecrated height behind, we soon reached the pretty little town of Nazareth, nestled at the foot of the lofty hills, and secured rooms at a very comfortable hospice, kept by the Franciscan monks, of the Latin convent.   I was weary, but after a short nap, I could not deny myself the pleasure of an evening walk to the top of the highest hill, from which the

view is magnificent.   Among the finest points of the prospect
is Mount Hermon, which is the highest point of Palestine.   It
is still covered with snow.   The church of this convent, it is
said, covers the place of the virgin's residence.   A column
marks the spot where the angel appeared to her, and under
the altar a star is placed to indicate the place on which she
stood as she heard the annunciation.   A room, very old and
immediately above, is shown as her place of abode—until she
went to Bethlehem to be taxed, etc.   Having no books with
me, I do not know on what authority she is said to have lived
here previous to her return from Egypt.   Joseph's shop is still
shown—and the table on which the Pascal Supper was laid.
This morning we set out for the summit of Mount Tabor,
three hours distant.   The top is covered with the ruins of a
church, and perhaps a very large convent, but the stupid ignorance of our dragoman, and every one about me, deny me
all knowledge that I do not already possess.   The blocks of
stone are very large, and the ruined arches indicate fine architecture.   The sole occupants are a Greek priest, who has undertaken to become a hermit, yet keeps a servant.   He came
to welcome me, and seemed heartily glad and willing to participate in our luncheon.   The view from the top is pano-
ramic.   The Mediterranean is seen on the west, and the Sea
of Tiberias, with the course of the Jordan, on the east.   The
village of Endor lies in front of the mountain of Gilboa—Nain
is also in view—and the village of Deborah lies at the foot of
the mountain.   The plain below, now so tranquil, has been the
scene of as many battles as those of Belgium or Lombardy.

MOUNT CARMEL (MONASTERY), *Tuesday, 20th.*
What would I not do to pass on to Beyrout and home.   I
found last night several sisters of charity, with their escort,
who are on their way direct to Beyrout, and we have accompanied them thus far, as our way coincides with theirs.   The
situation here is delightful, and the good fathers are kind as

15

old friends. It reminds me of olden times, when convents were the only inns for travelers.

TIBERIAS, SEA OF GALILEE, *Thursday, 22d.*

I sent off my packet of the last three weeks to you by an Englishman, who promised to put it in the mail at Marseilles, devoutly trusting that it may soon reach you. I was too weary last night to write. The position of the monastery is truly magnificent. I walked, at 6 A. M., to a place on the bold and lofty promontory, where a little chapel is built to designate the place from which the Prophet Elijah is said to have seen the cloud as "large as a man's hand." No position could have been better chosen for a distant sea view.

At ten o'clock, with real regret, I took leave, to return to Nazareth. The ride is truly charming; the harbor of the neighboring port of Kaifa contained several foreign vessels, and the beautiful gulf, with St. Jean d'Acre in full view, and the ships, and the palm trees, and the beautiful nature every-where, contributed to make this a memorable spot. On reaching our previous quarters, at the Latin convent of Nazareth, we found the fraternity in a state of delighted excitement, owing to the arrivals of the consul general and imperial of Austria from Beyrout, and his brother consul from Kaifa, and the consulesses. All the dignitaries, ecclesiastical and civil, of the pretty little Nazareth, were on the alert to deport themselves suitably on so important an occasion, and we willingly acquiesced in the diffidently made proposal of the monks to waive our right to the common dining-room in favor of these distinguished guests. Having already seen the shop of Joseph, we went this morning to visit a chapel which contains a singular table-looking rock, on which tradition records that our Lord frequently ate with his disciples, both before and after his resurrection. We then pursued our way thitherward, pausing a little while at Cana, and at the Mount of Beatitudes, where the Sermon on the Mount was delivered, and also at the place designated for the feeding

of the multitude with the loaves and fishes. Nearly all the
way the snow-crowned Hermon has been in full view, while
Carmel and Mt. Tabor were behind us. The low lands are
rich beyond belief, and are covered with barley and wheat.
The gardens around Cana are beautiful. I am now writing
at our tent door, some fifty feet from the shore of the Lake of
Galilee. The Jordan here is a mere brook. Water-fowl are
disporting themselves fearlessly; our horses and mules are
browsing around idly. A delicate haze softens the landscape,
and makes the outline of Hermon more beautiful, while the
flitting clouds give an additional touch to the charming
landscape. Except for the presence of our party, all is as
still as the desert. At Mt. Tabor we saw the first trees, except olives or figs, and, though they were not larger than
large apple trees, it is truly pleasant to see a shade. There
are also many trees near Carmel, but here at the Sea of
Galilee we have again lost them, and see little but bare
hills. The earth, however, is covered with beautiful flowers.
After writing the above, we mounted our horses to ride over
to the hot springs, about a mile below on the lake. There
are many marks here of volcanic action in the soil, and the
cinders spread around. The water is so hot as to blister the
skin if plunged into it. I could only touch the water and
snatch my finger away, and this, too, as it gushes in a copious
stream out of the hill-side. Ibrahim Pasha, when in power,
had a building erected over one of the fountains, which is the
best specimen of Syrian architecture I have seen; but, like
every thing else, it is falling into ruin and dirt. The ruins
of the old city extend a mile or more along the coast, and
columns lie half in the water at all degrees of angle, pro-
truding through the rubbish. There are many Jews here,
and at a tomb called Jacob's, near the springs, I saw many of
them entering the excavation on the hill-side to pray. It
gives one a strange feeling to see and feel how literally the
prophecies concerning them are fulfilled. The dragoman tells
me they are so fearful and timid in consequence of the op-

pressions which they suffer. Read, as I have done on this spot, the **XXVIII** of Deuteronomy, and also Matthew **XI**, 21st to 25th. From the promontory on which I write, the places where these cities once stood are all within view, and I see rubbish in the distance, but not a single habitation. No part of Palestine has so much touched me as this. It was the familiar place of our Lord's life, and here were most of those "mighty works" manifested which should have enlightened the whole earth. The very soil seemed consecrated, and now in the utter ruin and desolation of this once populous district we seem to be brought face to face with the causes which have wrought it. All are dead, and the sepulchers which remain all along the hill-sides are alone left to tell that men have lived, and wept, and sinned, and suffered. Jerusalem is trodden down by other races, and there one has a painful confusion of feelings. Here there is nothing to interrupt the profound contemplations which every thing calls forth. One wretched little fishing boat is the only occupant of the beautiful lake, and one squalid-looking town contains its sole population.

Friday, 23, Taafed.—This town, some six hours north of Tiberias, is perched upon so dizzy a height, it seems to over-look, as the common expression is, "all creation." The Sea of Galilee is spread at its feet; Carmel and the sea are at the west; Mt. Tabor rises above some dozen intervening ridges, like a regular cone, while the height called the Mount of Beatitudes seems to stand out in front, though really a day's journey on this side. Our day's journeys, however, are not to be calculated after the manner of American distances. We are awakened at five A. M., breakfast at six, and by seven are en route, with tents, kitchen, etc., moving at rather a slow walk. We proceed seven or eight hours to the next station (for there is no possibility of changing them), where we usually arrive about three or four P. M. for luncheon and rest, having passed over some fifteen or eighteen miles at most. This afternoon, after ascending a high place to see the view, we visited a synagogue and several houses, Jew, Mahomedan and Christian, and found them all of quite a superior order to the native population I had seen. The Jews come here from every land, fancying that this is the spot at which the Messiah will descend, and I suppose that some of them bring European civilization which the others imitate. This being the evening of preparation for the Sabbath, the Jewesses were *en grande-tenue*. At one house we found a bride.

April 25th, Tyre.—The Druses being in a state of insurrection on the east of the Jordan, we have made another zigzag. Last night brought us to the Christian village of Dibbel, where silk is produced. The people seem poor and lazy. The hills are covered with small trees, many of which are in bloom. From this to the Sea of Galilee, there is a succession of hills without plains, and the population is quite thin. Some two miles before we reached Tyre, we passed a very old tomb composed of stones of immense size, called the sepulcher of King Hiram. No vestige of the grandeur of the ancient city is left, except some broken columns which are chiefly half covered with water. The town is small, but rather decent, and contains some two thousand Christians.

26th, Sidon.—We have had a pleasant ride along the coast, but I am quite indisposed, and avail myself of so good an excuse to break my engagements and return homeward two weeks earlier. It is rather too much to give thirteen days to see Damascus only, and Baalbec, and I give them up. I decided to proceed directly to Beyrout to take the steamer of to-morrow, after which there would be none for two weeks. I set out alone with my dragoman this morning, and reached Beyrout in time to get money, passport, etc., in time for the Austrian steamer of to-morrow, but owing to Miss Howard's slow ways, and her detention of the luggage, which accompanied her, I came very near losing my passage at last. I, however, persuaded the captain to wait a little, and finally secured it, and am thankful that I shall soon hear from you all, for I am positively sick from anxiety. God grant you are all well. Our steamer is crowded with pilgrims, nearly five hundred, returning from Jerusalem, who are packed all along the sides of the vessel day and night like chickens in coops. If our voyage were to be a long one, I should fear pestilence. I am now, thank Heaven, on my way to civilized life, but chiefly am I thankful that I shall soon hear from you all. God grant that you are all well. The steamer is small. Our ladies' cabin, which contains four berths—all filled—is exclusive of the berths, about six feet long and four wide, having one window of four inches square! One passenger is the English wife of the Sardinian consul in Cyprus. Another is the noted Harriet Livermore, and there is also a little French girl, I making the fourth. There is a good circle of Americans and English, most of whom I met at Cairo or Jerusalem.

28th.—We have been all day coasting along the island of Cyprus, after having passed an hour or more at the town of Lavana. The island on this, the southern side, looks bare and dreary, but I am told that in the interior it is fertile. It was called, as you know, "the Isle of Venus," who sprang from the waves at Paphos.

29th.—We have rather rough winds, and are passing along the coast of Asia Minor with the range of Taurus in full view. Their tops are covered downward for a thousand or fifteen hundred feet with snow, and they have presented all day a magnificent outline. We were to have reached Rhodes tonight, but the rough weather obliged our captain to put into the harbor of Marmoritya, which is surrounded by magnificent mountain peaks. It rains heavily, and I am concerned for the multitude above (pilgrims) who are exposed.

30th.—We reached the town of Rhodes about seven o'clock, and remained some hours in the harbor. As we are supposed to have some infected persons, we are not permitted to land. The town lies beautifully on ground which gradually rises from the sea; the walls are very strong, and what is rare among Turkish possessions, they seem to be in good repair. The fine cathedral rises above all, but is now desecrated into a mosque.

May 4th.—The wind continued so high in the last two days of our voyage, that writing was impossible. We passed in turn quantities of small islands, which rose beautifully from the sea, and at last the gulf of Smyrna, where we entered the quarantine, to be confined three days in order (for there is pretense of nothing more) to pay a pound sterling for each room, etc., for our food per diem. I am in a wretched apartment, with two French ladies, who are pleasant enough, and Miss Livermore, whose oddities, etc.—but to-day is the last of the "durance vile," and to-morrow I hope to have a room to myself at Smyrna.

This Lazarretto is the strangest place that I have yet seen in its mixed multitudes of costume and manners, which indicate representatives of every nation under the sun: Christians, of course, from every part of Europe, Mahomedans and Jews, Greeks, Armenians, Maronites from Asia, even to Siberia. Of the "upper ten," we have a large proportion of our countrymen, of whom two are from Tennessee.

SMYRNA, *May 6th.*

At length, my beloved ones, I begin to see my way out of this oriental labyrinth, which I shall be glad to have seen if it please Heaven to have preserved us all in safety, but my anxiety about you is at times absolutely agonizing.

I go this afternoon to Constantinople, and I positively tremble for fear of bad news. I shall be obliged to remain there a week for the next steamer, and if from the letters I expect to receive, I am so blest as to find that all are well, I shall pass a week in Athens and Greece, and proceed by Trieste to Paris and England. I sent off a packet from Beyrout which I hope reached you safely. This will be taken by a gentleman who goes direct to Paris. I am quite well, but for my extreme anxiety to hear from you, in consequence of the endless delay I have been subjected to in common with all travelers in this land of infidels. I trust my dear Rufus is taking care to have a sufficient supply of money. Not knowing how much L. may have required, I am unable to say how much we shall want. May God bless you all, and bring us together in safety.

CONSTANTINOPLE, *May 9th.*

When I landed here yesterday, my anxieties had wrought so upon my fears that I dreaded to receive the letters I had so long hoped for, and when at length one was put in my hands from L., I positively feared to open it. You may judge of my relief when I found all were well up to the first of April. I was sadly disappointed not to find a letter from Rufus, as I had told my banker to send them to me, but L. tells me she had received late letters, and I am content. We sailed from Smyrna on the afternoon of the sixth, and I was truly glad to find myself the sole possessor of the little cabin appropriated to ladies. The same party of Englishmen are on board who came with me from Beyrout, and the pilgrims occupied the same places as before. There were also four of our missionaries, returning from their annual convention at Smyrna, and I found them a most agreeable addition to the party, so my short voyage here was a bright spot in my travels. We passed Troy at an early hour next morning, and so near the coast that every object was clearly visible. On the highest point is a cairn or mound not unlike many of ours at the west; this is called the tomb of Patroclus, or Achilles, but, of course, the name is altogether apocryphal. No other vestige of the past remains. It is, however, a beautiful soft landscape, especially after my sojourn among the harsh features of Palestine, and the still more rugged ranges of the Caramanian coast. We were soon at the Dardanelles, and passing Sestos and Abydos, we entered the pretty sea of Marmora, and were occupied all day in passing through it. At about nine o'clock we anchored for the night in order to reach the city in daylight, no vessel being permitted to reach it after sunset. It was a beautiful sight next morning as we approached. The bay is not so fine as Naples, and the city, though twice as populous, is altogether inferior in its architecture. Yet these orientals have the art of giving an air of beauty or grandeur to the distant view of their towns which no Europeans possess. This city is, probably, on first view, the most beautiful city in the world, beyond question the finest in Europe. On entering its narrow, ill-paved streets, however, the delighted traveler is disabused. My first care was to send to the bankers for my longed-for letters. My next for John Brown, who had heard that I was expected, and came immediately with his wife. Since then he has continued in every possible way to facilitate my wishes in all things. He soon put me in a fair way for sight-seeing, and, accompanied by the two Tennesseeans, Messrs. Ewing and Price, I set forth to mount a tower, and then to the bazaars, etc. This morning, Mr. Brown came to accompany me to the Mission Church, where one of my *compagnons de voyage*, Mr. Dwight, officiated, and then he kindly invited me to his house, where I saw his mother, who is not well enough just now to go out. He then took a carriage and we went up the "Golden Horn" to the "Sweet Waters," a place of great resort among the pleasure-loving citizens, where were assembled Turks, Jews, Gypsies, Greeks, and every body else, in family groups, for picnics, or any other form of amusement they liked best. To their credit be it said, that neither cards nor strong drink were among them—and afterward dined with my kind friends, the Browns, and returning about dusk. I close the day with this chat with my dear ones.

May 10th.

I doubt not you have all remembered that this is my birthday. Entirely among strangers, I have not mentioned it, for who would care? I had hoped before this to have been with L., but I have been disappointed. I have been, as usual, busy all day with sight-seeing, though with less success than usual, since it is raining. On my way to the bankers, I

called, first, at the Convent of the Sisters of Charity, a large
and extensive suite of buildings, containing a dispensary, in
which was gathered a large number of persons of both sexes
and all creeds who required medical or surgical treatment, a
large collection of orphans and foundlings of all classes, and
a large boarding and day school. All seemed contented and
happy. The sisters, forty-two in number, bear an unmistak-
able air of health and happy tranquillity, and received me
with great kindness. I traveled, as you may remember, with
their superior from Nazareth to Mt. Carmel, and the good
sisters were rejoiced to hear of her through me. Why is it
that Protestants fall so far short in these true labors of love?
Their vulgar fears of Popery drive them into a wicked extreme, and such bigots are justly chargeable for losing the
good which our women might accomplish if, like the Papists,
they were allowed a fair field in which to exercise their faculties. Returning from this busy and happy scene, I mounted
a horse, and, with the gentlemen above named, took a ride
around the ancient walls. The roads are impassable for carriages, and scarcely practicable for horses. The streets are
ill-paved and filthy, and they are, besides, so precipitous that
they are hardly safe for horses.

May 12th.

Being supplied with a firman from the Austrian embassy,
I accompanied a large party of various nations yesterday to
visit the places which can only be seen by this means. We
are, of course, in that part of the city called Pera, the Frank
quarter. Crossing the Golden Horn, which divides it from
Stamboul proper, we entered the seraglio gates and visited
the apartments formerly occupied by the harem. The Sultan
has, for many years, lived in a new palace, which is not visible to strangers. These apartments are pretty and very clean,
and have, through the gratings, the views of the adjacent
waters. We also saw the old divan, or place where state criminals are judged, the baths, library (small), etc., and then
we passed on to the far-famed St. Sophia, to adorn which the

finest temples were robbed by Justinian. But whether the vile taste of the Turks has spoiled it, or that it never equaled the wonderful accounts of its splendor, it now appears quite a common-place edifice, although one is a little startled to see columns from Ephesus and Troy and the Temple of the Sun. The mosques of the Sultan Achmet, Mahmoud and Sulieman the Magnificent are large, but they are Turkish. There are tombs in each, of the founders of these families, all covered with cashmere shawls of immense value. I counted fourteen on that of Mahmoud alone, which, besides, has at its head an old cap (tarboosh) with an aigrette of diamonds, which is worth more than I can tell. The dome over Sulieman is covered all over with precious stones, besides being covered with shawls. These valuables are, of course, strictly guarded, but all is barbaric. Nevertheless, at a little distance, nothing in Europe equals, in its way, the beauty of this picturesque city.

I send you this by the Austrian overland mail. The day after to-morrow I sail for Athens, where I shall remain for the next steamer four or five days, and then take the most direct route for Canterbury. In these barbarous climes it is impossible to calculate time or distance with accuracy. At Athens I hope to find a little improvement. May God bless you all.

CONSTANTINOPLE, *May* 15.

I sent off a letter two days since by the Austrian mail, which I hope will reach its destination in due season. The paper was not long enough to bring up my journal for the day before, when I made a memorable excursion up the beautiful Bosphorus. We took a pretty little caique, with three rowers, and emerging from the Golden Horn, by the point of Tophane, we passed the magnificent, but as yet unfinished palace of the Sultan, and close by the tomb of the famous Barbarossa, and the palace inhabited by the Sultan, and in an hour reached the pretty village of Belec, on European coast, where our missionaries have a station. They had kindly invited us to see their schools, and I availed myself of this occasion to

visit them. The students, male and female, are all either
Greeks or Armenians, and seem to profit in various ways by
their instruction. Visited Mr. and Mrs. Everett, and Mr.
Hamlin, accompanied by Mr. Bliss, whom I chanced to meet
on the way. After a pleasant hour, we proceeded to our boat,
another hour to Therapia, the residence of Mr. Marsh. This is
the spot rendered famous by Medea. Mr. and Mrs. M. received
us kindly, and offered luncheon; then I called to see Mrs.
Bliss, who is a grandniece of Mr. Rufus King, her father
having been a Porter. She and her husband are stationed
in Asia Minor, but are here on a visit. Mr. H., son of our
old Boston acquaintance, of this name, is second dragoman,
and I found Mrs. Brown at his house, next door to Mrs. Marsh.
The views from all these houses are magnificent. We then
passed Bayukdere, and then crossing the strait we ascended
the Gianti Mountain, on the top of which, guarded by dervishes, is the tomb—fifty feet long—of Joshua, who being a
great man, had a body, according to the Turkish legend, in
proportion to his capacity, and as he sat upon this mountain,
some thousand feet high, he bathed his feet in the Bosphorus
at its base! From this height, the northern portion of the
strait, and the adjoining Black Sea are all before you on one
side, Mount Olympus covered deep in snow on another, and the
beautiful heights covered with pretty kiosks and houses and
gardens, with numerous headlands and inlets, stretch away to
the south. I have seen many views more extensive, but none
so beautiful or so remarkable. We returned to our caique
delighted with our excursion. The next day was devoted to
Scutari and its views and its cemeteries, and the howling
dervishes, who perform of Thursdays. I can not undertake
to describe them—their rites are too horrible. They cut themselves without mercy, and seemed more like demons than men,
and I was glad to escape from the shocking scene.

Yesterday, Friday, the Moslem Sabbath, Mr. Brown again
accompanied me the whole day. Nothing can exceed his
kindness, and here, more than anywhere else, such a friend

is necessary. We went first to see the Sultan go in state to a
mosque. Some hundreds of soldiers were drawn up to receive
him, and at twelve o'clock, with cannons roaring on all sides,
and also from a war steamer full of troops on their way to
the Black Sea, he approached, preceded by several large boats
gaily painted, and filled by officials. Next came his own
splendid barge, with twenty-four rowers in white dresses. He
sat under a canopy of scarlet velvet, trimmed with heavy gold
fringes, mingled with lilac, and white silk draperies. He
wore a sort of loose frock coat of blue cloth, with a little gold
embroidery, and the eternal tarboosh, or red cloth cap (of
which I have grown so weary), and walked alone, preceding
all else, into the mosque, where we "Christian dogs" could
not enter. We then went to see the whirling dervishes, who
have the reputation of being learned. It seems their Asiatic
founder was of such ecstatic sanctity, that he was perpetually
tending toward heaven, by a rotary or spiral motion, by which
he was continually and involuntarily lifted from the ground.
His disciples, desirous to retain him on earth, were accustomed
to draw him hither by music, and they continue to aspire to
imitate him by weekly exercises in public. They have a circular floor, perhaps thirty or forty feet in diameter, surrounded by a railing, which divided them from the spectators,
with music from a sort of orchestra. The floor is bare, and
after various genuflections and movements, they extend their
arms and whirl for an hour or two. Their dresses are long, and
they are not ungraceful, and besides they are harmless. After
this we proceeded in a caique to the "sweet waters of Europe,"
where we found many thousands amusing themselves in innocent ways. There were gentlemen and ladies of high rank,
in numberless Turkish and European costumes, and thousands of little boats—this is the Moslem Sabbath. It is a picturesque and pleasing scene. Returning, I passed the evening
quietly with our missionaries, Mr. and Mrs. Dwight, who had
invited me the day before. Within an hour or two I go on
board the steamer for Syra.

SMYRNA.

We reached here about eight o'clock this morning, and I went on shore to request the American consul to send a box of relics from Palestine to Messrs. J. & J. Stuart & Co., New York, by the ship " Martha Clark," which sails in a day or two.

SYRA, *May* 18*th.*

We reached this port at half-past seven, and although every one is in perfect health, we must lie idle in quarantine till to-morrow evening. I am beginning, however, to see my way more clearly out, and on this day week I expect to return here to take the weekly Austrian steamer for Trieste. I should greatly prefer the French steamer, but it goes over only once in ten days; and so I hope to be in Paris a week after L. receives this. Unless I find her there, I shall remain but a day, and hasten to Canterbury. I send this by the boat which has brought us from Constantinople. Our voyage through the archipelago has been full of interest, to which the fair though cool weather has added much; but I begin to lose all desire to see or do any thing but to rejoin my family. I am in good health, though rather travel-worn, and this I suppose you have all discovered from the dullness of my letter. However, I spare no pains to see and learn all that is in my way; and to-morrow, as soon as we are released from this absurd quarantine, I shall run up the hill and explore Syra as vigorously as when I commenced my travels. May God preserve us all!

ATHENS, *May* 20*th.*

I little expected, on my arrival here before daylight this morning, the comfort and consolation in store for me. I had requested, on leaving Naples, that my bankers would forward letters here for a week or two, and therefore had no hope to find any letter so late as that of L.'s at Constantinople. All of your letters, however, are of inestimable value to me, and relying upon the early hours of the modern Athens, I sent off forthwith to Mr. Notaria, the banker here, expecting

perhaps two or three, at least three months old, when, to my
surprise and delight, there came back a large packet of
twenty-four letters, the last having arrived only yesterday,
dated at Cincinnati on the 14th of April; so that, instead of
pining away my visit here, I am refreshed by the latest intelligence from home. I must be careful of my paper, as well
as my time, both of which are scanty. After breakfast, I
went to call on Mr. and Mrs. Hill, where I found I was expected, where I was most kindly received, and invited for the
evening. From thence, with guide and companions, I proceeded toward the Acropolis, of which I have a magnificent
view from my window at the Hotel de l'Orient. Passing the
pretty temple of the winds at its foot, we wound along the
rude path, and pausing to look down at the remains of the
Odeon of Athens, we proceeded upward to the Parthenon,
where a guard is stationed to unlock the rude gate which pro-
tects the sublime ruins within. From this point, we looked
down on Mars Hill, the finely preserved temple of Theseus,
the Arch of Adrian, and the superb ruins of the temple of
Jupiter Olympus. Entering the door, we walked up along
the remnants of the ancient marble-paved ascent to the Temple of Victory, which has been so repaired as to be complete
in its proportions. Still moving onward, the majesty of the
Parthenon is displayed before the wondering eye in all its
severe and beauteous symmetry. I will not describe it here;
you can find it more accurately done elsewhere. I found it
less ruinous than I expected, and such views are unfolded of
the beautiful sea and islands that one could weep in meekness
and silence to behold such abounding loveliness lying all
around, while the remembrances of the illustrious past come
swelling over the memories of our lifetime. One feels it is
cruel to be silent, when each hill and inlet has of right such
histories to tell. I wandered about here and there, and then
crossed over to the Erechtheum, in a chamber of which,
it is said, was the grave of Cecrops. I remained among
these wonderful relics of the mighty past some hours, and de-

scending, mounted the spot on Mars Hill made sacred by St. Paul.

From this we crossed over to the prison of Socrates, and stood upon the Pnyx of Themistocles, and then to the other of Demosthenes, cut out of the solid rock, and on the Temple of Theseus, and the Stoa of Adrian, to our hotel, where I arrived in time to get a warm bath before dinner. This, Ascension Day, is one of the greatest festivals of the year. All the common people who can, and the better sort, at this season, climb on donkeys or horses the precipitous Hymettus the day before, with tents for the night, and then they attend mass in the neighboring convent, and pray, and sing, and dance away the night and morning. In the afternoon they descend to the spot near the royal palace, where refreshments of all kinds are sold, and where they amuse themselves during the evening. To this latter spot, then, I directed my steps, and, ordering a carriage, I went to invite some of the ladies at Mrs. Hill's to accompany me. Two of them accepted ; and, as we moved slowly along, we met their majesties, the king and queen, on horseback. He looks in very bad health ; she, like an English woman. It was a curious sight to see among the crowd such varied costumes. The Greeks, especially the men, are very fond of dress, and the whole resembles more the personages at a *bal costumé* than any thing in real life. Every costume in Greece, I think, must have been represented. This multitude was, of course, the industrial classes. We looked on for a while, and then drove by the Protestant cemetery, to the ancient Stadium, which, with the remains of a very ancient bridge, is near the now feeble rivulet of the Ilyssus. Near this are the ruins of a temple of Diana. We then sent the carriage to join us further on, while we visited the recently discovered substructures of the Temple of the Eleusinian Mysteries, among which are some fine mosaics. A little further on is the Fountain of Calirrhoe, with its nine outlets. The ancient Amphictyons were obliged to swear never to refuse this water to a confederate city in peace or war. Near this are the beautiful Corinthian columns, which remain of the Temple of Jupiter Olympus; and, as the ground was leveled for a large space around it, and the situation in all respects well fitted for the purpose, the pleasure-loving Greeks are accustomed to take ices, etc., under the columns, and I ordered a strawberry ice for each of our party, which was promptly handed to me by a young Greek in a rich costume, on a pretty silver waiter, having also a glass of ice-water with each ice—all being as good as I ever tasted. We then drove on through the Arch of Adrian and Theseus, and returned to Mr. Hill's to tea, where we found two missionaries of the Baptist Church, Mr. and Mrs. Arnold, and passed a quiet evening.

Friday, 21st.—I set out this morning with a party in two carriages, three of our countrymen, one Englishman, and the former Belgian minister at Washington, Mr. Serruys, who joined us at Constantinople. We went first to visit in turn each of the three ports of Athens and the ruins of the "Temple to the Unknown God;" then, taking a boat, we were rowed out of the harbor to the tomb and column of Themistocles (all in ruins), just opposite the scene of his glory at Salamis. The tomb was covered with water, and the various portions of the column are scattered around. We then crossed to the Bay of Salamis, and examined it with deep interest. Just above it, near Eleusis, is the mountain on which Xerxes was seated to witness the battle. We then returned, and, taking our carriage, we went to a spot marked out by a modern monument, where it is said poor Antigone took leave of Edipus, and where he was burned (supposed to be). Near this is the academy, where the legendary grave of Plato is marked by columns. On our way to the king's gardens we were stopped by a procession—an aged man had died the day before, and was now to be conveyed to the tomb. First, there was a long array of soldiers, with funeral music; then some half dozen young men, or, rather, boys, who carried banners and other Greek decorations, of course a large cross;

16

then followed fifteen or twenty priests chanting psalms; and then, seated in an arm-chair, covered with black velvet, and borne on the shoulders of men, appeared the dead bishop himself! He was dressed in full robes of state, with a gilded crown, or mitre (I do not know what to call it), on his head, his right arm leaning on the arm of the chair, while the hand was made to hold the crosier. The left lay in his lap, containing a copy of the Gospels. But for his ghastly face he might have been taken for one still alive. Another large troop of soldiers followed him, but I saw no friends. It was a painful sight, never to be forgotten.

Saturday, 22d.—This has been a very warm day. At seven o'clock we set forth in a carriage to Mount Pentelicus, 3,500 feet high. We drove to the foot and walked up. The height overlooks Athens and the gulf on one side, and Marathon and Euboea on the other, with the snow-covered Mt. Parnassus in the distance—one of the grandest views in the world. From the quarries of its sides the Parthenon was built. All the scenery around Athens is beautiful, and unlike any I have seen elsewhere. The outlines are bold and soft at the same time, and the exquisite charm which is lent by the ever-varying outlines of the sea-coast, and the soft, yet clear haze, that unceasingly veils it, are indescribable. Strange that, in the midst of so much natural beauty, which probably inspired the early Greeks to their expressions in art, the moderns seem positively insensible to either, for not even in our western villages is less taste exhibited in architecture. The royal palace resembles a factory, and the houses are inferior to those of our second or third rate towns.

Sunday.—I have been passing the day, by invitation, with the Hills. Went to the church with them, which is very small, yet too large for the congregation. I have just been to look from my windows over the beautiful blue waters of the Saronic gulf, stretching away to Egina, with Salamis on one side—then the eye runs along a soft, undulating line, some three or four miles, till it reaches the hill of Musæus, on the

top of which is perched the modern observatory. Just below this, in its clearly defined proportions, stands the temple
of Theseus—behind it is the height which contains the Pnyx.
Mars hill follows close upon the latter, and the towering hill
of the Acropolis rises abruptly near it, with the sublime ruins,
each column of which I can count as I stand.   Behind all, in
the range of Hymettus, carrying the eyes still further to the
west, the peak of Lycabettus rears its savage front, and but
for an obtruding little hill would close that portion of the
magnificent panorama.

Monday, 24th.—To-day I have seen Eleusis and Megara.
The drive is one of the finest in the world. We passed through
the beautiful valley of Daphne to the Gulf of Salamis, and
along the Via Sacra of the Eleusinian mysteries, on which the
marks of the ancient cars are deeply worn.   Next comes
some ruins of the city of Pisistratus, with inscriptions—then
the traditionary scene of Aristides' "Strike, but hear me."
Still passing along the charming sea coast, we reached Eleusis,
and wandered among the ruins of the once superb temple of
Ceres.   It is now a small village of sickly-looking people.
The men seem to be all engaged in cards or some other
amusement—the women in spinning cotton or wool with dis-
taffs, such as their ancestors used two thousand years ago.

We went into several houses, and all indicated great poverty and backwardness of improvement. Chairs are rarely
seen—bedsteads I believe are unknown.   I saw in one house
a loom.   The cloth (cotton) was well made.   Some ancient
mutilated statues are preserved in an old church.   Megara is
some two miles further along the sea coast, with apparently a
still more uncivilized population—less clean and industrious.
The most curious thing we saw there was some two hundred
sarcophagi, collected round a fountain, at which as many
nymphs were engaged in washing!   There are statues too, and
ruins scattered about.   Every inch of soil is covered with
historic memories.   The Hills are very kind, and are always
making me feel that they are taking good care of me.   On

Friday I will leave Athens for Nauplia, Argos, etc., to Corinth, and on to Corfu and Trieste, and then for our dear L. and the children. God bless you all. I am quite well.

Delayed two days. On Tuesday I packed a box of antique vases, which you will all like to possess. I visited what I had not seen at Athens. I dined with my kind friends, the Hille, and they took me a charming drive afterward, which was closed by ascending the Acropolis to see the sun set from the Parthenon. I climbed up the ruined stairway quite to the top of the front. The view is never to be forgotten. Such beauty, illustrated by such associations, the world does not contain.

May 25th.—I shall not forget the birthday of my dear R. I shall probably be in the Gulf of Lepanto. Write to Brown & Shipley, and thank them for me for their kind attention, and say that I have received here their second letter of credit. Pray do this forthwith. Yesterday I set forth, at 3 o'clock A. M., with the worthy Mr. Serruys, for Sunium, on which you have learned, from the noted extract of Cicero's letter, are majestic remains of a temple of Minerva. It is thirty-four miles there and back, part in a carriage and part on horseback, with three relays of horses, and yet I am not very tired. The grand monument is truly sublime in its solitary grandeur. Read descriptions of it, for it is all that can be said. In reaching it we traveled the finest part of Attica.

GULF OF ARGOS, NAUPLIA, *May* 27.

I sent off a letter from Athens yesterday, after which nothing occurred of much note except the arrival of my old friends, the Allens, of Providence, who are to join me in the Gulf of Corinth and proceed to Trieste. I set out this morning with Mr. Serruys and a young German, who has been with us from Beyrout, to make a tour in the Peloponnessus. The morning was beautiful, and the majestic ruins of the Parthenon, as the sun rose, were literally bathed in a glory of golden light. Behind it rose the graceful Pentelicus, on the

right Hymettus guarded the plain, and Parnassus flanked
the left. Never was city so honored by nature and art.
There is a grace and refinement, if I may so apply the word,
in the beauty of Greece. At the Piræus we embarked on
board of the Austrian steamer, and swiftly passed out of the
ancient port. A few minutes later and we turned the point
where once reposed the ashes of Themistocles, opposite Salamis. Within half an hour we neared Egina, on the summit
of which stands in solemn grandeur the remains of the once
magnificent Temple of Jupiter Panhellinius; twenty-six columns, with their architrave, remain. The captain kindly
lent me his telescope, and with this aid the Parthenon was
still clearly visible across the water, and I had but to turn
myself to look first upon one and then upon the other, and
all around the most beautiful seas and islands that can be
conceived but can never be described. Poros came next, with
its ruined temple, the death place of Demostheues; and then
we came to the modern isle of Hydra, where we paused to set
on shore some passengers, and then we passed on to Spezzia
to land others, for our steamer was full of Greeks—many of
them of the upper class—who speak Italian and French, and
who, seeing that I was the only stranger lady, chatted with
me in the most friendly way. Most of them were dressed in
the costume of their provinces. All were easy, and there was
not one awkward individual on board. There were no English. I wish I had room to write more about them. After
Spezzia, we entered the Gulf of Nauplia, leaving the Argo-
lide, or Argore, country on the right and Laconia on the left,
and a snow-covered mountain in Arcadia towering in the distance. The whole country is covered with mountains of the
most majestic outlines, on both sides, until we reach the upper
part of the bay, when the plain of Argos stretches out, and
from which rises abruptly the steep-pointed hill of the old
Acropolis of Argos, and the Acropolis, or citadel, of Nauplia,
which we ascended this afternoon, 720 feet high. Here we
saw many Venetian cannon, which belonged to that city when

she was mistress of Greece. The lion of St. Mark is stamped upon each. Argos and Tyreus, the birth-place of Hercules, are both in view, and as I looked upon them you may easily imagine how many legends rebounded in my memory. It was only last summer that L. and I heard Göethe's Iphigenia in Vienna. O, that I had an edition of the Greek Trag- edies with me! I sought in vain for a translation in any modern language in Athens. I write on the steamer where we sleep to-night for want of accommodation in the town.

MYCENE, *Saturday, May 29th.*

We set out this morning on one of the most memorable of my tours. First (in a carriage), some three-quarters of an hour to the Cyclopean ruins of Tyreus, and then on horse- back across the plain to Argos, now a pretty town full of gardens. The remains of the old theater, containing sixty- eight steps cut in the solid rock out of a hillside, are wonder- ful, and there are also other remains of magnitude. From thence we crossed over to the Lernean marsh to see the cavern of the fabled hydra of Hercules, which is the most remarkable cavern I have seen, fit for the abode of "chimeras dire." Some twenty yards below, issues from a single outlet a strong and rapid river, which almost deluges the valley. On our way to it, we coursed around a large portion of the east side of the beautiful vale of Argos, which is the freshest thing I have seen for a long while. We returned by the ruined citadel of Argos, and pursued our way across the extensive plain to Mycene, the ancient capital of the Atridæ, some eight miles further. I was disposed to try a little of modern Greek life, and I resolved to pass the night at Mycene, where there is only a *khan, i. e.,* a bare room, in which you are ex- pected to repose (if you can) on the floor, and furnish your own table. For this latter we had provided at Nauplia, and being luxuriously disposed, we purchased some fresh straw from a passing farmer, which (our cloaks being spread over it) furnished a not comfortless bed. There was but one room

for all, and, ensconced behind a row of umbrellas, I occupied
the same floor with the gentlemen, who, being quiet sleepers,
we got through the night without other disturbance than the
arrival at midnight of a flock of sheep and goats, each having a bell, which made a prodigious noise. But, before going
to bed, a good deal was to be done. We set out with our
guide, about three hours before sunset, to explore the pre-
cincts of this ancient royal abode. On the side of the
mountain, and commanding a view of the whole beautiful
vale, with the mountains of Laconia behind it, stand the
ruins of the ancient citadel of the "King of men." The
gateway is the finest specimen of Cyclopean or Pelasgic architecture extant, and proves that its founder must have had
taste as well as wealth. There are lions well sculptured over
the gateway, and immense blocks of stone are neatly sculptured and fitted. Much of the entire wall remains, though the
city was destroyed five hundred years before our era. The
Pelasgi seem to have built for eternity. At a little distance
from the citadel, and near the scattered ruins of the city, is a
remarkable vaulted dome, almost quite underground, called
the treasury of Atreus. A chamber adjoining it is called the
tomb of Agamemnon, all of fine masonry, yet beyond the
knowledge of all but traditionary history. At a considerable
distance, and outside the walls, is a smaller structure, well
executed, called the tomb of Clytemnestra, who, they say, was
denied a place near her kindred on account of her crimes.
Until in the neighborhood, I knew not of the existence of
these and other monuments of this remarkable region. Greece
has many of these records of better days scattered over it,
which are seen by few. The present race, I fear, hardly de-
serve a better fate than they endure, for in the country they
are quite barbarians. Every-where I have seen to-day (they
are just reaping the wheat) old men and women beating out
the grains with their hands, where, if they had the energy,
they could easily provide machinery.

CORINTH, *Sunday, May 30th.*

There was no avoiding it, so we traveled several hours this morning on our way here. Nemea was our only stopping place, where there are remains of a beautiful Temple of Jupiter, and also a theater. Not far off, in the sides of the mountains, are the caverns of the Nemean lions which the renowned Hercules subdued. The country is entirely uncultivated from Nemea here, though I am sure the soil would yield good harvests. We came across the height, about two thousand feet, of Acro Corinth, upon which the citadel is placed, and from which the finest view in Greece is obtained. Athens is quite distant on one side of Parnassus, and Helicon, and Sparta, and Arcadia, all before you. The isthmus, and all its historic places, are spread out at your feet. This is the last of my labors in climbing, I suppose, and I am less fatigued than you could think possible. The extreme heat in this climate makes it laborious. We descended into the modern village to a so-called hotel—Great Britain—equal to the taverns in our back-country villages, except the cooking, which is good (I fear we are the worst cooks in the world), but poor beds, and no carpets; neither is there any fruit, not even lemons, nor dried peaches, nor prunes. The open place in front of the house has been filled this afternoon with a multitude of Greek men in their absurd costume—red cap with immense blue and black tassels, a white petticoat, very full, coming down to the knees, under which is an embroidered shirt, open at the front, over which is an embroidered white cotton vest, and above this is a gay-colored jacket, red, blue, and green or purple velvet, richly embroidered in gold, and the sleeves open from the shoulder to the wrist. Under this appears the full open sleeves of the shirt; a sash of scarlet, or in gay stripes, is girded together to compress the waist, and below the petticoat are woolen gaiters (white, with gay garters below the knee) and scarlet or yellow shoes, complete the useless and vain attire. The women, for the most part, seem rather indifferent to dress, but the men are real cox-

combs in their exterior.   I fear they are, for the most part,
as idle as they are vain.

LUTROPE, PORT OF THE GULF OF CORINTH, *Monday, 31st.*

We came here, some six miles, this morning, to take the
steamer for Corfu and Trieste, and, thank heaven, I am now
fairly on my way homeward.   The Athenian passengers came
over to join us, one of them bringing two letters, from my
banker, of the 22d and 29th, from you and M., which had
arrived after I left Athens.   I am thankful that you are all
well, and glad to hear of your plan to bring Mr. Peter to you.
I am afraid some of my letters must have miscarried, that
you were so late in hearing from me at Cairo.   This is my
darling child's birthday.   You well remember, my dear
Rufus, that I was at the same age when I took you to Cambridge.   Now I can not dwell on birthdays; the thought
brings about such heart-breaking associations that I dismiss it
from my letter, but not from my meditations.   You will be
glad to hear that the Allens joined us to-day, and I shall
have the good fortune to have friends to Trieste.   May God
bless you all.

June 2d.—Since our embarkation, there has been so little
to write, that I have not taken out my pen.   We left port
about eight P. M., having been engaged all day in receiving
passengers and goods, who, for want of proper transportation,
occupy much time in accomplishing small ends.   The steamer
was at length full—over fifteen passengers in the first cabin,
and hundreds bivouacked about the decks, many of whom
are elegantly dressed in Greek costume.   There was a full
moon, and the grand outline of the Acro Corinth and the
snow-topped mountains behind it, on both sides of the gulf,
are lofty and precipitous heights, which afford magnificent
landscapes all along the coast.   On the north, Mt. Helicon,
and beyond, far away, stretches the snow-crowned Parnassus;
but these I saw from the Acro Corinth, and not from the

steamer. I was sorry to leave so beautiful a combination of earth and sky, and I went to bed reluctantly.

Not long after I rose in the morning, we reached Lepanto, where the great battle was fought in which the Turks were for the first time defeated, and where Cervantes was wounded. Two hours brought us to Patras, where we were to remain some hours. We went on shore. The town was all destroyed in the revolution, and is now new. We visited the churches, Latin and Greek, each claiming to be placed on the spot of St. Andrew's martyrdom. It was a double holiday throughout Greece, both as Whitsunday and the coming to the throne of King Otho. The public vessels in the port were streaming with flags and firing salutes, and the Greek church was strewed, as usual, with branches of baywood. It is covered with portraits painted on the walls, and well executed, of the apostles and martyrs; but what struck me most, on approaching the altar, was the little open coffin of an infant about six weeks old, supported on a tiny trestle. The pale, diminutive little face was tranquil, as if asleep; the delicate limbs were tied at the wrists and ankles with crimson ribbon, and a bouquet of fruits and flowers was laid upon the folds of the little white grave-dress, while a sort of aureole of gold and silver tinsel stood out above the head. This frail relic of mortality lay quite alone in the immense space; no creature was near it, and about the door of the church were only a *padre* and one or two men of the working class. I wondered why the little creature had been so deserted, and after gazing awhile at the touching spectacle, we moved on to examine a tomb, which the *padre* assured us contained the bones of St. Andrew. They claim to possess them at Rome, but who knows? As we were leaving the church, one of the men took up the tiny coffin, and, accompanied by the *padre*, hastily went forth. We followed, to see what would be done, and entering with them the adjacent cemetery, we saw a rude little grave opened by the side of a larger one newly filled up. There, we fancied, might rest the poor mother, and hence the desertion of her infant. The *padre* mumbled a few words as if in prayer; the man placed the open coffin in the shallow grave, and the *padre* taking up a shovel having earth upon it, the man poured it full of water, and this compound of mud was thrown directly upon the poor little face by the *padre*, as he mumbled other (to us) unintelligible words; a rude board was put over all, and the dirt thrown in until the grave was full, and then a bucketful of water was poured over it, and both *padre* and man moved hastily away, leaving me beside the harshly treated dead. Was it not a barbarous proceeding?

Near by was a large vineyard of Zante currants, which so closely resembled grape-vines that a stranger could not possibly perceive any difference. Before returning on board, we took ices and lemonade at a café—both quite good. I regret we did not touch at Missolonghi. We proceeded at once to Zante, but could not land for want of time. The town is beautiful from the sea, and I understand the island is the best cultivated in the Ionian group. It is called by the Italians, "Zante, the flower of the Levant," and, indeed, the largest and finest bouquet was brought on board I ever saw. The moon was brilliant. I went on deck this morning early, just as we were passing "Sappho's Leap," at the southern extremity of St. Maure, since when we have been coasting along Albania.

CORFU, *Friday, June 4th.*

We reached this beautiful island on the afternoon of Wednesday (the day before yesterday), and finding the two hotels full, the Allens and myself found quite comfortable lodgings in a private house. A gentleman by the name of Fellows, from New Orleans (formerly of Louisville), is also in the same house.

We took a long drive yesterday to the ancient ruins of Corcyra, and thence to the pass of Garuna, which affords one of the finest views on the island. After my long stay in lands devoid of trees, it is delightful to me to dwell on the perpetual verdure of the island. At first view, all seemed so prosperous that I rejoiced to find among Greeks the semblance even of thrift, but I was soon struck by the haggard faces of the common people. I learned, on inquiry, that they are suffering from famine, and are supplied with bread on allowance by the subscriptions of the charitable. The staple of the island is olive oil, and the crop having failed for three years, they have no other means of subsistence. A family owning a dozen olive trees are able to live, and as the trees require hardly any culture, the people acquire idle habits, especially since there is little demand for labor of any kind. This is the capital of the seven Ionian islands, who call themselves a republic under the protection of England, who furnishes a governor and some thousands of troops.

I mounted to the top of the citadel, which commands a magnificent view of the sea and land, which yet exhibits many remains of Venetian rule, *i. e.*, the winged lions over gateways, etc. It was near sunset, and in the very large square or planted area in front of the governor's palace a military band was playing, and large numbers of people, ladies and others, were enjoying the air among the trees and flowers which adorned it. I had a letter to the Countess Valsomachi (widow of Bishop Heber), but she was out when I called. I could not accept her very kind invitation to breakfast this morning, as our steamer promised to start at ten o'clock, but did not get off till one, so I might have been there after all.

COLOGNE, *Friday Evening.*

After traveling day and night from Trieste since Monday (except a few hours passed at Dresden yesterday to inquire about our pictures), I find I have a half an hour to write here before the trains go off.

I will begin where I left off. After Corfu we steamed up the Adriatic without interruption, passing in turn Zara, the ruins of Dioclesian's palace at Spalatra, etc. Trieste nestles around the head of the bay; behind are very high mountains. Our steamer anchored out in the bay and a medical man came on board to see if we brought any pestilence, and for the assurance that we were all clean, we were each mulcted a shilling. Next came the custom-house officers, for although Trieste is a free port, salt and tobacco are monopolies, and our luggage was examined to see if either was concealed in it. Some two hours having been thus usefully employed, we poor wights were at last permitted to land, and soon found ourselves in a capital hotel; but my desire was to get on, and I proceeded at once to the bankers for additional funds to proceed forthwith, but soon found myself again in Austrian coil, and was obliged to lose twenty-four hours simply because it is the pleasure of the government that all luggage is to be examined in the custom-house before twelve o'clock, and we had arrived in the afternoon, and therefore must wait till next day. The next afternoon, therefore, taking leave of the Allens, I got into a coach with three others, and, after riding all night, we reached Laybach and the railroad about eight o'clock. The views from the mountains behind Trieste are of immense extent over the Adriatic to Aquilaia, and nearly to Venice, and at the east to Capo d'Istria. The road passes through Styria and Moravia, and borders along the Tyrol, the mountains of which are capped with snow. The people of these districts have a good moral reputation, and their country indicates great industry and comfort. The men and women seem to work in common, and feel themselves very much on a par. They labored side by side in the fields and on the roads breaking stone, digging ditches, carrying heavy sacks, etc.; but after the civilization of France and Italy, seeing these German boors, one has the feeling of descending from the drawing-room to an ale-house. The Germans, doubtless, have their virtues, but they seem to be made of clay so innately coarse that they are incapable of refinement.

FONTAINEBLEAU, *Sunday.*

Before I had finished the last sentence at Cologne, I was hurried off to the railway, and now, after forty-eight hours—

me voici—in the ancient residence of the French king's. To return to our Styrian railway, which passes through the most beautiful scenery I have seen in Germany. Gratz is its capitol. Tycho Brahe passed many years near it, and there are many old Middle Age castles perched like eyries upon mountain tops all along, and until we were almost within sight of Vienna we are seldom out of sight of snowy mountains. We crossed one during the night of Tuesday in carriages, some 3,300 feet high. I was very desirous to have turned aside to visit Pesth, the Hungarian capital, as I thought you would like to hear about it, but I thought of our dear L.'s loneliness, and I passed on even through Vienna without stopping, and reached Prague the same night about seven o'clock. Having an hour at my disposal, I jumped into a little carriage and drove up the grand old hill of the Hradschin, which I described to you last year, and from that magnificent height I surveyed the well remembered and beautiful landscape as the setting sun lighted it up with his gorgeous rays. On my return, and near the Wallenstein palace, I met one of the sons of the family driving with a friend. He is a fine looking young man. I looked at the Schwartzenberg palaces (there are three near together) and remembered how full of life and ambitious hopes had been the chief when I last saw them ; already, in the fullness of his pride, he has gone down to an early grave. Prague is a place to dwell upon and never to be forgotten. I resumed my place in the railway, and proceeded to Badenbaden, on the Saxon frontier, where we were to wait three hours, and I profited by the time to secure my " nature's sweet restorer," not " balmy sleep," as Young says, but a good warm bath of soap and water.

At 7 o'clock we reached Dresden, where I had resolved to pause to inquire about our pictures. Worthy Mr. Kallmeyer was delighted to see me again, and loudly expressed his satisfaction. Not having been able to devise ways and means of getting the pictures to Hamburg, he had written to me months ago to inquire, giving no other address than Philadelphia.

These people are profoundly ignorant of commercial matters—more so than you can conceive. He, however, had faithfully preserved all I had ordered, and I have written out and placed in the hands of Mr. Bassange, banker, directions which I think can not be mistaken. I also decided to order other pictures, and accordingly drew up a contract with Kallmeyer for seven pictures, which will be delivered within two years—at three different periods—the first about this time next year. Seeing he could not wait longer, I paid him in full for the Cecilia and Magdalen; and as we shall have time enough to talk over the others, I will not now take up room about them. I have deliberated about them, and I am glad to have secured them—the porcelain pictures are to be paid for on delivery in Philadelphia. Brown and Shipley are to be furnished with money, and Mr. Bassange is to be authorized to draw on them as soon as the pictures are received. I am spending, I know, a good deal of money, but I am so persuaded of the beneficence of bringing works of art into our country, that I am willing to make some sacrifices. There are two or three great pictures here, which, if we could have copied for the Cincinnati Gallery, would give that place pre-eminence over all the eastern cities. The Madonna di San Sisto is, without doubt, the finest picture in the world. Will not the ladies of Cincinnati subscribe, and win the glory of possessing a *fac-simile* of the masterpiece? It would require two years to finish it, and would cost $1,000. How easily they might raise this sum by subscription. Do try if it can not be managed. Mr. Kallmeyer will undertake it. The copying at Dresden is finer than anywhere else. I left Dresden on the evening of Thursday, and passing through Leipsic, and Halle, Magdebourgh, and Brunswick, and Hanover, and to Cologne, took the express train, and flying on the wings of steam, scudded over Belgium, and reached Paris in nineteen hours from Cologne. From the railway I went to Hottinguer's to find letters from my dear ones, and had the comfort of re-

ceiving one from my darling Rufus. I am sorry you were all
so uneasy about me in Syria. I had forgotten that Mr. Spencer found so many hardships; but you know our clergy generally like to live softly, and would clamor about privations
which I should hardly think worthy of notice. As to danger,
there is none. Unless L. joins me I shall only stay long
enough to get some needful clothing, and then to Canterbury.

PARIS, *Thursday.*

I am getting myself refitted a little, and profiting by the
time, but I am anxious to see the dear children. I wish I
could guess what M. would like to have from Paris.

BOULOGNE, *June* 17*th.*

L.'s anxiously expected letter arrived at last, the day before
yesterday, and I should have left Paris yesterday, but for the
delay in cleaning some of my travel-stained habiliments,
which on account of incessant rain, could not be finished.
She is impatient at my long stay, but if she knew half how
much I had hurried myself to get on she would excuse me.
I am very anxious about what she says about Mr. Peter's illness, yet hope that he is entirely well before this.

When I left Paris this morning, I thought to have taken
tea with L., at Canterbury, yet find myself provokingly
delayed here twenty-two hours. There is, at present, it appears, no correspondence between the railway and the steamer
across the channel, and though I was assured at Paris I
should find the steamer here, it had departed two hours before our arrival. It is provoking. I profit, however, by the
opportunity it affords me to make up my journal for you.

Mrs. Peter here described a visit to the yet unfinished
tomb of Napoleon, now so familiar to visitors at Paris.
Having visited the Sainte Chapelle, founded by St. Louis,
to receive relics he had brought from the Holy Land,

and other objects of interest, she left Paris, taking Rouen in her way to Boulogne, and she says :

"Yesterday, I went to see Rouen and its numerous antiquities, which are so very remarkable. On the way we passed Rosney, the birthplace of Sully, minister of Henry IV. The country, like nearly all the north of France, is flat, but is so well cultivated that it is very pleasing. There is enough in these environs to keep one employed for a month, but I can not stay. I have sent off a fine old cabinet, by Livingston and Wells, which I hope will arrive safely; the transportation is to be paid. I have already paid for the cabinet."

Mrs. King and her little boys met Mrs. Peter at Folkstone, and after remaining a week at Canterbury, a week in London, short excursions to Oxford, Winchester, and the Isle of Wight, they embarked on the steamship Baltic, at Liverpool, and safely reached New York after a comfortable passage, to be met by Mr. Peter, and Mr. and Mrs. King. The whole party proceeded to Philadelphia, where, after a short stay, they decided to go to Newport for the few weeks of hot weather which still might be expected, to avoid for the children the risks of a climate to which they were not accustomed. Mrs. Peter was happy to settle herself again in her comfortable home, and to arrange the many treasures collected in her foreign travels, from the already arrived boxes. The idea of a future removal to Cincinnati, was already under discussion, for Mr. Peter was quite willing to change his place of residence, to secure the great advantage of a home near Mrs. Peter's son. This, however, had to be subject to certain conditions connected with his

17

official affairs, and for the present, Philadelphia was still the home for Mrs. King and her boys. But a short time, however, was to elapse before all should be changed

www.ingramcontent.com/pod-product-compliance
Lightning Source LLC
Chambersburg PA
CBHW020348030726
47496CB00007B/2060